Books in the D BRANCH Series
Razor Sharp
Too Sharp To Hold
A Sharp Edge

I0556265

Books in the TALBOT Series
Talbot
Fortuna
Return
Conflict

Books in the AGENCY Series
Eve of War
The Favor
The Cure
Marque
Reprisal

Books in the PANTHEON Series
Hecate
Tridyma

Books in the COLONY Series
QUANT
ARCADIA
GALACTIC SURVEY
SILK ROAD
LOST COLONY
EARTH

Books in the EMPIRE Series

by Richard F. Weyand:
EMPIRE: Reformer
EMPIRE: Usurper
EMPIRE: Tyrant
EMPIRE: Commander
EMPIRE: Warlord
EMPIRE: Conqueror

by Stephanie Osborn:
EMPIRE: Imperial Police
EMPIRE: Imperial Detective
EMPIRE: Imperial Inspector
EMPIRE: Section Six

by Richard F. Weyand:
EMPIRE: Intervention
EMPIRE: Investigation
EMPIRE: Succession
EMPIRE: Renewal
EMPIRE: Resistance
EMPIRE: Resurgence

Books in the Childers Universe

by Richard F. Weyand:
Childers
Childers: Absurd Proposals
Galactic Mail: Revolution
A Charter For The Commonwealth
Campbell: The Problem With Bliss

by Stephanie Osborn:
Campbell: The Sigurdsen Incident

A SHARP EDGE

by

RICHARD F. WEYAND

RICHARD F. WEYAND

ISBN 978-1-954903-24-1
Printed in the United States of America

Cover Credits
Cover Art: Luca Oleastri and Paola Giari,
www.rotwangstudio.com
Back Cover Photo: Oleg Volk

Published by Weyand Associates, Inc.
Bloomington, Indiana, USA
April, 2025

A SHARP EDGE

CONTENTS

Quandary

No matter which way he looked at it, Dominic Trask was at a complete loss as to what to do.

It was not a situation the multi-decabillionaire had much familiarity with. He had been decisive in building his first company and selling it off for a handsome sum. He had been well studied about the projects he and his investment group had invested their new wealth in and had made fantastic amounts of money.

Of course, Trask had missed the misuse of investment funds on one project to finance the startup of a piracy operation. It had made their interstellar shipping insurance and defense contractor investments do quite nicely, but had exposed him to terrible liability. But he had not been in the know and he had paid his penance.

The people who had been in the know had paid a higher price, all ending up dead at the hands of D Branch.

After Trask had made his money, most problems could be solved by simply throwing money at them. Sometimes those problems had even pointed the way to new investments.

But not this time. This one was beyond him.

Trask considered the matter over the course of several weeks, then put in a call request to someone who had become, as unlikely as it seemed, something of a friend. Acquaintance, at the very least.

Deke Sharp, Senior Field Operative and, though Trask didn't know it, Assistant Head of Field Operations, for D Branch.

The Call

Deke Sharp sighed and rolled over on the chaise out on the patio of their country house, in the far suburbs west of New Destin, the capital of Ariel, the home planet of D Branch. The sub-tropical climate, the warm, early afternoon sun, felt so good.

This was living.

It almost hadn't turned out this way. Deke Sharp had been cruelly injured in the first hit on his ship, *Circe*, in a battle with a division of pirate ships two years and more ago. The pirates were desperate to stop him escaping with information on their operations.

Sharp had been blasted with radiation, carved up with flying shrapnel, and then the wave front of the plasma cloud of the explosion had engulfed him. *Circe* had been disabled, her engines shut down. In the resulting zero gravity, and injected with adrenaline and pain-killers by his compromised vac suit, Sharp had barely made it to the medical life-support unit in his day cabin.

The rest of the crew of *Circe* hadn't been so lucky. The ship had been destroyed with all hands during the battle. Only Deke Sharp and the medical life-support unit had survived.

More or less, that is. It had taken D Branch – the intelligence arm of the Directorate of the Federation of Human Planets – the best part of a year to reassemble him. Much of the Deke Sharp who survived now was artificial parts, to make up for the parts that were missing.

Microphones for ears, cameras for eyes. Bioplastic skin grafts for ears, eyes, nose, and mouth. Realistic-looking facades for eyes, to cover the implanted cameras that lay beneath them. Prosthetic arms from just above the elbows. Prosthetic legs from just below the artificial knees.

Even his genitals were prosthetic, though, like the arms and legs, feet and hands, they had full sensation through neurally connected processors.

Once reassembled, Deke Sharp had sought out the pirates, and, later, the people who had financed them, and sent them all to hell.

Sharp had survived, had married Suzie Fuller, the kid sister of his best friend in high school, and was now the Assistant Head of Field Operations for D Branch. He would take over operations from Otto Pasha in another year or so.

In the meantime, he enjoyed the sunshine on the patio of his and Fuller's country house.

The call request came in that afternoon, as Sharp lay out on the patio. He almost ignored it, but checked the originating location. The planet Elizabeth. More, it was from the private address of Dominic Trask, one of – if not *the* – richest men in the Federation.

Dominic Trask had been a strange case. His investment group had funded the startup of the piracy operation, but he himself had not been in the know. The managing partners for that investment in their portfolio had kept the other members of the investment group in the dark. When Trask had found out what they had done, he was too compromised to go public with his knowledge.

Over the next twenty years, the investment group had broken up, the individual partners going their own way. They were all wealthy enough by this point to make big investments by themselves even while maintaining diversity in their portfolios.

But Trask had lived that entire time waiting for the other shoe to drop, knowing his investment in piracy could come back to haunt him.

When Sharp had shown up on Elizabeth last year, Trask had arranged a meeting, which had turned into a lovely dinner in Trask's penthouse condo in Gotham, the capital of Elizabeth and the financial capital of the Federation. Trask told Sharp what had happened with the funding of the pirates twenty years before.

More, he had cooperated with the investigation, providing the information Sharp's team needed to prove the guilt of the real culprits. Under a little-used section of Federation law, Sharp had executed four men for aiding and abetting piracy.

What could Trask be calling about?

Sharp doubted it was a social call.

"Deke Sharp."

"Hello, Deke. Dominic Trask here."

"Hi, Dominic. What's up?"

"I'm sorry for calling on the weekend, Deke, but I didn't want to make this call from the office. Too many ears about, and the subject is extremely sensitive."

"I understand, Dominic. Not a problem."

"Oh, good. Deke, I have picked up hints that someone is going to attempt, um, a hostile takeover of your employer."

D Branch? Sharp's confusion must have shown.

"Your *ultimate* employer," Trask added.

The Federation! A coup d'etat, or something of the kind?

"You're sure, Dominic?"

"Not sure, Deke, but the signs are there. Subtle, but compelling. I didn't know where else to go with it. I don't know, for instance, who all is involved. But I suspected that you, of all people, would not be. I also suspected that, were I to go to any other uninvolved person, it would come to you as an action item anyway."

Sharp nodded. That was certainly true. No matter who in the Federation Trask contacted, it would come to D Branch, then to Deke Sharp, to deal with it.

"How do you suggest proceeding, Dominic?"

"I would think you should probably come to Elizabeth, Deke. As my guest. I can provide you with all the information. All the things I am seeing. You can stay at my beach house while you and your team look into it."

That made sense. Sharp had looked into Trask's 'beach house' when he was investigating the piracy funding question. It was the size of a large country club.

"Very well, Dominic. I'll be in touch when I have my plans together."

"Thanks, Deke. It makes me feel much better to have you in the know about what I'm seeing. I've been afraid to tell anyone else."

Sharp cut the connection and considered.

The piracy funding investigation had begun when police tried to arrest Sharp and various of his familiars. He had ended up with his current ship, *Medea*, filled with refugees from the police on Humphreys, his own home planet. His now-wife Suzie Fuller, his high-school girlfriend Lydia Thompsen, her husband Paul Camden, and their three pre-school children Sarah, Matthew, and Michael, had all crammed into *Medea*'s one-man cabin and her two small shuttles.

Medea was a one-man ship with the tonnage of a frigate, which would normally have a crew of over a hundred. But

Medea was a D Branch ship. She had the engines of an attack-ship carrier twenty times her mass, which made her the fastest ship in space. She had the guns of a cruiser, which made her one of the deadliest ships in space. And those huge engines ran her shields, compressed to diamond hardness around the smaller ship, making her almost invulnerable to attack.

The money trail on the police attacks had led them to Elizabeth. Once there, Trask had become aware of Sharp's surveillance, and called Otto Pasha at D Branch to set up their meeting. Using Trask's files, tracking down the truly guilty had been easy.

That investigation had been made much easier by his companions. Suzie Fuller was a senior investigator of official corruption on Humphreys. Lydia Thompsen was a finance whiz. Paul Camden was a forensic analyst and cyber security expert. Together – and with D Branch tools – they had made short work of the investigation.

What about this investigation?

Thompsen and Camden could assist, but they were not trained as potential combatants, and they had their kids to worry about. Most of what they had done in the previous investigation, however, had been done in virtual terminal, and they could do that from Humphreys. OK, so count them in.

What about Fuller? She had also worked in virtual terminal for the investigation part of it, but she had done surveillance as well. And she was trained in various police skills, including with firearms.

Besides which, without her it would be a real separation, perhaps for months. Not fun.

Sharp didn't want to leave Fuller behind.

"How busy are you the next several months?" Sharp asked

Fuller over dinner.

"Why?"

"I got a call from Dominic Trask today. He wants me to come to Elizabeth. He thinks someone is going to attempt, and I quote, 'a hostile takeover of your employer.' Then he added 'your ultimate employer.'"

"The Federation? How would anybody even do that, D.K? I would think the Federation Navy would take a dim view of that sort of thing."

"So do I, which to me means it has to be from within the Navy, but I don't know."

"Wow."

"Yeah. Now, if it was anybody else other than Dominic Trask...."

"Right, D.K. Wild rumor. But I don't think Trask operates on wild rumors."

"I don't either. That's why I have to go."

"So, how long a trip, do you think?"

"Dunno, Suzie. It's a month round-trip to Elizabeth and back, so months at least."

"There's just so much going on right now. It's not a good time."

"Is any?"

"Probably not, D.K. And if this is a Navy coup attempt, that would be the official corruption investigation of the century right there."

"Yup."

Fuller sighed.

"Can I have till the end of the week to turn some things over?"

"Sure. We leave Friday night, then?"

"All right. And our venue while we're there? The Gotham

Astoria again?"

"No. Trask's beach house, at least at first. We're his guests."

"Oh, the beach. All right. I know how to pack for that."

She sighed.

"I hope this isn't a wild goose chase, D.K."

"Actually, Suzie, I hope it is."

On Monday morning, Sharp walked into Otto Pasha's office next door. Pasha spent the mornings here helping Sharp come up to speed in field operations, then spent the afternoons in an office next to Claude Allard, the current head of D Branch, as Pasha learned the ropes of being director.

"Hi, Otto. How about a walk?"

Pasha raised an eyebrow, but his response was matter-of-fact.

"Sure, Deke."

The two men went down to the back entrance of the building, out onto the path that led around the grounds. They stopped at a bench with a view out over the small lake on D Branch's corporate campus.

"What's going on, Deke?"

"I need to go to Elizabeth. Months, I think."

"Some more follow-up?"

"No. Otto, I got a call from Dominic Trask Saturday. He apologized for calling on the weekend, but didn't want to call from the office."

Pasha's eyebrows rose at that, and Sharp continued.

"Trask thinks someone is going to attempt a hostile takeover of our ultimate employer."

"Leave it to him to express it in corporate terms. Overturn the Federation, eh? Not a minor matter, Deke. I would think the Navy would have to be involved."

"I had already tentatively come to the same conclusion. Otto, what's your read of Admiral Jurgens?"

"The Chief of Naval Operations? Kurt's good people, Deke. I wouldn't expect trouble there. Then again, he won't have that position forever, either. I wonder who his heir apparent is. What his timeframe is."

Sharp nodded. That would be the most obvious place to look. Then again, he didn't actually know what Trask was seeing.

"Well, this is all wild speculation at the moment. Trask didn't give me anything. He's invited me to come out to Elizabeth. As his guest. Work out of his house, for that matter. If it were anybody else, I would think it fantastical, but not from Trask."

Pasha nodded.

"And Ms. Fuller?"

"I can't think of any bigger case of official corruption one could have, Otto."

"Right. And you still have virtual contact with the people on Humphreys. Thompsen and her husband. I never killed their D Branch accounts or access to tools."

"And they're two people I know I can trust."

"OK, Deke, go ahead. And you take care. You and Fuller both."

"And you watch your back, Otto. I can't imagine something like this doesn't have hooks into D Branch somehow."

Pasha sighed.

"Oh, yes. On the really serious cases, one must be somewhat circumspect. A shame, really."

During the week, Sharp and Fuller stayed at their condo downtown. They had packed Sunday night at the country house for anything they thought they might need on the trip.

During the week, Sharp went out to the New Destin Navy Shuttleport and performed maintenance and checks on his equipment aboard *Medea*'s shuttle. He could do a lot during the long, boring trip, but best to make sure things were at least in pretty good shape before they left. Weapons, special-purpose prosthetics, his dog suit. All ready to go.

Sharp also contacted the Navy's orbital Ariel Station and asked them to do a check of *Medea*, including her food stores and ammunition stores, per his inventory list. They also did a computer systems check, and brought her power systems up for system checks on engines, weapons, and shields. Environmental was started up and a system check performed, then it was left running.

Come Friday evening, they were all set.

Friday evening, they both got home from work, dressed down, and ate light from Piatti's, the little Italian restaurant around the corner. A heavy meal before weightlessness was not a good idea.

They took an auto-drive rental out to *Medea*'s shuttle at the Navy shuttleport. Sharp was in constant touch with *Medea* in orbit now, and the shuttle's engines were warming up.

"Just like old times, huh?" Fuller asked.

"Well, at least we don't have to run and jump in while people are shooting at us."

"That's definitely a plus."

Sharp opened the door and extended the ramp in virtual terminal, then they boarded the shuttle. They both took weightlessness pills, then Sharp got into the command chair and Fuller deployed a jump seat and belted in.

"We good to go, Ms. Fuller?"

"Anchors aweigh, Mr. Sharp."

Sharp chuckled and sent a message to *Medea*. The engines spooled up, Sharp focused the thrust and hit the oxygen, and the shuttle leaped into the air.

Once the acceleration had died down and the shuttle was on course for *Medea*, Sharp turned around and looked at Fuller. She was slumped forward in her seat, asleep.

Sharp chuckled.

The first time you went into space, it was very exciting.

Do it enough times, and it was just another bus ride.

The Trip

The shuttle docked to *Medea* and latched to its mother ship. Sharp undogged the hatches, and he and Fuller floated into *Medea*'s main cabin. The safety nets were deployed in zero gravity, and they pulled themselves along.

"Ah. Home sweet home," Fuller said.

"Let me double-check inventories before we space."

Fuller nodded and belted into a jump seat.

"I'll just stay out of your way."

Sharp did spot-checks on food and ammunition stores, environmental and water systems. He took almost an hour checking *Medea*'s readiness.

"Looks like we're good to go, Suzie. Ariel Station has always been pretty good."

"Well, I'm ready, D.K. Gravity sounds good to me."

Sharp chuckled.

He requested and received immediate departure clearance.

Once he had *Medea* on course for the envelope, Sharp and Fuller went to bed on the bigger bed in the main cabin. They had taken the smaller bed in one of the shuttles when there had been seven of them aboard on the last mission, to and from Elizabeth from Humphreys.

"Well, this is more comfy," Fuller said. "We have a little bit of room at least."

On that Friday night, tired after a long week of getting ready for the trip, they were both asleep in minutes.

The next morning – at least it was morning in New Destin, on Ariel, now falling behind them – they got dressed and had breakfast. Sharp serviced his prosthetics for the day, washing them and salving the skin around the connections.

"So how long is it to Elizabeth, D.K? You know, how long in the envelope?"

"A bit under two weeks."

"Now wait a minute. From Humphreys to Elizabeth was something like sixteen days. From Humphreys to Ariel was something like ten days. So why isn't Ariel to Elizabeth twenty-six days, or four days?"

"Two reasons, Suzie. One is that they aren't in a straight line. They're a big triangle in space. So it couldn't be more than twenty-six days, or less than four, but otherwise it could be anything in between, depending on the shape of the triangle."

Fuller thought about it.

"OK, D.K. That makes sense. What's the other reason?"

"The travel times aren't proportional to the distance."

"They're not?"

"No, because we're accelerating all the time. In normal space, at frigate power levels – no sense giving anything away – *Medea* accelerates at ten gravities. Pretty common. The engines only let us feel one gravity of it. But in the envelope, at her full power levels, *Medea* accelerates at something stupendous, like two hundred thousand gravities."

"But we still only feel one gravity of it?"

"Yes. I could set it for two gravities, or half a gravity, or no gravity in the cabin. But the envelope takes normal acceleration of standard power levels and makes it a large multiple greater."

"I don't understand that, D.K."

"Good. I don't either. Neither does anyone else. But it's the only reason we can get around in interstellar space."

"So why aren't travel times proportional to distance?"

"Because we're always accelerating. If you take, say, a ten day trip, and you accelerate for another four days, not only are you constantly going faster, those four days are on top of the speed you've already gotten up to."

"OK. I guess."

"That's why almost all trips are about two weeks. Humphreys and Ariel are pretty close, so ten days. But everything else is pretty much two to three weeks, because that third week, you are going really, really fast."

"Don't you have to decelerate, too? I know you turn the ship around when you get close to the destination."

"Yes, but the envelope is asymmetrical. You keep pushing on it, you will keep accelerating, but you are really something of an irritant to spacetime. When you start decelerating, you decelerate fast. Several million gravities at the same power level."

"Wow. And we only feel one gravity."

"Yup."

"It's magic, D.K."

"Might as well be, but that's just how strange the universe is, Suzie."

Fuller gave Sharp an old-fashioned look, and he shrugged.

"OK, D.K. I give. But it's a bit under two weeks?"

"Yeah. Twelve, thirteen days. Something like that. Once we get to the envelope. And another day to the planet on the other end."

"Anything on the agenda before we hit the envelope?"

"Well, you should download from Ariel anything you want on the way. And I need to call Trask and tell him we're coming. Other than that, no. Just the long wait, yet again."

"Trask."

"Good morning, Dominic. Deke Sharp here."

"Yes, Deke. Are you coming?"

"Oh, yes. We're on our way to the envelope on the Ariel end right now."

"Excellent. So that will be what, then? About a month?"

"No, Dominic. I'm in a D Branch fast ship. Which I would appreciate your confidence about, by the way. We should be on the ground in Elizabeth in thirteen or fourteen days."

"Wonderful. I'll plan to be out at the beach house that weekend. Let me know when you hit the Elizabeth system what your arrival time at the Gotham Navy Shuttleport will be, and I'll have someone pick you up."

"All right, Dominic. Oh, and I have Suzanne Fuller with me."

"The corruption investigator?"

"And my wife. Yes."

"Excellent."

"See you in a couple weeks, Dominic."

"Good spacing, Deke."

Two weeks in space is two weeks in space. There was no communications. There was no real gym, no walks outside, no view. Like any long voyage, it was mostly boring.

Sharp went several nights in a row with all his prosthetics removed. He could do that with Fuller around to help him get the last arm off at night and the first arm on in the morning. The issue was that necrosis of the skin covered by the prosthetics was a real potential issue, and, once started, it was a difficult recovery. He liked to occasionally give the skin a full recuperation to make sure there was no possibility of that occurring.

They made love, of course. The larger bed in the main cabin

was much more amenable to enthusiastic camaraderie than the smaller pull-down bunk in either shuttle. Just for variety, a couple of times Sharp adjusted the cabin gravity to zero and they made love tethered with an ankle strap to the zero-gravity nets.

They also caught up on the news. Sharp had downloaded all the news from Ariel, Elizabeth, and Meredith – the home of the Federation Navy – before they left Ariel. They read everything with an eye out for anything that Trask might be seeing, but came up dry, even in the business news that Trask likely concentrated on.

Both Sharp and Fuller worked out on what she called 'the rubber-band machine,' the universal gym on one side wall opposite the galley. No free weights or weight stacks on board ship; they were far too dangerous if they broke free. The machine allowed keeping up on the major muscle groups using rubber straps as the resistance element.

Sharp and Fuller worked over all the weapons on board, including her 8mm HP semi-automatic pistol. Every weapon was cleaned, lubricated, and the action checked. They had sat unused in the ship or the shuttles for months, and lubrication could thicken with age and hinder proper operation. Failure to feed on the second shot could be inconvenient.

It was a period of recuperation, preparation, and reflection, and they arrived in the Elizabeth system eager to be out of the ship.

Medea dropped out of the envelope on Thursday night of the second week spacing. Sharp had made his turn that morning and had the ship decelerating all day after the long acceleration within the envelope. They had one more day on approach before docking at the Navy's orbital Elizabeth Station.

"Somehow, the last day seems worse, because you're so close," Fuller said.

"Yeah. The last day definitely seems to drag."

Fuller sighed.

"Ah, well. Almost there."

When they got up Friday morning, they were about halfway to the planet, and Sharp had a hard estimate for their arrival. He called Trask.

"Trask."

"Good morning, Dominic. Deke Sharp here."

"Hi, Deke. Trip go okay?"

"Yes. We're about halfway to the planet from the envelope. I figure between six and seven for docking at Elizabeth Station, and between seven and eight to be on the ground."

"Excellent. I'll have my car waiting for you. Just message Gary Jones with your pad number when you have it."

Trask's chief of security. Sharp had met Jones when he and Trask had met for dinner the last time Sharp was on Elizabeth.

"All right, Dominic."

"Oh, and Deke? I have not shared my concerns with Gary. Just so you know."

Sharp nodded. That was an insane level of security. Sharp was apparently the only person Trask had told.

"I understand, Dominic. We'll see you tonight."

Medea docked at Elizabeth Station without incident. Sharp asked for, and received, clearance for an immediate shuttle departure for the planet.

On the way down, Sharp signaled Gary Jones their pad number.

Sharp had adjusted ship's time by about twenty minutes a day while they were in the envelope, so they were on Gotham time when they landed a bit after seven-thirty that evening. There was an armored limousine waiting at the pad.

Gary Jones and the shotgun got out of the car as Sharp and Fuller came down the ramp of the shuttle, both dragging their wheeled luggage bags behind them. Sharp also had a Navy-issue planet duffle over his shoulder.

At a gesture from Jones, the shotgun took their luggage and stowed it in the trunk of the car. Sharp walked up to Jones.

"Good evening, Mr. Jones. Good to see you again."

"Good evening, Mr. Sharp. Welcome back to Elizabeth."

"This is my wife, Suzanne Fuller," Sharp said, with a wave to Fuller.

Jones shook her hand.

"Good evening, Ms. Fuller."

"Mr. Jones."

Jones waved them to the open door of the car, then got in after them, sitting in the rear-facing seat in front of them. The shotgun closed the rear compartment door, and returned to his seat in the front compartment. The car moved away from the pad and headed toward the shuttleport entrance and the public highway beyond.

"Mr. Trask has left his office in the city and is also on the way to what he calls the beach house. He will arrive within an hour of you, Mr. Sharp. He was planning a late dinner."

"That works for me, Mr. Jones. One doesn't overeat when looking ahead to zero-gravity maneuvers."

"So he surmised, Mr. Sharp. His wife and daughter will also be in attendance, with business discussions delayed until a private meeting after dinner."

Sharp nodded. Sounded sensible.

"It will be about an hour's drive to the beach house from the shuttleport."

"Very good."

Having delivered his messages, Jones remained silent for the rest of the trip. He appeared to be monitoring something – their security status? – in virtual terminal.

Sharp watched the scenery go by. They were heading farther down the coast, away from Gotham. Let's see. An hour further from Gotham than the shuttleport would be pretty far out in the country. In contrast, the beach resort where they had stayed during Sharp and Fuller's last sojourn on Elizabeth was in the other direction.

It was a quiet trip. The plush, cushioned interior was a welcome break from the spartan, utilitarian furnishings of a space ship or shuttle.

The limousine pulled up in front of what was clearly a side entrance to the huge estate house.

"This is the entrance to the guest wing. Mr. Trask has no other guests in residence at the moment. As an aside, Mr. Sharp, I will note that our security here is pretty good. Walled enclosure, intruder alarms on the wall and around the property, video monitoring, and a ready squad in addition to posted guards."

"Thank you, Mr. Jones."

The shotgun opened the door, and Jones escorted them into the house, the shotgun following behind with their luggage.

Jones led them into the primary guest suite, a three-room arrangement with living room, bedroom, and its own kitchen. All the rooms had window walls with an expansive vista of the beach and the ocean beyond. The exquisite rooms were expensively decorated in the modern style.

"Very nice, Mr. Jones."

"Thank you, Mr. Sharp. There is a call button on the light panel for each room, as well as one on each night stand. With guests in residence, the staff desk in the guest wing will be manned twenty-four hours a day."

Sharp nodded. Quite a setup.

"If there are no questions, Mr. Sharp, someone will be by to escort you to Mr. Trask when he arrives. Dress code for dinner is casual, though not beach casual, as it is for breakfast and lunch."

"Understood, Mr. Jones. Thank you."

Jones nodded and turned to Fuller, nodding at her.

"Ms. Fuller."

Jones and the shotgun then left, closing the door behind them.

"Nice setup," Sharp said.

Fuller was looking around.

"I'll say, D.K. Even the Gotham Astoria didn't have a bar in the room that stocked the Dufort *Esprit*."

"Really?"

"Oh, yes," Fuller said, holding up the distinctive bottle.

"Well, that would seem a good place to start, then."

Dominic Trask

The butler found them out on the patio of the guest suite, nursing the dregs of their snifters. It was too dark to see the ocean, particularly with the lights of the house behind them, but they could smell it. It was a comforting smell, much like that of their own ocean, back on Ariel.

"Mr. Sharp, Ms. Fuller. Mr. Trask has arrived, and invites you to join him in the salon," the butler pronounced.

"Why, then we should go," Sharp said.

They both got up, carrying their empty snifters into the house, and dropping them at the bar. The butler nodded approvingly, and led them off down the hallway to the main part of the house.

"Mr. Sharp and Ms. Fuller," the butler announced as he waved them into the salon.

"Deke! Come on in."

They shook hands, then Trask turned to Fuller and shook her hand.

"Ms. Fuller. Pleased to meet you."

"And you, Mr. Trask. Please call me Suzie."

"And you must call me Dominic. Let me introduce my wife, Janine Dubois, and my daughter, Marie Dubois."

Janine Dubois was younger than Trask, but not by much. Not as much as a decade. Not a trophy wife, then. She was dark, and lovely. Marie was clearly her daughter, in her upper twenties, also dark, and beautiful.

There were handshakes and pleasantries all around, then Trask motioned to the bar.

"We're ahead of you, Dominic," Sharp said. "Please, go ahead."

Trask nodded, and poured drinks for the others. He then waved a bottle of the Dufort *Esprit* – the best cognac in the Federation – in the air.

Despite the fact that the Dufort *Esprit* was over three thousand credits a bottle – if you found it on sale – Trask had bottles of it lying around like some mass-market beer.

Every cognac maker had various grades of product, including VS (Very Special), VSOP (Very Special Old Pale), and XO (Extra Old), but their top grade – their very best and most expensive cognac – was named, like Dufort's *Esprit* product.

Sharp enjoyed it, but he only ever had it at Maxine's, when Pasha was buying.

"You sure I can't entice you with a little splash, Deke?"

Sharp acquiesced, and all five of them sat with their drinks in a conversation circle of comfortable overstuffed sofas in front of the stone fireplace.

"Was your trip pleasant, Deke?" Trask's wife asked.

"Space trips are never pleasant, Janine. Mostly, if one is lucky, they are boring. Ours was without incident."

"Wonderful."

"I would think space travel was exciting," Marie said.

Fuller snorted.

"You sit around in a small, bare room with absolutely nothing to do, waiting for the weeks to pass. You have a bed, a single gym machine, and a small kitchen. Couple of chairs. That's it. There's nothing to be excited about, Marie. Truly, there isn't."

"Wow. It always seemed so glamorous."

"It's more fun watching shuttles take off for a few minutes, and thinking about where they might be going. Actually going, however, is the most boring thing ever."

The butler appeared at the door and made a small noise.

"Yes, Robert?" Trask asked.

"Dinner is ready, sir."

"Ah. Excellent. Come along, everyone. Bring your drinks with you. I hope you and Suzie like orange roughy, Deke."

"Sounds delicious, Dominic."

At the beach house this evening, it was a seafood meal. A white clam chowder with fresh baked bread started them off, followed by a garden salad. The entree was pan-fried orange roughy with a dill sauce. Sides were blanched asparagus spears and angel-hair pasta in a butter and caper sauce. Dessert – with more of the cognac – was an assortment of chocolate dainties.

As at their previous meeting, the dinner was superb. Trask kept an excellent kitchen.

Conversation did not resume until dinner was complete.

"You're going to spoil me, Dominic. That was truly wonderful."

"Excellent. I don't want to give you any excuse to leave before your work here is finished, Deke."

"Oops. Someone mentioned work," Janine said. "Come along, Marie. Let's decamp and leave them to their business."

"And we should move to the lounge or the patio," Trask said.

"The patio is very nice this evening," Fuller said.

Trask turned to the butler.

"Robert, cigars and amaretto on the patio."

"Very good, sir."

Everyone got up from the table. Janine and Marie left to go deeper into the house, while Trask led Sharp and Fuller out onto the patio.

"What do you do when it's raining, Dominic?" Fuller asked.

"Ah. I have a smoking lounge in the house. Completely separate air system. I am permitted to smoke there, as long as I keep the room doors closed."

Fuller laughed. The idea of the wealthy Trask submitting to his wife's demand in such a way struck her as funny. Then again, she appeared to be Trask's first wife – clearly Marie's mother – and she had been with him throughout his long climb to extreme wealth. In a long-term marriage, accommodations must be made.

Trask waved them to seats around a patio table, then sat himself. Robert, the butler, appeared with a tray containing a humidor of cigars, a lighter and cutter, a bottle of amaretto, and three glasses.

"Thank you, Robert. We'll serve ourselves. I won't need you any longer this evening."

"Very good, sir."

The butler disappeared, and Trask turned to them, looking back and forth between Sharp and Fuller.

"I'm very happy the two of you went to all the trouble to come here. I just hope it isn't a wild goose chase."

"Given what you've told me, Dominic, I'm hoping it is a wild goose chase. The alternative could get very nasty."

"Indeed, indeed. Let me tell you what I am seeing that raised the hackles on my neck.

"Most investors buy stocks or mutual funds and hang onto them. That's the typical behavior of the individual investor. They may sometimes jump out and buy back in, but they almost always do this at the wrong time. When stocks go down, they sell, and when they go up, they buy back in. They jump on the bandwagon, and that costs them.

"More sophisticated investors often buy things like puts and calls. That is, they buy the option to sell or buy a stock at a given price in the future. If you think a company is going to go down, you buy a put. If you think it will go up, you buy a call. If you have some visibility into the company's business, you can make a lot of money that way.

"Especially if you buy a put, and the company stock falls, you can make a lot of money, because stocks go up on the escalator, but they go down in the elevator."

"Unless they jump off the balcony," Fuller put in.

"Yes, Suzie. Nicely stated. Unless they jump off the balcony. In which case you make a great deal of money.

"Now, some investors sell puts and calls. If you think the stock won't change much for the next ninety days, say, you can get paid free extra money for an option the option purchaser will never exercise. There is a great deal of danger in that strategy, because you can lose a great deal of money if it goes against you, especially selling naked puts and calls, but if you are a large institutional investor, you have a very diverse portfolio already, so it can make sense.

"Are you with me so far?"

Sharp looked to Fuller, and she was nodding.

"OK, Dominic. At least one of us is with you."

Trask chuckled.

"It gets easier from here, Deke.

"As an investor, I pay a lot of attention to the markets, especially the people who are buying puts and calls. As I say, that's where the more sophisticated individual investors are, and their purchases signal what they think is going to happen in the next thirty days, ninety days, or a year.

"Now, one has to be careful. People buy puts and calls every day. What I am looking for is developing consensus, where the purchases of calls or puts are outside of their recent historical norms. I also look at the expiration dates, because that gives me an idea of the timeframe of people's expectations.

"We good?"

"I'm following you, Dominic. My degrees are in finance," Fuller said. "What are you seeing?"

"There is unusual activity in both directions, on different stocks. There are a lot of puts being purchased against stocks like defense contractors, luxury goods, durable goods. The list goes on. Calls are being purchased on surveillance system manufacturers, small weapons manufacturers, manufacturers of police equipment – everything from tactical equipment to armored vehicles to armed drones – and on alcoholic beverage makers, particularly the mass market ones.

"What does that all say to you?"

Sharp turned to Fuller.

"Downturns in luxury goods and durable goods look like a recession signal to me, Dominic. Military as well, perhaps. But those purchases are things people put off or don't buy when money is tight."

"Right, Suzie. And the police equipment? Alcohol?"

"Somebody's planning on setting up a police state," Sharp put in.

Trask nodded.

"That's what it looks like to me, Deke."

"Why alcohol?" Fuller asked.

"Escape," Sharp said.

Trask nodded.

"Police states have historically had high rates of alcoholism. It's the one way out. The way to forget about one's plight."

"Why a threat to the Federation, though, Dominic?" Sharp asked.

"The stocks involved are all companies in Federation space,

Deke."

"What expiration dates are involved?" Fuller asked.

"The one-year calls and puts, Suzie. Not the shorter-term contracts."

"And how unusual is the activity?"

"They are all trading outside their ten-year ranges."

"Oh, my."

Sharp raised an eyebrow to Fuller.

"Stocks bounce around, options bounce around. The ups and downs of a short period don't mean much. Being outside their ten-year ranges means a real move."

"Indeed, Suzie," Trask said. "Trading outside their ten-year ranges is one of my criteria for significant movement."

"Where is the money coming from?" Sharp asked.

"I don't know, Deke. I can't see that in my systems. But I suspect some of it is coming from outside the Federation."

"Why?"

"Because I haven't heard of anything. These are some pretty big moves, Deke. Rich people tend to talk to each other. Send mails and messages back and forth. If I have some lead, and I get in with some pretty cheap put or call options, it's no skin off my nose if you go in after me and buy some at a somewhat higher price. Doesn't hurt my position, and, if it works out, you owe me one.

"But nobody's talking. I haven't heard a peep. That's very unusual. So I wonder if it's even Federation actors working this."

"But why would they take financial positions?" Fuller asked. "They're just signaling what's coming, giving us a heads up."

"Yes, that had occurred to me as well, Suzie. The people buying the options may not be the real players in this game. But people who are part of the plans, who know something's coming, might be making plays on their inside knowledge without the real actors knowing about it. I imagine they wouldn't be pleased about it."

"OK, that would make sense. And you have a data package for us?"

"Yes, Suzie. I have set aside all of what I have found. You can likely do better than I, given your access to databases I can't see. But I have what I've seen for you."

"Excellent, Dominic. Then we have our work cut out for us, D.K. First thing tomorrow, I'll be hard at it."

"After breakfast, surely," Trask said. "I insist on a full breakfast for myself every morning, and the morning staff here is wonderful."

Fuller laughed.

"All right, Dominic. After breakfast."

"One must be civilized, after all," Trask muttered.

Sharp and Fuller both laughed.

Evidence

Sharp and Fuller both woke about sunrise. With very little axial tilt, Elizabeth's day was just over twelve hours long all year, running from sunrise before seven to sunset just after seven every day.

Sharp went into the bathroom to perform his morning ritual of servicing his prosthetics and their connections, while Fuller put on a long T-shirt and walked out on the patio to watch the sunrise.

After fifteen minutes or so, Fuller went into the kitchen of the guest suite to make a cup of coffee. The kitchen had an espresso machine, and she made one for herself and another for Sharp, then went back out on the patio to sip her coffee in one of the chaises there.

Sharp came out on the patio. He was wearing swim trunks.

"That's a fetching outfit," he said.

"I didn't want to shock the staff. Besides, it covers more than a bikini."

"Is that an espresso?"

"Yes. I made one for you as well."

"Excellent."

Sharp went inside and fetched his espresso, then came out and sat on the chaise next to hers.

"Looks like breakfast is buffet on the patio this morning," Sharp said, gesturing toward the main house.

"Sounds good to me. I can't believe I'm hungry after that dinner last night, but I am."

"I don't see the Trasks yet, so you probably have time for a shower."

"OK. I'm off. Be right back."

Fuller left, and Sharp lay back on the chaise and sighed. He had half-hoped this trip was a milk run, that they would find nothing, but it didn't sound that way. Trask's logic was solid. Ah, well. They would find what they would find when they analyzed his data. What to do then was an open question.

Fuller came back out on the patio wearing some sort of stretchy short-shorts and a bikini top.

"Oh, that feels better."

She sat on the chaise and resumed sipping her espresso.

"So you think Trask's worries are real, D.K?"

"I'm afraid they may very well be."

"And then what?"

"I don't know, Suzie. We'll see."

"Oops. There's Marie."

"OK, Suzie. We should probably wander down that way."

They got up, leaving their empty espresso cups on the side table between them, and headed across the patio to the breakfast setup. Marie was just working her way down the buffet.

"Good morning, Marie."

"Hi, Suzie. Sleep well?"

"Wonderfully. And you?"

"Good."

The buffet was small – just for the five of them – but it was enough to feed a dozen hungry people.

"What do they do with all the rest of this food?" Fuller wondered.

"Staff has breakfast after us," Marie said. "It works out."

The buffet included waffles – the big Belgian style – with fruit or syrup, French toast, eggs Benedict, eggs over easy, blintzes, both cheese and fruit, several kinds of toast, and both bacon and ham. Orange juice, grape juice and coffee rounded out the offerings.

"This is wonderful," Sharp said. "We're never going to be hungry."

"I'm gonna gain a ton," Fuller said.

"There's a gym in the house," Marie said. "Any of the staff can show you there."

"That's good," Fuller said. "I'm gonna need it."

Trask and Janine came out and started down the line behind Sharp.

"Morning, Deke."

"Good morning, Dominic. Janine."

Janine was apparently a person of few words in the morning, as she just nodded.

When Marie went off to sit at a table, Fuller followed her. Janine also went to their table, but Trask caught Sharp.

"Sit with me, Deke."

"Sure, Dominic."

They sat at another table.

"Janine's not much of a conversationalist in the morning, although I did get two grunts out of her already."

Sharp chuckled. He knew the type.

"That's all right, Dominic. I understand."

"Now that you've slept on it, Deke, do you think my concerns are well founded?"

"Actually, I do. I had hoped you were wrong, but I suppose I should have known better. We'll just have to dive into the data and see what we find."

"I can't ask for more than that."

At that, they both turned their attentions to their breakfast.

Sharp and Fuller walked across the patio back to the guest

suite after breakfast.

"Well, in addition to the gym, they have a fencing piste, a shooting range, and horses."

"Do you do any of that stuff, Suzie? I mean, other than shooting."

"Oh, yeah. Daphne's been teaching me fencing and horseback riding. Marie will probably kick my ass in fencing, but it's great exercise. Nothing to get you moving like someone coming after you with a sword."

Sharp chuckled.

"Yeah, I can see that."

"And horseback riding along the edge of the ocean? In the shallow water and wet sand? That is so much fun. This is gonna be great."

"We have work to do, too, Suzie."

"Oh, yes. I know. Speaking of which, what did you and Trask talk about?"

"He just wanted to know if, on reflection, I thought his concerns were justified, and I said I regretted that they probably were."

Fuller nodded.

"Yeah. Me, too. Well, I guess there's nothing to do but get into it. Oh, the other thing Marie told me is that there's a high-speed secure link here, so we won't have any problem connecting to D Branch and doing the analysis from here."

"Excellent."

They took comfortable seats in the living room of the guest suite and logged into D Branch. They met in the data visualization engine.

"So let's see what we have," Fuller said.

Fuller loaded Trask's information file, and a rat's nest of

entries appeared in 3-D before them.

"DV. Show interconnections."

Lines criss-crossed the space, connecting entries.

"DV. Arrange entries by the links between them, rubber-band style."

The entries jostled themselves in front of them, and the lines between entries now varied in thickness by the number of interconnections. The heavier lines were shorter, as if they were rubber bands, and the heavier rubber bands pulled things closer.

Expanding an entry, it was a transaction record of the purchase of a put option on a company stock.

"OK, so these are transaction records?" Sharp asked.

"Looks like. And they're grouped."

The entries were in clusters, with heavy links between cluster members and light links between clusters.

"What are the links?"

Fuller expanded a number of links to show their contents.

"OK, so most of the lighter links look like they're companies. That is, a bunch of different people bought options in the same companies, and those show as links."

"And the heavier links, Suzie?"

"Are investors. See. Here's the investor account, here's the contact information, here's the reconciliation account."

"Reconciliation account?"

"The bank account to put proceeds into, D.K."

"I see. DV. Retrieve account information for investor accounts and reconciliation accounts in the entries."

"You can do that?"

"Sure, Suzie. D Branch has access to those kinds of things."

"Wow. I could do the bank accounts, I think, through Ariel DoJ, but not investor accounts."

"Yes, but that would create some perhaps inconvenient communications records between DoJ and D Branch."

Fuller nodded.

"So what have we here? Yes, the account information is now all filled in, you see? Oh, look at this."

Fuller opened a bunch of other entries, then pointed to them.

"D.K. Look at these entries. What do you see?"

"The name on the investor account doesn't match the name on the bank account."

"Right. DV. Search names in investor account information and bank account information. Determine alias names and highlight."

The names on the investor accounts were now all highlighted.

"Ha!" Fuller said.

"What, Suzie?"

"I was wondering how people from outside the Federation could be trading options, D.K. Setting up an options account from a foreign entity should not be possible with a Federation-based broker. What they did is set up the account with aliases. But the reconciliation accounts – the bank accounts where the money goes – can be outside the Federation if you want."

"Got it. So where are they?"

"DV. Analyze investor account addresses and determine whether these are valid addresses. Highlight non-existent addresses, or addresses of known people or institutions that do not match investor names."

The addresses associated with the alias investor names all highlighted.

"You see?"

"Yes, Suzie. But where are the reconciliation accounts? That's what I want."

"Oh. Right. DV. Indicate bank and planet of origin of reconciliation accounts."

The information filled in.

"Looks like they're all banks and planets within the Deneb Republic, D.K."

"Oh, lovely."

"What's the matter?"

"They're not exactly a hotspot of libertarian thinking. Let's leave it at that."

"But aren't they far away?"

"Yeah. Something like fifteen hundred light-years, so they're not usually trouble."

"That's what? Something like thirty weeks in the envelope?"

"No, Suzie. You keep going faster, so travel time isn't linear with distance. The travel time goes as the square root of the distance. Fifteen times farther is more like four times the travel time."

"So eight weeks?"

"For *Medea*, yes. For a normal ship – like a warship – more like twice that. Figure sixteen weeks."

"So we have sixteen weeks, more or less."

"Not if they've already left. And it could be more than that if they haven't left yet."

"Oh. Right. Now what, D.K?"

"Are any of Trask's options investors located within the Federation?"

"Don't know. DV. Highlight entries with Federation bank reconciliation accounts."

About two-thirds of the entries lit up.

"DV. Generate a list of names and locations from the highlighted entries. Mark if those locations are valid."

A list popped into existence in front of them. Sharp scanned down it.

"I don't recognize anybody right off, Suzie."

"DV. Enhance list by including titles, if any, and employer."

"Ouch."

"Yeah. That makes it clear, D.K."

Maybe half of the list was Federation Navy officers, many of flag rank.

"DV. Show star map of Federation. Highlight area of operation for each listee of flag rank."

Fuller was on to where Sharp was going.

"DV. Expand map to show Deneb Republic," she said.

"Well, that tears it. They command the forces we would expect to repel an invasion."

"How can they do that, D.K? Subvert all those officers?"

"Maybe they were Deneb plants to begin with, Suzie. Fifty-year plan? Could be."

"So will they stand aside when Deneb invades? Or will they fight on Deneb's side?"

"I would think the latter would be hard to pull off, Suzie. Rank and file isn't going to go along with anything like that. But they may just arrange to be in the wrong place at the right time."

"Geez, D.K. Now what the hell do we do?"

Reaction

The analysis they had performed so far had taken the whole morning. They dropped out of virtual terminal and just looked at each other.

"I need to talk to Otto," Sharp said.

Fuller just nodded. She checked the time.

"Just about time for lunch, D.K."

She walked over to the patio doors and looked down the patio.

"Looks like something on the grill for lunch. They're getting set up. Oh, and there's Trask."

"We better head down there."

They walked across the patio from the guest wing to the main house. Staff was cooking up hamburgers and bratwurst on the grill.

Trask waved to them as they walked up. He was sitting at the table with a beer. It was a premium beer, of course, in a chilled glass. Condiments and sides on a lazy susan were the table's centerpiece.

"Hi, Deke. Suzie. You're just in time."

Sharp and Fuller sat down, and Trask looked back and forth between them.

"What's the matter? You guys look like you just got back from a funeral."

"Worse than that," Sharp said. "We just did the preliminary analysis on your data, resolving references with my employer's database."

"That bad, Deke?"

"No. Worse."

Janine and Marie came out on the patio then, and they dropped the subject.

"Hi, everybody," Marie said.

Robert took orders and poured soft drinks or beer for everyone. Then hamburgers and bratwurst were served, with buns that were buttered and toasted on the grill.

Sides were a creamy potato salad and baked beans. The beans were very thick, and had lots of onions and bacon pieces, with subtle tones of Dijon mustard.

"The hamburgers are really good," Sharp said.

"They make them like meat loaf, then grill them," Trask said. "So they've got onions and egg and all that stuff in them."

"The brats are good, too," Fuller said.

"They boil them in beer first, then finish them on the grill."

"They're remarkable."

Trask seemed pleased his guests enjoyed lunch so much, despite the dark nature of the earlier conversation. After Janine and Marie left, he went back to it.

"Anything you can tell me about what you're seeing, Deke?"

"Not much, Dominic, but I will tell you that you were right to be concerned."

"You're seeing a pattern that tells you what's going on?"

"Yes."

"Should I take their position as well? With calls and puts, I mean."

"You might be better off taking a contrary position. I can't guarantee success against coming events, but I'm going to do my damnedest."

Trask nodded.

"Perhaps a modest contrary position."

He looked to Fuller, and she nodded. He turned back to Sharp.

"Thanks for that, Deke. Let me know what you can as things go along, if you would."

"I certainly will, Dominic. We owe you one."

"What now?" Fuller asked as they walked back to the guest suite.

"I need to call Otto. They're three hours behind at the moment, but he'll be in the office now."

"You know, we could have done this analysis back at D Branch. Now we're here on Elizabeth, two weeks from home, and out of touch."

"That's the wrong way to think about it, Suzie. I don't need to be in personal contact with Otto and the D Branch agents. We all know each other well enough I can operate from here. But I wanted to meet with Trask personally. I can't read infrared over a visual call. Those frequencies aren't carried over the system."

"Ah. And is Dominic telling the truth?"

"Yes, near as I can tell. I didn't pick up any of the signs of prevarication when we spoke with him. That data is real, as far as he is concerned. At least to him. That was critical to know."

"OK, that makes sense. I was thinking that coming here was the wrong move. It left us in the wrong place."

"No, I had to be able to see Trask when we talked. I can operate from here just fine. We're closer to the Deneb frontier from here, for that matter."

"Pasha."

"Hi, Otto. It's Deke."

"Hi, Deke. You made it to the planet OK, I take it."

"Oh, yes. And we've done a preliminary analysis of Trask's data."

"Ah. He had a data packet ready for you then?"

"Oh, yes. It's in my account, Otto. You really need to take a look at it. You know about options trading? Calls and puts and such?"

"Enough to get by, Deke. Is that what signaled Trask something was up? Unusual options activity?"

"Yes. People are taking positions hedging against a depression and reduced military expenditure, but betting on increased policing and surveillance activity."

"A dreary police state, huh?"

"That's what it looks like, Otto. But take a look at who's behind it."

"All right, Deke. Give me a couple hours. I'll call you."

"Talk to you then, Otto."

Pasha found the analysis in Sharp's D Branch account and entered it in the data visualization engine. He found the entries for people making unusual options purchases separated into two groups, a third of them being high-ranking Federation Navy personnel. Another third were from the Deneb Republic.

Well, that explained why the Deneb Republic, typically a hotbed of trouble for the Federation, had been quiet lately. They didn't want anybody looking too closely in their direction.

Pasha sighed. Was this the big one? It sure looked like it.

D Branch resources in the Deneb Republic – D Branch's most dangerous posting – were not as robust as Pasha could have liked. It was difficult to get people in there. There wasn't much tourism or immigration in that direction. Who would want to live in the police state of the Deneb Republic if the Federation was their alternative?

Still, D Branch did have some people in the Deneb Republic,

but they hadn't seen this coming. Oh, there had been some buildup of navy capacity, but that was typical stuff. Mostly they used their navy against their own people.

In the other direction, there was a small but steady stream of visitors and refugees from the Deneb Republic to the Federation. Pasha suspected most of them were Deneb spies and government agents, but the Federation Council refused to bar them.

Their naval vessels one-on-one were about the par of the Federation's – mostly due to technology theft – at least on paper. They had not been tested against each other in a long time.

It looked like that was about to change.

They were sitting out on the patio, sunning and waiting for Pasha to get back in touch.

"Hey, D.K."

"Yeah," Sharp said lazily, not opening his eyes.

"I was wondering. The Deneb Republic is basically a closed society, yes?"

"More or less, yeah."

"And they've been separated for several hundred years, right?"

"Yes. What are you getting at, Suzie?"

"Has there been enough genetic drift we can identify Deneb agents from DNA?"

Sharp sat up, opening his eyes, and looking at her.

"I don't know. That's an interesting question."

"Maybe we should find out."

With Sharp off-planet, Pasha was holding down operations all day, not spending the afternoons upstairs with Claude

Allard in the director's office. He sent Allard a meeting request now, and Allard accepted.

"Good morning, Claude."

"Good morning, Otto. What's going on?"

Pasha brought Allard up to speed on what Sharp had turned up on Elizabeth, and his own review of the data.

"So they're finally going to do it, huh?"

"That's what it looks like, sir."

Allard sighed.

"And I was going to retire."

"Sorry, Claude."

Allard thought about it, then brightened.

"Actually, I think this is a perfect opportunity to hand over more responsibility. The Navy is going to be involved in this, and you already have a relationship with Admiral Jurgens. On Elizabeth, Sharp is closer to the threat axis, and all our field agents already know him. So I think you need to take the lead on this at an agency level, and Sharp can run operations from there."

"And our other operations in progress, sir?"

"You need to look at those closely, Otto. Prioritize them. Drop or delay those operations we can to go after this. In particular, I think we need all the Medea-class ships available for this operation."

"How would that work?"

"Well...."

They talked for an hour about possible scenarios and responses, but Allard made it clear he was just brainstorming. The decisions were Pasha's to make.

Still sunning out on the patio, Sharp and Fuller entered the data visualization engine in a new blank workspace.

"DV. Load DNA signatures of known spies and immigrants from the Deneb Republic," Sharp said.

"Define probability to query word 'known,'" a voice came back.

"DV. Ninety-five percent."

Perhaps a hundred entries stacked up in front of them.

"DV. Is that all?" Fuller asked.

"Required confidence level limits the available dataset," the DV voice answered.

"Good enough, Suzie. If a specific DNA feature is useful, this ought to allow us to find it."

"That's probably fair."

"DV. Import diverse sample of one thousand DNA signatures of Federation citizens."

"Refine definition of query word 'diverse,'" DV said.

"DV. Samples from all Federation planets. Samples of multiple name ethnicities. Exclude any signatures – at even five percent probability – of suspected spies or immigrants from the Deneb Republic."

Another array of entries appeared, perhaps ten times larger.

"DV. Analyze DNA signatures for any feature or features or combination of features that distinguish Deneb Republic import signatures from Federation import signatures."

"This will take time for a complete analysis. DV can notify you when processing is complete."

"DV. Estimated time to complete analysis?"

"Three hours."

Sharp looked at Fuller, and she nodded.

"DV. Notify us when processing is complete."

They logged out.

"Well, that will be interesting to see, D.K."

"And very helpful if it pans out."

"Well, we'll have to wait and see."

Sharp rolled over.

"Time to sun the other side."

The call request came while they were still out on the patio.

"Deke Sharp."

"Hi, Deke. Otto here."

"Hi, Otto. What do you think?"

"I looked at the data, and I agree with your assessment. I talked to Claude about it, and he wants me to handle D Branch response, and you to run operations from there."

Sharp nodded.

"Makes sense. This and the aftermath could run on for a while."

"That's what he figures, and his mind is more and more on the mountains lately. I already have the Navy contact with Jurgens, and we get along pretty well, so I can handle the issues there."

"On that front, I have an analysis running right now. Suzie's idea. We're looking for a DNA marker that someone's from the Deneb Republic."

"Oh, that would be terrific, Deke. It's unlikely that everyone involved is playing the options market. But if we knew who the other possibles were, we could look at their finances really closely, see if they're getting paid from outside. Short of some other evidence, though, that's probably not something we want to do."

"Understood. We're waiting on that analysis. Should be another hour or two."

"Let me know. In the meantime, Claude and I were tossing around ideas."

They talked for another hour, with Sharp throwing in some

ideas of his own.

As Sharp had actually taken a Medea-class ship into battle – and no one else had – his insight into the matter was valuable to Pasha.

When he got off the call, he looked over to Fuller.

"That was Otto."

"Well, we better go inside to talk about it, D.K. We've been out here a while, and we're getting pretty red, even as tan as we are."

Sharp had just finished filling in Fuller when they both got a message from the data visualization engine that the DNA analysis was done. They logged into the workspace.

"DV. Report results of analysis."

"There is no single DNA marker or group of DNA markers that differentiates people known to have been born in the Deneb Republic from those known to have been born in the Federation of Human Planets."

"Damn," Fuller said.

"There are, however, two combinations of DNA markers that do provide that differentiation."

"DV. Explain."

"Consider three DNA markers, A, B, and C."

A close-up of three comparisons appeared in the workspace, one for each DNA marker. In each, on the left was a portion of a sequence with the marker identified by being highlighted, and on the right was a portion of a similar sequence without the marker. It was all gibberish to Sharp – strings of the letters A, C, G, and T – but Fuller nodded.

The DV voice continued.

"If marker A is present with marker B, or if marker A is present with marker C, then the person was born in the Deneb

Republic, for these samples. If marker A is present alone, or markers A, B, and, C in any other combination, then the person was not born in the Deneb Republic."

"DV. These are definitive? That is, if the stated combinations are present, that identifies all the persons in the Deneb Sample and none of the people in the Federation sample?"

"That is correct."

"I wonder how that came about, D.K."

Sharp shrugged.

"Some combination of the people that moved there, some dominant gene perhaps, and enough generations to spread the gene."

"I suppose. Still, it's nice to know."

"Wait a minute. I have an idea. DV. Do you have DNA samples for all Navy flag officers?"

"Yes."

"DV. Do you have DNA samples for all Navy ship captains?"

"Yes."

"DV. Import DNA samples for all Navy flag officers and ship captains and determine whether they were born in the Deneb Republic or the Federation."

Another big sample set appeared in front of them. They watched as a number of them started being highlighted. When the highlighting stopped, there were perhaps five percent of Federation Navy senior officers indicated as born in Deneb.

Or born to parents who were both from Deneb, Sharp supposed.

"Look at that, D.K."

"DV. Highlight command areas of the Deneb-born officers on a Federation map."

Once again, the axis of approach to the Federation from the

Deneb Republic was controlled by Deneb-born officers, although this time it was more complete. There were no gaps this time.

There were also a number of dots on Meredith, the location of Federation Navy headquarters.

"DV. List area of responsibility for Deneb-born officers on Meredith."

"Well, there you go, D.K. The heads of promotions and assignments are both Deneb-born."

"As are their chiefs of staff. Well, that explains how their people got promoted, and how they all ended up assigned to the commands where Deneb wanted them."

"Now what?"

"I call Otto again. We can use this. Oh, can we use this."

The Scope Widens

"Pasha."

"Hi, Otto. It's Deke."

"Yes, Deke. Did the DNA analysis finish?"

"Yes. We have a way of identifying whether the DNA is from someone born in the Deneb Republic, or whose parents were both from the Deneb Republic, as opposed to those born in the Federation."

"Excellent. That's going to come in handy."

"It already has, Otto. The Navy has DNA profiles of all the senior officers."

"I think they have DNA profiles of everyone, Deke. It helps in identifying remains if there's a battle or an accident or something."

Sharp nodded.

"We ran the differentiation against the captains and flag officers of the Navy, and it's illustrative of the problem. You want to join me in the DV engine?"

"Sure."

They both logged into Sharp's new analysis. Sharp pointed out the markers first.

"There is no one marker or group of markers that differentiates. But I asked for a deeper analysis. Looking at these three markers, A plus B or A plus C identifies the Deneb-born, but is not present in any of the Federation-born."

"So if someone did a normal analysis, they wouldn't see this?"

"That's right."

"Which means they may not know there is a way for us to

A SHARP EDGE

tell."

"Probably not. The analysis I did took the DV engine over three hours to perform."

"Which is a lot of processing. Got it."

"Now here we have all the high-ranking officers in the Navy. Captains and flags. This subgroup off to the side show up as being Deneb-born."

Pasha nodded. Sharp directed him to the map.

"These are their command areas."

"They've hollowed out the entire volume of the Federation on their approach vector."

"All the way to Meredith and Diane."

"The headquarters of the Navy and the Federation Council."

"Yep. And here's how they did that."

Sharp walked Pasha over to the list of captains and flags on Meredith.

"See here, Otto? The head of personnel promotions and the head of personnel assignments."

"And their chiefs of staff. Remarkable."

"Oh, yes. Very effective penetration. That's the problem with being an open society. We have nothing like that in Deneb space."

"No. Nothing close."

Pasha sighed.

"All right, Deke. I'll talk to Jurgens."

"Tell him to be careful. He has people in his own office he can't trust. See here and here?"

"Yes. I see."

Pasha stared at the entire display, looking back at all the DNA samples and analysis results.

"Deke?"

"Yes?"

"We have DNA of everyone in D Branch, too, don't we?"

"I think so. Yes."

"Let's run this on D Branch. Let's find out where our problems are."

"If you move against them, Otto, they'll know we're onto them somehow."

"Oh, we won't. Not right yet. But it needs to be part of our plan."

"About that plan. I have some more ideas."

"OK. Back to our offices. I want to hear them."

They logged out of the DV engine and talked for another hour.

When Sharp came out of virtual terminal, Fuller was waiting.

"We have another analysis project," Sharp said.

"Can it wait? Robert was just here to announce dinner."

"After dinner is fine."

Dinner tonight was inside in the dining room. Sharp changed quickly out of 'beach casual' into 'casual' clothes, then followed Fuller down the interior passages to the dining room.

Dinner was on the table, but Trask had held seating everyone until they arrived.

"Sorry I'm late," Sharp said. "I was on the phone to home."

"A productive call, I hope," Trask said.

"Oh, yes."

"Good. It's only been a couple of minutes. Let's be seated, everyone."

Dinner tonight was Italian-themed. They started off with a minestrone soup, once again with fresh bread, this time of a more Italian bent. The entrée was diner's choice, either chicken parmesan or veal parmesan. Sharp took the veal, while Fuller selected the chicken. Sides were rigatoni with a Bolognese sauce and a garden salad with a balsamic vinaigrette dressing. Dessert was tiramisu, while the wine was a flavorful chianti.

As the night before, conversation nearly stopped during dinner. Afterward, Trask, Sharp, and Fuller retired to the patio with cognac and cigars as Janine and Marie left them alone.

"Anything you can tell me, Deke?"

"I'd rather not, Dominic. There is no small amount of danger. I will tell you this, though. The deeper we dig on this thing, the deeper the hole gets. We haven't hit bottom yet."

"So my warning was well founded."

"Oh, yes. The Federation may well hang in the balance."

"As serious as that?"

Sharp nodded. Trask turned to Fuller, and she nodded as well.

"Well, I'm glad I called you, then. I thought about it quite a while, you know, Deke. Before I called you. Be careful when you pull a weapon. It ups the ante all around."

"A weapon, Dominic?"

"Yes. You, my friend, are the weapon."

Once back in the living room of the guest suite, Sharp and Fuller logged into the data visualization engine and loaded a new blank workspace. As before, Sharp handled the machine.

"DV. Load the criteria for determining Deneb-born individuals from the prior workspace."

The illustration of the three markers appeared.

"DV. Load the DNA signatures of all D Branch employees."

"There is a person present who does not have clearance to see this data," DV said.

"DV. Override on my authority."

This was a big dataset, composed of tens of thousands of

individuals.

"My word. D Branch has that many employees?" Fuller asked.

"Oh, yes. Headquarters is pretty big, and we have people splattered around all over the place. DV. Run DNA criteria for Deneb-born individuals against D Branch employee data. List positives separately."

Perhaps a hundred individuals formed another dataset of entries.

"D.K. Look at that."

"Yeah. Not good. DV. List individuals. Add current work assignments. My authority."

They scrolled down the list.

"Some of these people are in the Deneb Republic, D.K."

"Well, that explains why it's so hard to get good actionable intelligence out of the Deneb Republic. More than half the people we have assigned to spy *on* them are working *for* them."

"That sucks," Fuller said as she continued scrolling.

At one point, she stopped.

"Oh, no."

She pointed out an entry. 'Matthew Deckard.'

"Fuck me," Sharp said. "DV. Re-run DNA scan on Matthew Deckard. Confirm prior results."

"Prior results confirmed."

"Shit."

"Now what, D.K?"

"Well, this says he's Deneb-born. Or both parents were. Or all four grandparents. It doesn't say he's in their employ."

Sharp thought about it.

"DV. Analysis on Matthew Deckard financial accounts. Look for outside income. That is, income from some other source than D Branch and common investment accounts. Display results."

"No known outside income sources found for Matthew Deckard."

"DV. Run the same analysis on remaining Deneb-born entries. Separate into three datasets. Known outside income, no known outside income, and financial data not available, in whole or in part."

The dataset of Deneb-born D Branch employees in front of them separated into three groups. Matthew Deckard was in the 'no known outside income' group.

"What about bank accounts we don't know about, D.K? Under an alias or something?"

"DV. Look for people living bigger than their known income would suggest likely. Analyze real estate records, automobile purchases, credit purchases, current loans outstanding, and other financial data. I'm looking for people with an outside source of income we don't see. All three groups. Highlight results."

"Why loans, D.K?"

"If someone likes an expensive car, and he has a big loan on it, it means he didn't pay cash."

"Ah. Right."

Two people in the 'no known sources of outside income' were highlighted. Neither of them was Matthew Deckard. A majority of those with 'financial data not available, in whole or in part' were highlighted. Almost all of the 'known outside income' group were highlighted.

"Geez, D.K. Now what do you do?"

"Turn it all over to Pasha and see what he thinks. But that's a job for tomorrow. I'm pretty beat."

"Yeah. All that time outside. Fresh-air poisoning."

Sharp chuckled. They logged out and got ready for bed.

Later, they discovered they had some remaining energy, after all.

Sharp did send a message to Pasha that evening before bed, and Pasha saw it when he came in the next morning. He logged into the new workspace and surveyed the data.

It was dismaying. A big part of intelligence was counter-intelligence, but no matter how much you did, foreign agents slipped through.

It was something of a tightrope walk. You couldn't disdain counter-intelligence. You would be overrun with foreign agents. Yet you couldn't analyze everyone's financial and personal data at the level Deke Sharp had done on the Deneb-born. You alienated your loyal employees. Made the workplace something that reasonable people with other opportunities left, losing your superstars.

That was why you kept things compartmentalized. Worked within need-to-know guidelines. No one person had the whole picture, about anything.

Pasha looked at where the likely guilty were posted within D Branch. No department heads at least. Damaging enough as it was, though, even with compartmentalization.

"DV. Search all stored communications for all Deneb-born D Branch employees. Highlight employees with significant encrypted message streams."

Yes, that made sense. All those previously identified as likely guilty.

"DV. Beginning with those encrypted message streams with most recent traffic, submit message streams to the factoring engine for decryption."

"Define 'recent.'"

"DV. Two years."

"Submitted to factoring engine."

That would take a while. What else? How else could the Deneb Republic create chaos and promote an ineffective response to invasion?

How about Deneb agents acting under color of law?

"DV. Do we have access to DNA signatures for police on Federation planets?"

"Most of them, yes."

"DV. Import DNA signature data for all police on every planet of the Federation. Differentiate Deneb-born."

Very large datasets began appearing further down the display, one for each planet of the Federation.

"This will take time for a complete analysis. DV can notify you when processing is complete."

"DV. Notify Deke Sharp as well."

Pasha logged out.

When Sharp got up the next morning, he performed all his maintenance chores on his prosthetics. He then went out on the patio to wait for breakfast. Fuller joined him from her shower. She brought out two cups of coffee, setting one down by him.

"Thanks."

"Sure. Anything new?"

"No. I sent Otto a message last night, but he won't have seen it yet. New Destin is still behind us."

"I wonder what he'll think."

"So do I."

The only tide on Elizabeth, like most planets, was due to the local sun. Planets with moons as large as Earth's was, when compared to its primary, were very rare. Now at sunup, the ocean was at slack tide, just heading into flood tide. High tide would be at solar noon, around one in the afternoon here. A couple of feet higher.

They watched as household staff got breakfast ready, then Trask appeared.

"Looks like it's time for breakfast, D.K."

"I'm good. Let's go."

They walked across the patio to the main portion of the patio behind the main house.

"Morning, Dominic."

"Good morning, good morning. How goes it this morning, Deke? Still digging?"

"No bottom in sight yet, Dominic."

"My word."

"Yes, it's a real rat's nest."

Janine and Marie came out, and they all went through the breakfast line. Today it was traditional crepes, as opposed to blintzes, and eggs over easy and coffee cake rather than eggs Benedict. All the other traditional favorites were there, including bacon, toast, and those big Belgian waffles.

After breakfast – with Janine and Marie gone, and the staff clearing the buffet – they sat with their coffee at the big round table.

"Tomorrow is Monday, Deke. We would normally go back into town so I can go into the office, and Janine and Marie can attend to their social activities. You are free to stay here, or go into town with us this evening."

Sharp looked at Fuller, and she shrugged.

"I think I would rather stay here, if that's OK with you, Dominic. I like the security, I like the isolation, and it's closer to my shuttle at the shuttleport. Lots to like, from my point of view."

"That's perfectly OK, Deke. I don't shut the house down when I'm not here. Enjoy yourselves when you're not working.

Just let the staff know anything you need."

"Will do, Dominic. Thank you."

Trask nodded.

"Given that we head back tonight, the big meal today will be luncheon, in the dining room at two."

"We'll see you then."

Trask nodded, and Sharp and Fuller headed back to the guest wing.

"Anything yet, D.K?"

"I would think it's still too early, Suzie."

Sharp checked in virtual terminal. His messages, his files.

"Nope," he said, shaking his head.

"Then I'm going swimming with Marie. She has a raft."

She went in from the patio and changed into a skimpy bikini bottom, with a shirt thrown loosely over. Sharp settled down on one of the chaises on the patio.

Then the most remarkable thing happened. A vehicle – looking for all the world like a wooden swimming raft – drove out from under the patio of the main house. It had four drive wheels with big rubber tires, two of which steered, and two propellers on the rear side. Sharp thought it must be electric, with a basement under the main house to charge and service it.

The thing stopped at the water's edge and the two young women climbed on, then it motored out into the sea. At a hundred feet out, it dropped anchor. The breakwater – perhaps a half-mile out – made the sea behind it pretty calm, so the raft would have no trouble maintaining its position.

The women laughed and jumped off the raft into the water.

Sharp lay back and enjoyed the view of two beautiful, topless young women splashing and diving from the raft.

He drifted off to sleep to the sound of women's laughter echoing off the water.

The Plan

"D.K.," Fuller said as she touched Sharp's shoulder.

"Hmpf? Wha'?" Sharp mumbled as he came awake.

He woke to Fuller's bare breasts hanging over his face.

Nice.

"D.K. You should check on status back home. Has Otto done anything?"

"Oh. Yeah. OK."

Sharp logged into his account and looked at his files. The analysis file on D Branch employees had been modified. He entered the DV workspace, looked around, and then sent a message to Fuller to join him.

"What have you got, D.K? Holy criminy. What's all this?"

"Apparently it's a DNA analysis of every police officer in the Federation."

"And those police forces are riddled with Deneb Republic agents?"

"Looks like. A few of them, anyway."

"Wow. That'll contribute to the overall chaos. Delay a proper response. Confuse everything."

"Absolutely."

"I need to talk to Otto. Some response to this has to be part of the plan."

"Call him in here. I'll hang around."

"OK."

Otto's avatar appeared in the workspace. It was the first time Fuller and Pasha had seen each other, even in a video call. D Branch didn't really have any social events.

"Hi, Deke. Good morning, Ms. Fuller."

"Suzie."

Pasha nodded and turned to Sharp.

"What do you think, Deke?"

"Well, we're going to have to deal with all of this. We need to build our response into the plan."

Pasha nodded.

"So let's review. What all have we got?"

Sharp ticked them off on his fingers.

"First, we have to see them coming. I think we have that covered."

"Agreed."

"Second, we have to follow them, because we won't know where they are going to drop out of the envelope until they start decelerating."

"Right."

"Third, we have to meet them where they drop out, and detain them there until larger, slower forces can arrive."

"Right."

"Fourth, now, we need to clean up D Branch and the police before the ball drops, but without giving them an opportunity to withdraw their force to try again later."

"And how do we do that?"

"Once they're in the envelope, I think we can move against their people here. I don't think they can communicate to their fleet in the envelope. That would give us days – probably weeks – to pick up all of these people. We probably don't need to start that until their fleet crosses into Federation space."

Sharp waved at the display in the workspace, and Pasha nodded.

"I think that covers it, Deke."

"What do we do afterwards, Otto?" Fuller asked. "Do we space to the Deneb Republic and teach them a lesson?"

"That's not part of our assignment here, Suzie. That would have to come from the High Commissioner."

"And what's his position?"

"We don't know yet, because we haven't told him anything about this."

"Really? Nothing?"

"No. The only people who know anything are the three of us and Claude Allard. Unless you've told Dominic Trask?"

Pasha looked at Sharp, and Sharp shook his head.

"No, Otto. Just that his warning was justified. That there is something very serious going on."

"OK. So it's just us for now. The police chiefs and Admiral Jurgens will be told once their fleet is in motion and it crosses into Federation space. Not before. There's too much chance that it will leak."

"Wow."

"There's no reason to say anything, Suzie," Sharp said. "There is no policy decision involved. Our standing orders are to protect the Federation against espionage and invasion. If we told the High Commissioner, he would just tell us to counter the invasion. That's what we're doing anyway. Telling him just gives another potential leak, from his staff or something. There's no guarantee we have all the Deneb Republic spies uncovered."

"I suppose, D.K. It just seems like an awful lot of responsibility to assume."

Sharp shrugged.

"That's the job. That's always been the job."

"Deke's right, Suzie. I'll note that Claude has not told me to inform higher of what's going on. Not yet."

Fuller looked back at the display before them and sighed.

"What a mess."

"I have another question for you, Otto," Sharp said.

He highlighted the entry of Matthew Deckard among those D Branch employees who were Deneb-born but who had apparently not been receiving payments from the Deneb Republic.

"What about Matt Deckard?"

"Him I'm not worried about, Deke. Parents were a bit too outspoken against the regime. They were arrested when he was a toddler and tortured. His mother was released, but his father was released only after nearly ten years in a work camp.

"The Federation took them in as political refugees. His father, a broken man, died a few years after they got here. Not unlike your case, D Branch recognized his talent and sent him to college. There's no one more loyal to the Federation."

"I see. Well, that's good. I would hate to lose him."

"No need, Deke. Plus, there's a little wrinkle I hadn't yet told you about."

Sharp raised an eyebrow, and Pasha shrugged.

"There is a demolition aboard every Medea-class ship. Built into the engines. It's on its own communications channel. If someone goes rogue with a Medea-class ship, we can just blow it up."

Sharp stared at him, while Fuller laughed. Sharp looked at her and then back to Pasha.

"On *Medea* as well?"

"Oh, yes."

"And you never told me about it?"

"It never came up."

Sharp's look was priceless, and Fuller was in full giggle now.

"Look. Deke. We were dealing with pirates then. In Navy ships. The Navy was happy to let us design our own ships, but the problem with a one-man ship of that power is, What do you do if your agent goes rogue? Is a double agent and you don't know? So we built in a little safeguard."

"And who has the communications channel and the codes?"

"I do. Just me. I set the codes and no one else knows them. They're not recorded anywhere."

"But you could blow up any D Branch ship anywhere, at any time."

"Yes. Of course. It's always been that way, Deke."

Sharp's face had sort of a congealed look.

"OK, Otto. We'll catch you later. It's time for lunch here."

"OK, Deke. See you. Bye, Suzie."

"Bye, Otto."

They all logged out. Fuller looked at Sharp on the other chaise. He still had the congealed look on his face. Fuller laughed again.

"Get over it, D.K. You think they weren't going to have a way to disable a Medea-class ship to rein in a rogue agent?"

"I suppose, Suzie. Just a bit of a surprise, is all."

"Well, it shouldn't have been. C'mon. Let's go join our hosts for lunch before they all head back to the city."

It was just before two in the afternoon when they arrived in the dining room. The glass wall was open to the patio and the ocean beyond.

"Deke. Suzie. Come on in. Let's be seated, everybody."

They were seated around the table as always, with Trask at the head of the table, Sharp to his right and his wife to his left. Fuller sat next to Sharp, and Marie sat next to Janine.

Sunday lunch was like a dinner most nights. Today's appetizer was lobster bisque with fresh bread. The entrée was baked salmon, slow baked in aluminum foil on the grill and served with a lemon vinaigrette. New potatoes and a garden salad rounded out the meal, served with a solid full-bodied Chardonnay. Lemon meringue pie was the dessert.

"Thanks for showing me the gym, Marie. I'm going to need it."

"And you can take the raft out as well, Suzie. Swimming is great exercise."

With dinner over, Janine and Marie went to pack. Trask, Sharp, and Fuller went out on the patio. Robert served cognac and cigars.

"You were a little subdued at dinner, Deke."

"Just a lot on my mind, Dominic."

"I know you can't tell me much if anything about what you are finding, Deke, but I will ask you this. If there is anything I absolutely must know, or if there is any way I can help, you will be in touch, all right?"

"That I can promise, Dominic. We owe you one."

"I can live with that. And now, let's enjoy the afternoon before I must be off to the city. It's three hours in the car, and we mustn't arrive too late."

"I'm surprised you don't take a helicopter, Dominic."

"It doesn't save that much time, Deke, and it's expensive. More to the point, however, I read in the car, catching up for the week ahead, and I can't read while in the air. It would actually cost me time."

Sharp nodded.

It was a pleasant afternoon, with a sea-salt breeze off the ocean, and cigars and cognac on the patio was delightful.

Sharp and Fuller saw the Trasks off at the front entry of the main house. There were handshakes and hugs. Then they went back to their suite in the guest wing.

About a half hour later, Robert the butler showed up.

"Yes, Robert."

"I was wondering, sir, what your meal preferences would be. Normally, the master of the house makes his selections well in advance, but you will be our sole guests here until Friday evening."

Sharp looked across to Fuller, who came to the door.

"We have simple tastes, Robert. As much as we enjoy Mr. Trask's elaborate meals as an occasional thing, simpler fare is our normal diet. With the master of the house gone, I suspect whatever you are making for staff will be fine with us. Just make enough for two extra diners."

Robert nodded.

"Steaks, chops, Italian, ma'am? Perhaps pot roast. A garden salad. A soup and bread. Some small sweets for dessert. Hot sandwiches for lunch. A subset of the normal breakfast choices."

"All of that sounds fine, Robert."

"We can also serve you here – either indoors or out – if you would prefer it to the main dining room or the main patio, ma'am."

"That would be wonderful, Robert. Saves us the walk."

"Very good, ma'am. Sir. Thank you for the guidance."

He nodded and left. Sharp closed the door behind him.

"We could probably just eat with the staff, for that matter, Suzie."

"No, D.K. Never mess with someone else's household staff. Notice I just said 'simpler fare' and agreed with whatever he said after that."

Sharp nodded. He had no experience with household staff situations. Fuller clearly did. He wondered where she had picked it up.

It Begins

Michael 'Red' Tucker drew a beer and took it down to the chief petty officer sitting at the bar. There were perhaps a dozen people in the bar this evening, all service members. The chief was a regular.

"Thanks, Red."

"No problem, Chief."

Tucker looked around the bar.

"Sure is quiet for a weekend night."

"Yeah. The Navy canceled all planet leave couple days back."

"Some alert or something, Chief?"

"Nah. Some bullshit. Maneuvers or somethin'. That's all it ever is."

"And you're immune?"

"Yeah. I'm not ship-based. I got outta that shit."

Tucker nodded.

"Lucky you."

"Yeah."

Once he got home, Tucker turned on his coffee machine and made himself a cup of coffee. While it was on, he sent a message.

For the coffee machine contained an extra feature, a quantum entanglement radio. He would be executed if the Deneb Secret Police ever discovered it.

For Red Tucker was a D Branch agent, and had been living in the Deneb Republic, tending bar near the navy base on Gloucester, for nearly twenty years.

The deep agents in D Branch were not under operations. Operations handled the field operatives. The deep agents were handled by the intelligence group. Just one more way to compartmentalize information within the organization.

Pasha had advised analysis to discount the reports received from suspect agents within the Deneb Republic, and rely on the reports received from those agents within the Deneb Republic who were not Deneb-born.

Several of those agents had noticed canceled or reduced planet leave for Deneb Navy ship's crews, and had reported it.

Pasha put in a call request to Deke Sharp.

Sharp got the call request the Wednesday of his second full week at Trask's beach house.

"Hi, Deke."

"Hi, Otto. What's going on?"

"It's started, Deke. They've recalled crews to their ships."

"Preparatory to departure?"

"That's what it looks like. It's probably time to start the plan."

"Can I see the intelligence, Otto?"

"Of course. Here's the pointer."

"Thanks, Otto."

"Sure, Deke. From this point out it's all reactive, I think, and the point organization is operations. It's on you. Just let me know anything you need."

"Got it. Thanks, Otto."

Pasha nodded and cut the connection.

Sharp checked the data and couldn't fault Pasha's conclusions. It was a recall of crews to their ships over a broad cross-section of navy facilities in the Deneb Republic. All reliable, non-Deneb-born sources.

Most of the Deneb-born sources, of course, reported nothing out of the ordinary was going on. Yawn, move along, nothing to see here stuff.

Sharp nodded, then placed a call request to Larry 'Berk' Berkshire and Theodore 'Ted' Lanham, both D Branch field operatives, for a conference call. Both accepted right away.

"Hi, Berk. Ted."

"Hi, Deke."

"Everything I will tell you on this call is being held closely at the highest level."

That got raised eyebrows. Such warnings were unusual in D Branch, because they were understood. To say it explicitly raised the stakes. Sharp continued.

"The Deneb Republic has launched, or is in the process of launching, an invasion of the Federation with the intent of overturning the Federation government and installing a police state. This is not speculation.

"The Deneb Republic has highly placed operatives in D Branch, the Federation Navy, and Federation police forces who are expected to disrupt operations here to assist this goal. As a consequence of that, your orders will come only from me or Otto for the duration of this event."

Sharp looked up, and both field operatives nodded. That precaution only made sense given what Sharp had said.

"The two of you are to man a picket to detect the Deneb Republic fleet when and where it crosses into Federation space. Berk, you are to take *Acala*, and Ted, you are to take *Baldr*, to set up this picket. You will circle in place, just inside Federation space. You will do this while in the envelope. I will send the spacing plans to you.

"When the Deneb Republic fleet is seen, you will follow

them, while keeping D Branch informed of their location and course via the envelope communications system. Those messages will be encrypted, as detailed in your spacing plan. We don't normally encrypt envelope communications, because only D Branch has it, but this time we are, because we believe we have Deneb agents in D Branch.

"While Otto and I both appreciate the initiative and operational flexibility field operatives use to accomplish their missions, this is not the time for either. That time will come, but not for this portion of the mission.

"Do you both understand these instructions?"

"Yes, Deke. Got it," Berkshire said.

"I'm with you, Deke," Lanham said.

"Very good. You should space within the week. Be sure to inventory your supplies against a potentially long space deployment. It may be several months before the fleet arrives in Federation space, after which point you will be involved in the response.

"That is all, gentlemen. Good spacing."

"Thanks, Deke."

"See you, Deke."

Berkshire and Lanham independently reviewed their spacing plans. Both were surprised by their instructions.

The two ships were to travel to the envelope at their maximum acceleration, then space to the Deneb-Federation border. There they would convert their forward velocity into a circular orbit, maintaining acceleration toward the center. While in the envelope, and at the velocity they would have achieved by that time, their circular orbit would be some ten light-years across. They would arrange their two circular orbits to be twenty light-years apart.

The axis of rotation of those orbits would be parallel to the Federation-Deneb border, so they would form two giant circles in space, looking like wheels of a vehicle bound for Deneb. This meant that achieving and then breaking from that circular orbit would not require they make a high-speed turn to right or left. They would go into the orbit heading away from the Federation, and leave the orbit headed back toward it, at the tangent velocity of the orbit.

This would ensure that the Deneb Republic fleet, itself at high velocity by that point, could not outpace them.

While it was difficult to impossible to accurately determine the position or course of a vessel in the envelope – the envelope itself sent ripples and echoes across spacetime – it got easier as a vessel approached.

Such a large disturbance as dozens of envelopes approaching would also be easier to localize. Both ships should see them coming. Using the sensor readings from both ships, so far apart, would allow D Branch headquarters to more precisely determine location and course.

Berkshire and Lanham were both currently on Ariel. They tidied up their personal affairs for a long deployment, then called down the shuttles from their assigned D Branch ships. Within four days of Deke's call, they were both aboard their ships and adjusting inventory to their liking for a months-long deployment.

Within six days of Deke's call, both ships were accelerating to the envelope at their boat flank speed. They hit the envelope within hours and set course for the frontier, almost four weeks' spacing away.

When Deke got off the call with Berkshire and Lanham that Wednesday, Robert was just setting out dinner on the small dining table on the patio of the guest suite. Tonight was pot roast and mashed potatoes with brown gravy, a garden salad, and apple pie. By some quirk of fate, it was comfort food, well chosen to fit Sharp's mood.

"Well, it's started," he said to Fuller as they sat down.

"Really?"

"Yes. Their fleet is assembling. Or has already assembled and left. We're not quite sure of the timing there."

"And you've set the plan in motion?"

"Yes. Pickets will leave Ariel within the week."

"Excellent."

They were quiet during dinner. After dinner, staff came with a bus cart, bused the table, and left. Sharp and Fuller sat alone on the chaises on the patio.

"Why, Suzie?"

"Why what, D.K? Why set pickets?"

"No. Why does the Deneb Republic space against us? Why can't they just leave us alone?"

"We challenge them, Deke."

"How?"

"How does a police state justify its existence, D.K? 'If it weren't for us controlling things, everything would sink into chaos and you would be lost.' And the counter? 'Well, what about them?' Our mere existence challenges their own justification for their control."

"And if they pull us down?"

"Then they say, 'See. We told you. That system can't work.' It's crab mentality, D.K. If one crab tries to crawl out of the bucket, the others will pull it back."

"They'll pull us down to their level to prove we aren't better than they are."

"Of course."

"But we are better than they are."

"Of course, we are, D.K. That's why you'll succeed in defeating them."

"You sound so certain."

"I'm positive. Oh, they could have sucker-punched us if we didn't see them coming, and that would have made it messier and harder. But the fact is, we did see them coming. Or Dominic Trask saw it. And he called you. That's the point."

"I don't get you, Suzie."

"Dominic Trask saw it coming. Saw the options buys. Predicated on something bad happening to the Federation. Did he wonder, 'How could I make this work for me?' No. He called you. If there was a threat to the Deneb Republic, would someone there have called the secret police and told them about it? Hmm?"

"OK. I think I see."

"We're a better system, D.K., which means we have antibodies. People like Dominic Trask, and Otto Pasha, and you, who are looking out for the system. Who think it's better than other systems, and who will intercede for it. The Deneb Republic doesn't have them. Not like we do."

"So we'll win."

"Of course. Because our system is worth dying for, and theirs isn't. It's just that simple."

Trask and his family came out to the beach house that Friday night, as they had the two previous weekends Sharp and Fuller had been there.

That night, Sharp and Fuller came to the salon early, well before dinner. Trask was there with a cognac. He greeted them and waved them to the bar. When Sharp and Fuller sat down, he gave Sharp a piercing look.

"It's started, hasn't it, Deke? Whatever it is?"

"Yes, Dominic. It's started."

"And you can't tell me what it is?"

"Not yet. Another month or two."

"But I will know ahead of time? Before it comes to a head?"

"Yes, Dominic. I can promise you that. But not yet. There's too much in play right now."

"All right, Deke. I can live with that."

Janine and Marie showed up then, and business talk was off the table.

Later that evening, after dinner – which had been a rich beef bourguignon – over cognac and cigars on the patio, Fuller was curious.

"Dominic, how did you know things were underway?"

"Deke will never be a good poker player, Suzie. His tells are too obvious, at least if you know him at all well."

Trask turned to Sharp.

"I assume you've programmed your avatar to ignore your tells?"

"Yes. Of course."

Trask nodded.

"Smart."

He turned back to Fuller.

"For communications, Deke's avatar masks his tells. But, in person, I can read him now, at least on something as large as this. Something is weighing on him, as if his attention isn't fully in the moment. As if he's on watch."

"Interesting," Fuller said. "Thanks, Dominic."

"Of course."

"I had another question for you, Dominic," Sharp said.

"Yes?"

"Can I move my shuttle here? You do have a helipad, which is usable as a shuttle pad as well. When the ball drops, I would be advantaged by having the shuttle closer to me. And I can make sure my equipment is ready at my leisure."

"Of course, Deke. Go ahead. I don't use the helipad much. I'm seldom in such a hurry, and I don't care for helicopters much."

"Thanks, Dominic. It's a small thing, but small things may make a difference in what lies ahead."

The next day, Saturday, Sharp instructed *Medea* to warm up the shuttle, then he remotely piloted it to the beach house. The shuttle came down lightly on the helipad, which was a short walk from the house.

The helipad was made with a concrete dyed grass-green, so as to provide the least visual disruption of the large lawn in front of the house.

Trask, for his part, was interested in his new lawn ornament, and Sharp gave him a tour of the shuttle once it had landed and the pad had cooled down.

"Pretty Spartan," Trask said as he looked around the cabin.

"It's just for getting back and forth to orbit. Anything extra you carry, you have to lift. And it's going to what is effectively a one-man ship."

"Understood, Deke. Yet you had a number of people on the ship last time, yes?"

"Seven. Four adults and three children. We used the two shuttles as extra bedrooms."

"Two shuttles? On a one-man ship?"

"Redundancy, Dominic. One needs to be able to get to the planet, even if a shuttle fails."

"Yes. Of course. That makes sense."

Trask looked around one more time.

"Well, thanks, Deke. I've never traveled in space, and I was just curious to see it."

"You've never traveled in space, Dominic?"

"Oh, no," Trask said, shuddering. "I don't even like helicopters. Besides, one cannot do business while in the envelope. How would one keep an eye on one's investments?"

Sharp chuckled.

Trask might be stupidly wealthy, but he was also, in some ways, stupidly parochial.

First Contact

Weeks passed. This was not unexpected, as it would take weeks for the pickets to be in place.

It also took some time to muster a fleet and get it under way, plus the fleet had to achieve the envelope at no more than fleet flank speed, and space some way toward the border, before the pickets might see them approaching.

Sharp and Fuller remained in the guest suite of the guest wing of Dominic Trask's beach house, some three hours by car outside the capital city of Gotham on the planet Meredith.

Sharp and Fuller enjoyed having the estate to themselves during the week. They swam and sunned, and enjoyed the simpler meals prepared by the staff for guests and staff both.

Dominic Trask, his wife Janine, and his daughter Marie joined them every weekend from Friday evening until Sunday evening. Marie and Fuller went horseback riding and swimming on the weekends, with Sharp an appreciative observer from shore.

Sharp also made sure the shuttle was good to go at a moment's notice, and that all his weapons, devices, and prosthetics were in top condition.

It was as quiet and idyllic an existence as one could have while waiting for war to descend on the Federation.

That all changed in the ninth week of Sharp and Fuller's presence on Meredith, the second week of the pickets being in place and watching for the approach of the enemy.

Ted Lanham reflected that this had to be the most ludicrous assignment ever. His assigned ship, FNS *Baldr*, accelerated continuously toward the center of a huge circle, ten light-years in diameter. At the tangent velocity he had achieved before arriving at the frontiers of Federation space in four weeks of spacing, *Baldr* traveled the thirty-two light-year circumference of that circle every twelve hours.

Lanham was going very fast, and getting nowhere in a hurry.

But, that was the assignment. That and scanning envelope space continuously, looking for the Deneb Republic fleet or messages from D Branch.

No messages came, and no fleet showed up. He and *Baldr* just went around and around.

Lanham had brought plenty of reading and viewing material, and he whiled away the days, waiting for something to happen.

At least, with the ship under acceleration, he had gravity.

Lanham had been on picket just over two weeks when an alarm interrupted his reading. He switched channels in his virtual terminal processor to the message center to check on an incoming message, but there was no message.

The alarm sounded again. Wait. That was the scanning alarm.

Lanham switched channels to the scanning system. There, just to the right of center in his field, a large, fuzzy image was circled.

Of course, at any range, it would be large and fuzzy. Trying to locate anything in envelope space was very difficult, because the waves and echoes of an envelope bounced all over the place. Only as it got closer would it resolve.

This had resolved somewhat already, to be a single fuzzy image. That resolution was what had triggered the alarm.

Whatever it was, it was getting closer or it wouldn't be getting more localized.

Lanham requested the bearing to the center of the fuzzy object from the center of his orbit, and *Baldr*'s navigation system returned the vector.

Lanham encrypted the bearing per instructions, and transmitted it via the envelope communications system to D Branch.

It was early Tuesday morning when Sharp received the notification of an encrypted message from the envelope communications system.

That woke him up. D Branch operatives never encrypted messages in the envelope communications system, because only D Branch ships could pick up the signal. If it was encrypted it could only mean one thing.

A message from Lanham or Berkshire.

"What is it?" Fuller asked as Sharp rolled out of bed.

"It's show time."

"No shit."

Sharp began servicing his prosthetics while Fuller went out to the kitchen and started the espresso machine. With two espressos made, she passed Sharp coming out of the bathroom.

A quick shower, dressed, and Fuller took her espresso out onto the patio where Sharp already had his sitting on the table. He was in virtual terminal.

Sharp dropped out of virtual terminal, picked up his espresso, and sipped. He turned to her.

"Not much yet. A single bearing of an envelope beginning to resolve. From Lanham."

"So it's getting close to the pickets."

"Oh, yes. Oops. There's another alarm. That one's likely

Berkshire."

Sharp went back into virtual terminal, then dropped back out.

"Yep. A bearing now from Berkshire as well. Still fuzzy as hell, though."

Fuller stared out to the ocean as she sipped her coffee. Wait. Something on the edge of her brain. What was it? Oh. Oh!

"D.K., I thought the point of having two pickets twenty light-years apart was to gain aperture."

"Well, yes, but this is really early, Suzie."

"Let's check. Join me in DV."

They both logged into a blank workspace in D Branch's data visualization engine. Sharp started off.

"DV. Import bearings and known locations of D Branch picket ships *Baldr* and *Acala* from file Tracking."

"File locked. Eyes only. There is another person present."

"DV. My authority."

The raw numbers appeared in an entry in front of them. Fuller took over the analysis from here.

"DV. Use coordinates and bearings to generate three-dimensional display."

A black void opened in front of them. There were the two picket ships, there the vectors of the two bearings. The picket ship orbits were shown as dashed circles. The two bearings almost intersected.

"DV. Show stars within this volume. Label the stars."

The black void filled with stars, hundreds of them.

"DV. Begin vector at Deneb Republic's largest naval base, pass that vector through the near-intersection of the two bearings, and project into Federation space."

A line appeared, from much deeper in the volume of the display, passed through a small volume that both bearings passed though, and toward them.

"DV. Back display out to show Federation space. Label Federation planets."

The previous portion of the display moved away from them, and Federation space filled in between them and the picket ships. The vector from the Deneb Republic's largest naval base, through the intersection volume, and into Federation space, halted at a planet.

"There you go, D.K."

"Meredith."

"Looks like."

"Makes sense, Suzie. Take out the Navy first, then go after the government unopposed."

"Now what, D.K?"

"Start arresting people, I think."

"Well, let's see how much time we have."

She pitched her voice to the machine again.

"DV. Assume Deneb Republic Navy ships have the same acceleration profiles as Federation Navy ships. Assume Deneb Republic Navy ships at intersection volume of the two bearings as of the time the bearings were reported. Display travel times along the vector shown assuming departure from Deneb Republic's largest naval base. Project travel time to Meredith."

A set of tick marks with dates appeared along the vector.

"Assuming velocity obtained from continuous acceleration at Federation Navy acceleration rates from Deneb Republic's largest naval base on Gloucester to Meredith, arrival at Meredith will be in twenty-five days."

"Boy, they're clocking right along," Sharp said. "It took our pickets four weeks to get out there, at twice the acceleration."

"But that's including the slower first part, D.K. The rest of their trip to Meredith is at their current velocity and above."

"True enough. And our pickets kept their velocity, they just turned it into tangent velocity."

Sharp nodded, then considered.

"DV. Will the picket ships at their current tangent velocities be able to keep up with the Deneb Republic Navy ships when they pass along that vector?"

"Yes. The picket ships' tangential velocity will be approximately thirty percent higher than the velocity of the Deneb Republic Navy ships when they pass."

Sharp nodded. Good. Just one more question. Sharp asked this one.

"DV. When will the Deneb Republic Navy ships pass into Federation space?"

"At approximately noon on Saturday."

After Deke Sharp brought him up to speed on the detection and their analysis of it, Otto Pasha called Admiral Kurt Jurgens, Chief of Naval Operations of the Federation Navy.

"Hi, Otto. What's up?" Jurgens asked.

"Hi, Kurt. Some serious business today. This call will serve as a war warning."

"What?"

"We have detected a sizable naval force of the Deneb Republic spacing toward the Federation. We believe its target is Meredith."

Jurgens reoriented himself quickly.

"Arrival time?"

"They will arrive in Federation space about noon Saturday, with arrival at Meredith three weeks later."

Jurgens was doing mental arithmetic on travel times and disposition of forces.

He nodded.

"There's more, Kurt. D Branch, the Navy, and Federation police forces have been infiltrated by Deneb Republic agents. We have a list of these agents, for immediate arrest. They will otherwise try to disrupt or confuse your response."

"That I want."

Pasha nodded.

"Deke Sharp will be handling D Branch's response to the incursion and coordinating with you. He is head of operations for this event, while I am handling the agency-level issues. Sharp has the current Navy list for you, as well as location and bearing of the Deneb Republic forces."

"All right, Otto. Thanks."

"No problem, Kurt. You take care."

"Deke Sharp."

"Hello, Mr. Sharp. Kurt Jurgens here."

"Good afternoon, Admiral."

"Otto Pasha has just filled me in. I understand you have some data for me. Mr. Sharp."

"Deke will do, Admiral. Yes. I have the location and bearing of the Deneb forces. We do not have size of the force yet. I also have a list of Federation senior officers who should be removed of command and detained pending investigation."

Sharp sent the information, and Jurgens looked over the list.

"These are all Deneb agents, Deke?"

"We're not sure, Admiral. They are all Deneb-born. That's from a DNA analysis, and it is positive. If they did not disclose their correct birth location or ancestry on their Navy records, I would assume they are agents. For the current emergency, were it me, I would detain them all pending a later investigation."

Jurgens nodded.

"That seems wise. And you will keep me updated?"

"Yes, Admiral."

"Call me Kurt, Deke. How did you detect the Deneb fleet?"

"We were given a heads up by someone who noted something fishy in the options markets here on Elizabeth. We currently have two D Branch ships set as pickets on our frontier with the Deneb Republic. They detected the incoming envelopes. Still fuzzy, but as they get closer, we will be able to refine our estimates."

"All right, Deke. I'll talk to you soon."

"Good luck, Kurt."

Immediate Response

A lieutenant commander with an MP armband entered the flag bridge of the attack-ship carrier FNS *Indomitable*. He had four non-com MPs with him.

"Yes?" Rear Admiral Charles Beeman asked.

"If you would come with me, Admiral."

"Am I being arrested?"

"You are being detained, Sir, on the orders of Admiral Jurgens."

"Ridiculous."

"Nevertheless, Sir."

"Oh, very well."

The lieutenant commander turned to Beeman's chief of staff, Captain Jacques Cotillard.

"You as well, Commodore. If you would come with me, please."

The MPs led the two officers from the flag bridge to their quarters.

"You are both confined to quarters pending further instructions from Admiral Jurgens."

Beeman, shaking his head, went on into his quarters. Cotillard did, too, though without the theater. The MPs closed the sliding doors on their compartments, posted a guard on each, and departed.

Cotillard looked at the door control panel next to the door, and noted the inside door controls had been remotely overridden and were inoperative.

He tried his virtual terminal processor, and he had access to the ship's library, but all of the comm channels leading off-ship were blocked. He checked for his disguised quantum-entanglement radio to the Deneb Republic, and it was missing. Someone had searched his quarters before confining him.

Cotillard knew what it was about, of course, and so did Beeman. It wouldn't make any difference. The battle group was on unscheduled – and unauthorized – exercises well clear of the Deneb Republic Navy's advance. They were three weeks from anywhere.

If the Federation had seen the Deneb Republic fleet, it was already too late to move them into position.

They had done their part.

It only remained to be seen whether they would be shot for treason.

Captain Alan Corliss, flag captain of the FNS *Indomitable*, was sitting in his command chair listening to the routine hum of the bridge around him.

The lieutenant at the communications station turned to him.

"Sir. Priority One message from Navy Headquarters. Patching to you."

Corliss raised an eyebrow. He didn't think he had ever received a Priority One message before. Surely he'd remember.

It was encrypted. He decrypted the message with his private key and read:

> ***** **THIS IS A WAR WARNING.** *****
> **RADM Beeman and CAPT Cotillard have been removed from command and confined to quarters on suspicion of espionage. CAPT Corliss is in command of BG-14. The elements of BG-14 are to proceed ASAP at boat flank speed to Meredith. All ships are to be at battle stations when dropping out of the envelope,**

prepared to engage ships of the Deneb Republic that may already be on scene. Elements of BG-14 arriving at Meredith are to place themselves under the command of VADM Chester Matthews.

Well, there's something you didn't see every day. It must have shown on his face, as his first officer, Commander William Monroe, was looking at him quizzically. Corliss motioned him over.

"That was a war warning, Bill. We're to space to Meredith at boat flank speed."

"*Boat* flank speed."

"Yeah. The Deneb Republic. And Beeman and Cotillard are confined to quarters on suspicion of espionage."

"Well, that explains unscheduled maneuvers out of our patrol position."

"Indeed it does. How long to Meredith?"

Monroe shrugged.

"Three weeks? Something like that."

"Let's see if we can't beat that. Get the ship ready to go soonest while I pass on orders."

"Aye, Sir."

Corliss added his own orders to the end of the headquarters message: 'Proceed independently to Meredith at your best speed. Note battle stations directive. – Corliss.' He then re-encrypted the message with the public keys of the battle group's other captains.

He also composed a reply to headquarters, consisting of their departure coordinates and a simple 'Wilco.' Will Comply. There was nothing else to say, really.

Corliss walked over to the communications station while the first officer had everybody else busy.

"Four to go, Lieutenant. Priority One."

The lieutenant gulped.

"Aye, Sir."

Corliss sent him the messages, then went back to his command chair and watched his command prepare to space.

Battle Group 14 was composed of four ships: the attack-ship carrier FNS *Indomitable,* the battle cruiser FNS *Callisto,* and the destroyers FNS *Mace* and FNS *Saber.* It was a small ship complement, but a lot of power for all that, and the typical complement of a battle group in the Federation Navy. By now, people would be scrambling to get underway on all four ships.

Damn Beeman and Cotillard to hell. The battle group was out of position, with no way to intervene, and three weeks' spacing from Meredith. Well, they would make what speed they could, and hope to help out.

A call request came in from Captain Morton Sprigg, the captain of *Callisto.* Slower than *Indomitable,* and much slower than *Mace* and *Saber,* she would be last to arrive at Meredith.

"This is a hell of a thing, Alan."

"Yeah. And Beeman took us out of position to help out his buddies."

"That's true then?"

"MPs show him in custody. Confined to quarters."

"Damn."

Sprigg ran his hand through his hair and sighed.

"Well, leave some for us, Alan. We'll get there as soon as we can."

Corliss nodded.

"See you at the party, Mort."

Otto Pasha also called the Attorney General of the Federation Department of Justice. Claude Allard had introduced Pasha months back as his replacement as head of D Branch, and D Branch and the FDoJ had worked well together in the past, so it was not a call out of the blue.

Pasha turned over Sharp's list of police officers suspected of being Deneb Republic agents within the police forces of various planets and cities within the Federation.

The Attorney General, for his part, sent each list to the appropriate agency, with a request to arrest and hold them on pending Federation charges.

Police typically protected each other. It was a difficult and dangerous job, and mistakes were sometimes made, but they would defend each other against potentially career-ending mistakes, even egregious ones. The thin blue line held.

With one exception. Espionage on behalf of a foreign power.

When the Federation Department of Justice called for the arrest of police officers on suspicion of espionage on behalf of the Deneb Republic, whose navy was even now entering Federation space, most local and planetary cop shops didn't hesitate.

Almost all of the police officers and officials on the lists were arrested within days, and detained pending investigation of their finances and communications.

One police chief hesitated, and his assistant chief released the list to the rank and file anyway. They arrested everyone on the list. When the annoyed police chief threatened disciplinary action against his assistant chief, a police captain suggested that perhaps the finances and communications of the chief should be investigated, and the matter was quietly dropped.

Arrests of the suspicious Deneb-born in D Branch were mostly at headquarters. There were just a few arrests of local resources, especially on Diane, Meredith, and Elizabeth, the political, military, and financial centers of the Federation.

The arrests at headquarters were handled by sealing the building and then arresting everyone on the list. One person was home sick that day, and they were arrested once the building was sealed.

The arrests of local resources were put in motion once headquarters personnel were locked in.

By the close of business on Friday afternoon, all of the suspicious Deneb-born on Sharp and Fuller's lists had been confined or detained. Almost a thousand people.

Even at that, Sharp didn't think they had turned up them all. There had to be agents of the Deneb Republic that didn't show up on their lists. They simply didn't have DNA signatures on everyone in the Federation. Not by a long shot.

But local and planetary police now knew what was going on. They knew that the police they had arrested so far couldn't be all the foreign agents in the Federation. They would be watching for disruptions to aid the invasion.

So would D Branch and the military.

It was the best they could do.

Trask, Janine, and Marie arrived at the beach house Friday evening, as usual. Perhaps a little earlier than normal. It looked like Trask had left his offices in the city before the rush hour, rather than wait until it was over.

Robert arrived to advise them of before-dinner drinks in the salon, and Sharp and Fuller followed him down the hall to the main house.

When they arrived, Trask saw the looks on their faces and became concerned.

"Deke, is everything OK?"

"Yes, Dominic. And I can finally tell you what's going on. It will take a while, though, so that conversation is perhaps best left until after dinner."

"All right, Deke. As long as everything is OK."

"It should be. Here's hoping."

Janine and Marie arrived and they turned to polite conversation. What each had done that week, with Sharp and Fuller leaving out their work activities.

Dinner tonight was what Trask called luau pork chops, sautéed with a teriyaki sauce and crushed pineapple. Sides were fried apple slices and new potatoes, with a Caesar salad. The fruity character of a Gamay wine was a good fit, while dessert was a haupia pie, the pudding filling made with coconut milk and topped off with a chocolate drizzle and whipped cream.

It all fit well with the semi-tropical climate and the fresh ocean smell drifting in through the open window wall.

"Dominic, we've been here well over a month, and your kitchen continues to amaze us," Fuller said.

Trask beamed at the compliment.

"I like to eat well, there's no doubt about it. And Georges is a great chef. I stole him from one of my competitors."

"But of course," Sharp said.

Trask laughed.

"He didn't feel appreciated there. Here, he does, because he is appreciated here."

Janine and Marie left, and Trask, Sharp, and Fuller went out on the patio for cognac and cigars. Robert served them, then closed up the window wall to the dining room to keep the smoke from drifting into the house.

"All right, Deke. I've been a good boy. Very patient, all in all. What's going on?"

"Do you want me to jump to the conclusion, Dominic, or do you want the story?"

"Oh, I want the story, Deke. We have the time."

Sharp nodded.

"First, we took your options data, and filled in the account name and address and the reconciliation account."

"Yes. I couldn't access those."

"Many of those names and addresses were fake, but many of the reconciliation accounts – the ones with the fake names and addresses – were to banks in the Deneb Republic."

"Not surprising. One has to have bank transfers between us and the other star nations in order to balance books when trading with them. Watch those guys, though, Deke. I don't trust the Deneb Republic. I don't do business with them. They're too slippery for an honest businessman."

"Understood, Dominic. But why would people in the Deneb Republic be buying options as a bet against the Federation? And the accounts that didn't have fake names and addresses were people here in the Federation. In our own Navy."

"Ouch. People in cahoots with the Deneb Republic?"

"Yes. I began to suspect there could be an invasion from them. That the Deneb Republic was, once again, growing militarily adventurous. And that some of our people were Deneb agents."

"Makes sense."

"So we posted pickets on the border to watch for any incursion."

"Smart."

"Then we went looking for a DNA signature for those born in the Deneb Republic."

"That was my idea," Fuller said.

Trask looked at her, then back to Deke.

"Some uniqueness?" he asked. "Some genetic drift?"

"Yes, exactly. We had the DNA signatures of people we absolutely knew were born in the Deneb Republic, and we compared them to those of people we absolutely knew were born in the Federation. And we found a unique combination of markers."

"No shit. That's surprising to me, Deke."

"Yes, Dominic. I agree. But it's there."

"And now you can identify Deneb Republic agents."

"With two caveats, yes. One is that being Deneb-born does not make you their agent. We need to look at their finances and communications logs and the like. The second is that we don't have DNA signatures for everybody in the Federation. We do have, however, DNA signatures for all planetary and local police, all military servicemen, and everyone in D Branch."

Trask nodded.

"So you ran them all. What did you find?"

"Almost a thousand agents in D Branch, the Navy, and the police."

"Fuck me."

Trask turned to Fuller.

"Sorry."

She shrugged. Not like she hadn't heard it before.

Trask turned back to Sharp.

"So now what, Deke?"

"In the last three days, all of them have been arrested and detained. Their radios for communicating back to the Deneb Republic have been confiscated."

"Won't the Deneb Republic notice that they're not receiving communications from their agents anymore, Deke?"

"Yes, Dominic, but it doesn't matter anymore. We've seen

their fleet approaching the Federation. They're in the envelope, and the Deneb Republic can't recall them while they're in the envelope."

"Of course. That's why I don't like space travel. One is out of touch with one's investments. So they're committed."

"Oh, yes."

"And do you know where they're going to strike first, Deke?"

"We believe so. Meredith."

Trask nodded.

"Makes sense. They have to take Meredith anyway if they want to take down the Federation. Might as well do it first, before you have losses anywhere else, while you are at your full strength. And will we win?"

"Oh, yes. We saw them early enough. They didn't plan on that. Navy assets are rushing to Meredith right now."

"And they'll be enough?"

"We think so, Dominic. We don't know how big their force is yet. But we think we're OK."

"So we win."

"Yes. Because of you, Dominic. That's why we saw them so early, and can be prepared for their little surprise. Because you didn't like what you were seeing, and called me."

Sharp picked up his glass and lifted it to Trask.

"To Dominic Trask."

Fuller followed suit.

"To Dominic Trask," she said.

Trask picked up his glass and lifted it to them.

"To victory."

The Crossing

At nine in the morning on Saturday, after breakfast with the Trasks on the main house patio, Sharp and Fuller were laying out on the guest suite patio, nursing cups of coffee.

"Oh, that breakfast was too much," Fuller said.

"Well, you could hold back a little, you know."

"But I love blintzes."

"And Belgian waffles."

"Well, yes. And bacon, too. Ooooh."

Sharp chuckled, then he got an alarm message. Fuller saw him go into virtual terminal and pop right back out.

"They just passed the border, Suzie."

"Shit. That's what? Three hours early?"

"Yeah."

"From Tuesday, we have Wednesday, Thursday, Friday, Saturday. Four days. Call it fifty hours. Six percent faster than we thought?"

"Yeah, which means twenty-five days to Meredith just became twenty-three and a half."

"Is that going to work, Deke?"

"It's closer than I'd like. That's for sure."

"So what do we do now?"

"I need to send some messages."

Larry Berkshire was orbiting in his picket position when he saw the Deneb Republic fleet – its dozens of envelopes – cross the border in front of him. It wasn't very long later that he got a message alarm. He pulled up the display of the incoming message, watching as the message streamed.

A SHARP EDGE

WHEN DRN PASSES YOU, EXIT ORBIT & SHADOW THEM. DECELERATE TO MATCH THEIR SPEED. TRY TO LOOK LIKE A SENSOR GHOST. TRY TO IDENTIFY DRN FLEET SHIP TYPES AND NUMBERS. DROP OUT OF ENVELOPE AT THESE COORDINATES. – DEKE

He looked up the coordinates tacked on the end of the message. The Meredith system. He advanced the astronomical time by twenty-three and a half days so the planets were all in the correct positions for when they arrived. Those coordinates were about a quarter of the way toward the planet from the commercial safe distance for dropping out of the envelope.

OK. Fair enough. That distance had a lot of safety margin, because the two gas giant planets of the system were in conjunction from Meredith at the moment, on the other side of the sun, and *Acala* was tough. Much tougher than a freighter, or even a warship. Probably a bit of a bumpy ride, but not bad. Not without the gas giants making the system's gravitational field all wonky on this side.

Berkshire started setting up the navigation problem so *Acala* could do it all on automatic. That would make it look much more like a sensor ghost.

Aboard *Baldr*, orbiting twenty light years away, Ted Lanham was working the same problem.

Matt Deckard was relaxing in his apartment this Saturday when he got a call request. He wouldn't necessarily have answered it, but it was a special tone.

The one he had assigned to Deke Sharp.

"Hi, Deke."

"Hi, Matt. I'm sending you a briefing, but I need you to leave for Meredith soonest. We're on a twenty-three-day schedule."

"Not a problem, Deke. Meredith is like, what? Less than two weeks."

"Yeah, but I need you to do something tricky on the way. Get moving. Get to orbit, emergency departure, and I'll talk to you on the way to the envelope."

"You got it, Deke."

Sharp cut the connection and Deckard checked the assignments board. *Osiris* was his, and her shuttle was at the shuttleport.

Deckard called *Osiris* and used her remote to get the shuttle's engines warming up. He set the shuttle to land on the front lawn of the apartment building. He could apologize later. In D Branch, soonest meant *soonest*.

Deckard started throwing clothes into his Navy planet duffle.

At multiple locations across New Destin and its suburbs, shuttles landed in unlikely places. Lawns, parking lots, parks, beaches. One person ran aboard each, and the shuttles leaped into the sky.

An hour later, small ships began leaving the Navy's orbital Ariel Station on emergency departures. *Osiris*, *Shangdi*, *Minerva*, *Baalham*, and *Ninhursag* all made for the envelope at war emergency power. No loping along at frigate speed here.

In D Branch, soonest meant *soonest*.

On several other planets of the Federation, similar actions played out. Soon *Danann*, *Frigg*, *Hachiman*, and *Lakshmi* all sped to the envelope in the various systems where they had been located.

The D Branch ships, each named after a god in a different pantheon, made their best time to the envelope wherever they were located. They had work to do.

Deckard was on the way to the envelope when a recording came in. It was a briefing, by Deke Sharp and Suzie Fuller, whom Deckard had met before, when he ferried her from Humphreys to Ariel to take up her new position as Principal Investigator for Official Corruption in New Destin.

Deckard was shocked to see the Deneb Republic fleet on the way into the Federation. Already across the border, in fact. Their course lined up with a least time transit to Meredith, hoping to take the Navy by surprise.

At the end of the briefing, the recording cut to Deke Sharp.

"Matt, I need you to intercept the Navy's Battle Group 14 on this heading toward Meredith. Don't slow down. Overhaul them and transmit the following orders via whisker laser to each ship. They are at boat flank speed, so the battle cruiser FNS *Callisto* will be in the rear, attack-ship carrier FNS *Indomitable* will be in the middle, and the destroyers FNS *Mace* and FNS *Saber* will be in the lead.

"Then you need to head on to Meredith and drop out of the envelope at these coordinates. BG-14 vector and estimated positions follow. Message follows. Coordinates follow."

"Got it, Deke."

Sharp cut the connection. He had other calls to make.

Deckard mapped the vector and estimated positions. Yeah, he could do it and still get to Meredith before the party started. As long as he didn't slow down.

He'd never tracked down ships under way before, but the ship's navigation computer should be able to handle that. He thought.

Deckard started working the problem.

The captains – and sole crew – of eight other D Branch ships were working the same problem, for other battle groups.

At lunch that Saturday, Trask picked up on Sharp's mood.

"Deke. What's the matter?"

"Their ships are faster than we thought."

"Or they're pushing them very hard," Fuller said.

"So we have less time than we thought," Sharp said.

"Will it be enough, Deke?"

Sharp looked at him blankly.

"I don't know, Dominic. I hope so, but I just don't know."

"Admiral, we're picking up two ships flanking us."

"Flanking us? At our velocity?"

"Yes, sir. They actually came up from behind us, slowing down to match speeds."

"Let me see a time lapse of those sensor readings."

"Aye, Sir."

Vice Admiral Trent Hardesty looked at the sensor readings. The ships' signatures – they looked like frigates from the mass readings – came in from either side and behind their course, decelerating as they came. They were now a couple tenths of a light-year to either side of his formation, and paralleled it.

That was very curious.

Hardesty estimated the energy signature from their deceleration. Equivalent to an attack-ship carrier. What?

Then comprehension dawned.

"They're sensor ghosts."

"Sensor ghosts, Sir?"

"Sure. You don't get them with small formations. But our wake in envelope space is so big, we're seeing reflections of our own ships on that density wave. How else do you get a frigate apparent mass, an attack-ship carrier's apparent energy readings, and ships that are coming in faster than us when we've been accelerating for what? Five, six weeks now? Nah. It's just our angle on the reflection changed."

"Yes, Sir. That makes sense."

"For the time being, ignore them. If something changes, let me know."

"Aye, Sir."

The Deneb Republic was a group of two dozen inhabited planets clustered in a region of space around Deneb, a blue supergiant star. While Deneb had no habitable planets, it dominated the night sky of habitable planets in the vicinity, and that's how the Deneb Republic was named.

John Robertson, the Chairman of the Central Committee of the Deneb Republic – and the all-but-in-name dictator of same – considered the reports coming back from the Republic's agents in the Federation.

Or, rather, the lack of reports.

"Is our fleet sailing into a trap?" he asked.

"I don't think so, sir," High Admiral Hugo Biarritz said.

Robertson raised an eyebrow, and Biarritz continued.

"Consider, sir. The fact that they may have tripped to our spy network – and how they could have done that so completely, I don't know – doesn't mean they know anything about the fleet.

"Second, the fleet has been accelerating at emergency power levels for six weeks by this point. They are going very fast, sir. And it is very difficult to resolve ships in envelope space unless one is close. The Federation is unlikely to even know we are there for another week or two.

"So I have to consider the timing of these arrests – if that's what has almost silenced our network, and I'm not sure it is –

to be purely coincidental."

Robertson nodded. That was his tentative conclusion as well. He had been extensively briefed on the invasion plan before he had approved it, and he understood the issues.

Then again, reality had a way of running up and biting you in the ass when you weren't paying attention.

"We have all the standard denials prepared?"

"Yes, sir. Of course."

"Very well. Keep me informed."

"Yes, sir."

The estimates of enemy strength came in to Deke Sharp late Sunday afternoon. Twenty-four envelopes. Mass readings indicated eight attack-ship carriers, eight heavy cruisers, and eight envelopes with mass readings twice that of a destroyer.

Hmm. Their destroyers were likely envelope sharing.

So that made eight battle groups.

Normally, there would be two or three battle groups at Meredith, with several others close enough to respond in a timely way. Various Deneb Republic agents had moved those battle groups out of position so they weren't able to respond in a timely way.

There were still three battle groups at Meredith, one in the process of changing out personnel, plus ground-based attack ships. The issue was to keep from being overcome by such a large force as the Deneb Republic fleet by being defeated in detail – letting the enemy beat you by confronting your smaller forces one at a time.

The Deneb Republic fleet needed to be delayed long enough for larger Federation forces to arrive, and Sharp was working out just how to make that happen.

Sharp sent the force estimates on to Admiral Jurgens. He

would give Jurgens time to think about it, then call him later in the week.

Assembling Forces

"Sir, we're being overtaken by another ship."

"Excuse me?" said FNS *Indomitable*'s captain, Captain Alan Corliss.

"Yes, Sir. We're being overtaken by another ship. Her velocity is higher, and she's out-accelerating us – by a lot," *Indomitable*'s sensor tech answered.

"Mass and energy readings?"

"She reads as a frigate, Sir, but she's displaying an energy signature equal to ours. Coming up on us now."

Who the hell could even do that? Destroyers were faster than *Indomitable*, but not that much faster.

"She's hitting us with a whisker laser now, Sir. Identification is FNS *Osiris*."

Corliss didn't recognize the ship name.

"Recite ship registry, FNS *Osiris*."

"Yes, Sir. FNS *Osiris*. Configuration: Classified. Weaponry: Classified. Acceleration: Classified. Tonnage: Classified. Assignment: D Branch."

"No shit. Acknowledge identification by whisker laser. Include identification FNS *Indomitable*."

"Aye, Sir. Acknowledging."

Corliss waited to see what came back. Everybody knew D Branch had capabilities it didn't talk about much, but this was a new one by him.

"Message from *Osiris*. Priority One. Encrypted. Eyes Only. Patched to you, Sir."

Corliss decrypted the message with his private key and read:

A SHARP EDGE

Drop out of envelope at coordinates indicated. Be at battle stations. Deneb Republic forces may already be present in system. If so, launch all attack ships on arrival. – David Sharp, Acting Head of Field Operations, D Branch.

Corliss pulled up a chart of the Meredith system, and advanced the date to their likely arrival. He plotted the coordinates attached to the message and stared at it a while, then slowly nodded.

His designated drop-out point was a bit further from the planet than the normal drop-out point, the drop-out point he would normally use. The published drop-out safe distance, on a line from the Deneb Republic.

If he dropped out at these coordinates, he would come into the Meredith system behind the arriving Deneb Republic forces.

"The old hammer and anvil trick, eh?" Corliss muttered.

"Sir?"

"Acknowledge message: 'Roger. Wilco.'"

"Aye, Sir. Acknowledging Roger Wilco."

The stupidly fast ship was already in front of them and disappearing ahead. Corliss hoped they saw his message.

Matt Deckard watched the attack-ship carrier disappear behind. The computer displayed an incoming message as she fell behind *Osiris*.

'Roger. Wilco.'

Good enough. He could report that to Deke. Battle cruiser. Attack-ship carrier. All taken care of.

Now, where were those destroyers?

"Captain, we're being overhauled by a ship."

"What? Helm, are we at war emergency power?"

"Yes, Ma'am. Power levels at one-hundred-ten percent of nominal."

"Overhauling ship is making perhaps twice our acceleration, Ma'am. Mass reading is frigate. Energy reading is—"

Her sensor technician turned to her on the cramped bridge of the destroyer FNS *Mace*.

"Ma'am, she reads at attack-ship carrier energy levels."

"Well, I guess if you put an attack-ship carrier's engines on a frigate, she would go like hell, right?" said Lieutenant Commander Beryl Dent, captain of *Mace*.

There were chuckles on the bridge.

"Yes, Ma'am. Whisker laser contact, Ma'am. Ship IDs as FNS *Osiris*."

"Readout on *Osiris*?"

"Configuration, weapons, tonnage, acceleration all classified, Ma'am. Assignment is D Branch."

Oh, no shit. Got some new tricks, I guess.

"Acknowledge contact. Transmit identification as FNS *Mace* and FNS *Saber*."

"Acknowledging, Ma'am."

What new wrinkle now? With D Branch, one never knew. Dent had once dated a guy who she guessed was in D Branch.

He didn't talk about work much.

"Message from *Osiris*. Priority One. Encrypted. Eyes Only. Patched to you, Ma'am."

Dent decrypted the message and nodded. Made sense to her. Come in behind the bastards. Pinch them up against the planet.

"Acknowledge. 'Roger. Wilco.'"

"Acknowledging Roger Wilco, Ma'am."

"Whisker-laser *Saber* once that's gone. I need to talk to Roger."

"Aye, Ma'am. Opening a channel to *Saber*."

A friendly and familiar face appeared on her display.

"Hi, Beryl. What's going on? What the hell was that?"

Matt Deckard smiled. Three intercepts, three Roger Wilcos. It didn't get any better than that.

He sent a message to Deke Sharp over the envelope communications system.

Osiris bored on through envelope space, heading for her own rendezvous ahead.

Sharp contacted Admiral Jurgens when he started to get acknowledgements back from his agents that they had successfully conveyed his orders to the battle groups under way.

"Jurgens."

"Hi, Kurt. Deke Sharp."

"Hi, Deke. What's the latest?"

"We have a fleet size. Eight battle groups, running in twenty-four envelopes. It looks like their destroyers are envelope sharing."

"That makes sense. We always deploy destroyers in pairs. What about timing?"

"The Deneb Republic fleet crossed the border sooner than we expected. We think they're running about six percent faster than we estimated. They may be pushing their safety margins harder than we normally would."

"Ouch. Are we going to be in place?"

"It's going to be close. So I took the liberty of giving orders to the incoming battle groups about where to drop out of the envelope."

"How did you manage that, Deke?"

"I had D Branch ships intercept them in envelope space and communicate by whisker laser as they overtook them."

"That's some nice spacing right there. Can I ask what orders you gave my Navy?"

Sharp winced.

"Sorry, Kurt. I was in a hurry. I had nine sets of orders to cut and my ships were on the way to the envelope at their best speed, which is measured in hours."

"I understand, Deke. What were the orders?"

"I have eight battle groups dropping out of the envelope behind the Deneb Republic fleet, and one dropping out behind the planet from them. There are three battle groups on Meredith already, which makes four, plus the ground-based attack ships."

"Hammer and anvil, huh? That makes sense. That's likely how we would deploy them once they got here, assuming we had the time. Assuming that everyone was here before they showed up."

"Right. But they won't be."

"What do we do in the meantime, Deke?"

"We'll hold them."

"Twelve frigates, Deke? Against eight battle groups?"

"Very special frigates, but yes. We'll take our losses, but they won't get to the planet before everyone shows up."

Jurgens nodded. He had read Sharp's AARs about the pirate engagements, and he more than suspected what those very special frigates were capable of. They would get hurt, though.

"All right, Deke. For the record, I approve of your actions. Going through channels when the enemy is in your living room isn't a recommended strategy. But we do need to clean up the chain of command a little bit if this is going to work.

"Your field operatives have effectively held Navy rank as

commanders, and senior field operatives as captains, for a long time. Otto is taking over D Branch, and you're moving up to head of field operations, I understand."

"Yes, that's right, Kurt. For this operation, that change has already taken place. Claude's stepped out of it."

Jurgens nodded.

"All right, Deke. Your effective rank in the Navy is now vice admiral."

"Not rear admiral, Kurt?"

"Every battle group incoming is commanded by a rear admiral, Deke. Except for those where we removed a Deneb agent, anyway. We don't need people arguing with you when they show up. You'll be there with combat forces first, and, as others arrive, they need to integrate into a battle already under way. Vice admiral works for me."

Sharp nodded.

"All right, Kurt. I can make that work."

"In the meantime, I'll make sure all three battle groups here are ready to go. Probably hide them behind the planet as well. And we'll get all the ground-based attack ships up to operational status. Pull some on-leave pilots back in."

"That would help a lot, Kurt."

Jurgens nodded.

"Good spacing, Deke. I'll talk to you when you get to Meredith."

While Sharp was dealing with all the redirection and coordination issues, Fuller was active in the DV engine. After Sharp's call with Jurgens, they sat on the patio and talked. It was now Thursday, with just over two weeks to go before what Sharp already thought of as the Battle of Meredith.

"So Jurgens gave me a little grief, but not much."

"A little grief, D.K?"

"Yeah. He asked me what orders I had given his Navy."

"Ouch."

"He said it with humor, Suzie. He didn't really have a problem with it. In fact, he upped my effective rank in the Navy to vice admiral."

"That will avoid some problems, I imagine."

"Yes, but if I change my avatar to reflect that rank, I won't have any honors on the uniform. That was always a problem, but worse now."

"Construct your avatar wearing a shipsuit, D.K. No honors on a shipsuit, but rank insignia apply."

Sharp considered.

"That's probably a good idea. In battle, it will just seem normal."

"I would think. Meanwhile, I have something to show you. Join me in DV."

They logged into the data visualization engine. They were in a blank workspace.

"DV. Load battle space," Fuller said.

The display leapt to life with ship icons all over the place. In the middle were the planet Meredith and its sun. There, the gigantic footprint of the Deneb Republic fleet, inbound to Meredith. Around Meredith were nine more, smaller footprints inbound, the battle groups of the Federation Navy.

Closer to Meredith, the D Branch ships were inbound as well.

"DV. Wind the time forward, four days per minute."

The time lapse estimated the positions of all the ships as they bore down on Meredith. The D Branch ships arrived at the position Sharp had specified. Then the massive footprint of the Deneb Republic fleet arrived. Seconds later, the Federation battle groups started dropping out of the envelope.

"DV. Stop."

"There's your battle space, D.K."

Sharp stared at the display for several seconds.

"This is remarkable, Suzie. How long between the arrival of the Deneb Republic fleet and the arrival of our battle groups?"

Fuller reached out to a control hanging in mid-air and wound it back until the enemy fleet was back in the envelope, then forward just a touch. She zeroed a timer that appeared in mid-air. She then wound the control forward until the Federation battle groups had all appeared.

Fuller looked at the timer.

"Maybe seven, eight hours, D.K."

"During which we need to keep them out of missile range of the planet."

"Yup. That would be a good thing, I think."

"Yes. Absolutely."

He thought about it.

"It's too bad I can't pilot *Medea* from within the DV."

"But you can, D.K."

A pilot's command chair and panel appeared in front of them, looking out on the battle space. There was another command chair alongside of it.

"Wow. Nice. Why two command chairs, Suzie?"

"Because I'm coming along, D.K."

"Suzie..."

He turned to her.

"We're going to get hurt. The D Branch ships. Some of us aren't coming back. I don't want to put you at risk."

"Oh, no, you don't, Deke Sharp. You are not going to space off into oblivion and leave me a widow. If we die, we die together. Period. End of statement.

"Besides, you need me. You need a chief of staff, Mr. Vice Admiral. You are going to have twelve battle groups – forty-eight ships – plus hundreds of attack ships under your direct command, plus the D Branch ships. You can't do all that directly, and pilot *Medea*, without help."

"There aren't two command chairs on *Medea*. It's going to be a rough ride. Too rough for a drop seat."

"There's a command chair in each of the shuttles. Stop making excuses. I'm going with you or you aren't going."

"Or I'm not going?"

"Yes. You'll be too busy here trying to save your failing marriage. I will not be your widow because you won't let me help you when you need help. That's not a marriage. I don't know what it is, but it's not a marriage."

Sharp had always known Fuller had a core of steel. She had shown it before. She showed it again now, and he knew there was no arguing with her.

Their relationship stood or broke – forever – right here, right now.

"All right, Suzie. I don't want to put you at risk, but I do need the help, and we both know it."

"So I'm going."

"Yes. I give."

"Good. When do we leave, Admiral?"

To Meredith

Sharp and Fuller spent the rest of Thursday and all day Friday adding enhancements to her battlespace display in DV.

In front of Fuller's command chair, they added buttons for communication to each battle group, as well as buttons for Force A, the four battle groups collecting behind Meredith, Force B, the eight battle groups coming in behind the Deneb Republic fleet, and Force DB, the D Branch ships.

They added the ability for Sharp to manipulate ship icons in the display, automatically generating movement orders Fuller could transmit to the individual commands.

They also analyzed the strengths and weaknesses of the ships of the Deneb Republic fleet, generating firing solutions for the Force DB ships as they spaced through the enemy formation. For attack-ship carriers, the attack-ship launch rails, to trap the attack ships in their carriers. That was the highest-priority target of all. Stop the proliferation of threat sources.

The attack ships themselves were the secondary target. They would be hard to hit, but hit them anywhere and they were likely out of the action. They would be the primary force projection of the Deneb Republic fleet.

For the cruisers, whose shields hardened over their guns, the targeting solution focused on their targeting sensor arrays. Without the arrays – with the guns in local control – their accuracy would be perhaps ten percent of what it was with the arrays.

For destroyers that got in the way, the targeting solution was their engines. Engines were normally shielded too hard to take out, but the engines of a mere destroyer could not shield against the battle-cruiser guns of a D Branch ship.

They built one enhancement after another into what would be their battle center. They ran the simulation, worked the battle, and automated or optimized everything they tripped over. By Friday evening, they were ready.

Friday evening, the Trasks came out to the beach house for the weekend. Dinner that evening was beef stroganoff, with the beef so tender the pieces cut with a fork. In addition to the egg noodles it was served over, the side dishes were roasted Brussels sprouts and a fruit salad. The wine was a Cabernet Sauvignon, the unfiltered private reserve of an excellent Elizabeth winery. Dessert was a multi-layer lemon mascarpone sponge cake.

Trask, Sharp, and Fuller retired to the patio for cigars and cognac after dinner. Once they were served, and the staff dismissed, Trask began the conversation.

"What's your status this week, Deke? Are things working out after all?"

"It's going to be close, Dominic. I will have some forces there when the Deneb Republic fleet arrives, but most of my forces will arrive late."

"Your forces?"

"D.K. is acting vice admiral for the invasion, Dominic," Fuller said.

Trask looked to her, then back to Sharp.

"Truly?"

"Yes. It will be D Branch ships that hold the line until everyone else gets there. Admiral Jurgens decided the only way to make it work was to put them under my command as the battle would already be joined."

"Ah. Yes, that makes sense. Can you hold them, though,

Deke? Until everyone else gets there?"

"We should be able to. We're going to get hurt, but we should be able to trip them up long enough."

"When do you leave, Deke?"

In answer, Deke signaled *Medea* to start the engines on the shuttle currently parked in Trask's front yard. The sound of the shuttle's engines carried over the house to the patio.

"Suzie and I leave in about fifteen minutes, Dominic."

Trask turned to Fuller and raised an eyebrow.

"You're going as well?"

"It's my fight, too, Dominic, and I won't send Deke off to die alone. He needs a chief of staff, so he needs my help."

Trask turned back to Sharp, and Sharp shrugged.

Trask nodded.

"She laid down the law, did she?"

"Yes, in a manner of speaking."

Trask nodded.

"Well, I wish you both the best. For yourselves and the Federation."

"We'd better go collect our planet duffles."

"And I will collect Janine and Marie to see you off. They would otherwise never forgive me."

There were hugs and well wishes all around under the porte cochere of the main house. Members of both parties – those leaving and those staying – knew they might not see each other again, but there were no tears. Not quite.

As the sound of the shuttle's engines grew more insistent, Sharp and Fuller headed across the lawn to the shuttle. It was far enough away from the house that the Trasks remained outside under the porte cochere for the takeoff.

Sharp and Fuller stowed their planet duffles in cabinets, then a final wave out the hatch. The hatch closed and the ramp retracted.

The shuttle's engines spun up the rest of the way. When Sharp focused the thrust and added oxygen to the mix, the shuttle leaped off the ground and headed to space.

As the shuttle narrowed to a bright point in the night sky and disappeared, Dominic Trask offered up a prayer for his friends.

"May God protect both you and the Federation from our enemies," he muttered.

Janine nodded.

"Amen," Marie said.

Sharp requested emergency departure and traffic clearance from the Navy's orbital Elizabeth Station while they were still on the way up to *Medea*. Unusually, it was granted without question.

Then again, his request had been from 'VADM David Sharp.'

The shuttle arrived at *Medea* and latched on to the ship. Of course, Sharp and Fuller were weightless. They stayed on the shuttle while Sharp disconnected *Medea* from Elizabeth Station.

Medea maneuvered away from the station on low thrust, and then Sharp engaged war emergency power, heading for the envelope.

With gravity returned, Sharp and Fuller moved on into the main cabin.

"All right, D.K. We have what? Twelve hours to work on the simulation before we get to the envelope?"

Sharp looked at the display.

"More like ten. And it's eleven o'clock at night now. We're tired."

"And we'll be more tired before the battle's over. Come on, buddy. Let's get to it."

Sharp sighed and they logged into the DV engine back on Ariel.

"One thing I worry about is these dark quadrants."

Fuller made a gesture and the upper and lower portion of their vision of the battle space, from their point of view on their virtual command deck, grayed out.

"We can see those areas, though, Suzie."

"Yes, but we can't fire at them. The maximum ascension and declination on the guns won't allow it."

"I guess we could rotate the ship. That way, we would bring fire on any target within a quarter-second or so."

Sharp made adjustments, and the ship started rotating on its long axis about once per second. The view of the battle space rotated crazily about their viewing position.

Fuller gulped.

"Oh, I don't think I could take much of this, D.K."

"But we don't have to. DV. Maintain rotation, but stabilize battlespace view to eliminate rotation in the command view."

The rotation of the space around them stopped, but the lightly grayed-out areas continued to rotate about their position.

"OK. That's a lot better. This is OK, and we can still see what we can and can't shoot at."

Fuller continued to look at the display, considering.

"You know, D.K. I think we ought to build a one-man setup like this for the other D Branch ships. We'll probably have some time in Meredith – a couple days – for them to practice with it before the enemy fleet shows up. Let's build a setup for them."

Sharp nodded.

"Makes sense."

"DV. Duplicate workspace, name 'D Branch Ship Console.' Make it re-entrant for multiple users to each have their own instance. Put us in the duplicate workspace."

The view remained the same, but the small header line changed to the new name.

"OK, what do we do now, Suzie. Only one command chair, right?"

"Right. But we need to consolidate controls. They need a comm button back to us, for example. And a comm button to the whole group, I think.

"They need to see maneuvering vectors we apply from the command ship. So if you draw a vector for a ship on our screen, their intended path shows here. And an 'Accept Route' button for that, so the ship just automatically follows what we put in if the pilot decides to follow it."

"If he decides to, Suzie?"

"Sure, D.K. He may see something, concentrating on his own ship, that gives him a better way to accomplish the goal. None of your people are stupid. Or insubordinate, for that matter."

"OK, Suzie. That's fair."

They made changes to the console display for the primary command chair.

"OK, Suzie. That looks right."

"DV. Eliminate secondary command chair and console."

The second chair disappeared.

"Nice," Sharp said. "And this has the same anti-rotation view and all?"

"Yes. It should, anyway."

Fuller rotated the ship, but the battlespace view remained the same. The lightly grayed-out areas that the guns couldn't hit now circled the battle space.

"Excellent," Sharp said. "I think the guys will like this."

Sharp and Fuller went back to their own battlespace view and practiced maneuvers within the battlespace. For right now, they set the other ships to accept routes from the command ship so they could do group maneuvers.

By the time *Medea* hit the envelope, they were exhausted but well practiced in the maneuvers they thought would be necessary in facing the Deneb Republic fleet.

Especially in taking out those attack-ship launch rails.

Once *Medea* was in the envelope, and their communications with the DV engine on Ariel were cut off, they relaxed and enjoyed the trip. They ate healthy, regular meals. They slept regular hours, and tried to relax as much as possible, in order to be in the best possible shape when they arrived at Meredith.

They were receiving, over the envelope communications system, regular updates on the location, speed, and likely arrival time of the Deneb Republic Fleet. They adjusted the ship's clock a little every day to be in their own mid-morning when the Deneb Republic fleet arrived in Meredith.

They would fight the enemy fleet during their own best part of the day, with the Federation Navy battle groups arriving late in the afternoon.

That timing had nothing to do with the actual time in Meredith's capital or at Navy headquarters.

Training

Medea dropped out of the envelope short of Meredith, at the location Sharp had specified for the D Branch ships. There was a loud 'CLUNK!', and the ship shook.

"What happened, D.K? Did we run into somebody?"

"No. Just dropped out of the envelope a little closer to the planet than recommended. I wanted to make sure we were planetside of the enemy fleet when we arrived."

Now back in touch with DV on Ariel through QE radio, they both logged into the battlespace display. The Deneb Republic fleet showed in the display, in the envelope, still a couple days away.

"Well, they're not here yet, but we're in position."

So were seven of the D Branch ships: *Shangdi, Minerva, Baalham, Ninhursag, Frigg, Hachiman,* and *Lakshmi.*

"*Osiris* and *Danaan* not yet present," Fuller said. "*Baldr* and *Acala* as well, of course."

Sharp nodded. *Osiris* and *Danaan* had had the hardest battle-group intercepts, with battle groups the Deneb agents had had the farthest out of position. *Baldr* and *Acala* were still shadowing the enemy fleet. He could see all four ships on the display.

"All right. Let's get everybody acknowledging."

Fuller nodded and sent out a Force DB message for acknowledgement. Several seconds passed before she spoke up.

"All Force DB captains acknowledge, Admiral."

Fuller was businesslike, clipped speech, no frills. This could work out. He looked over to her sitting in the secondary chair –

the chief of staff chair – in the display.

Where Sharp's avatar was wearing a grey shipsuit with three stars on the collars, Fuller was wearing a grey shipsuit with two stars on the collars.

"Rear Admiral?" he asked.

"Yes, D.K. Chief of staff to a vice admiral is a rear admiral. You have a bunch of rear admirals incoming. You need them to follow your orders and mine. Civilian – or even captain – won't cut it. I've also designated this ship 'Fleet Flag', making it superior to the flag ships of the battle groups."

Sharp nodded. Fair enough.

"Where are the Meredith battle groups?"

"Hiding on the other side of the planet, Sir. Tying in to Meredith satellite data now."

Three battle groups appeared in the display on the other side of Meredith. Sharp could see them as the planet display went to fifty-percent transparency.

"OK, Suzie. Let's get those Force DB captains in the D Branch Ship Console simulation and start training."

"Aye, Sir."

Fuller set the D Branch Ship Console simulation to multiple logins – rather than re-entrant logins – and invited the Force DB captains present into the workspace. They all showed up in their avatars in civilian clothes, but, seeing her in shipsuit with insignia, they all changed to shipsuit with captain or commander insignia.

'Good morning, everyone. The Federation Navy is on the way. You can see nine battle groups incoming, here, here, here. We also have three battle groups hiding on the other side of Meredith here. The Deneb Republic fleet, being shadowed by two of our ships, is here. What's the first thing you notice?"

"The Deneb fleet gets here first," Captain Prudence Rialto of the *Ninhursag* said.

Prudence Rialto wore a captain's collar tabs. She was a senior field agent, and a good one, though her actions in the field sometimes belied her given name.

"Correct, Captain. The enemy gets here first. So what's our mission?"

"Keep them away from the planet until the cavalry shows up?" Commander Clyde Matthews of the *Frigg* said.

"Again, correct. We can't let enemy attack ships within missile range of the planet. We have to hold them here until the Federation Navy shows up in force large enough not to be defeated in detail. That is known as losing, and we don't intend to lose.

"We will do that by acting in coordination. Vice Admiral Deke Sharp is in command of all Federation forces shown here. Force A, Force B, and Force DB. D Branch ship *Medea* is the Fleet Flag. My name is Rear Admiral Suzanne Fuller. I am Admiral Sharp's chief of staff for the duration."

Fuller highlighted each of the Federation forces in the display as she named them, then highlighted *Medea*.

"We will fly our ships from within these simulations. The ships will answer to the controls just as they do in your normal command chair. But there are advantages.

"The first is that the flag can lay in a route for you from his own display, like this."

A route for the ship which was presumably connected to the simulation appeared in the display.

"You can accept that route with this button here. If you see something, from your perspective, that you consider a better route, you need not push the 'Accept Route' button. I will caution you, however, that the flag will have a better view of the whole battle than you do, that you may be routed in support of someone else or have the support of someone else for yourself. You are all noted for your ability to act independently. This, however, may not be the time. Consider that when you make that decision.

"Also, your guns cannot hit these areas."

The lightly grayed-out areas appeared above and below the battle space.

"You will therefore spin your ships on their long axis."

The battlespace display spun madly about them. Several people swore or swallowed hard.

"This simulation stabilizes your view."

The battlespace display came to rest, but the grayed out areas now rotated about them.

"Your ship is still rotating, but your own view does not. Note the active area of your guns rotates about the display. This is something you cannot do in your normal command chairs, and will be crucial in the coming engagement.

"While you all logged in to this same simulation today, this simulation is normally re-entrant. You will each have your own. You log into it and give it your ship's credentials, and you will be in control of your ship through the DV engine on Ariel."

One of the pilots – a captain – held up his hand.

"Admiral?" Captain Ralph Mueller of the *Hachiman* asked.

"Yes, Captain?"

"Have we reserved the DV engine and sufficient bandwidth to Ariel, Ma'am?"

"That's a good question. We will, before the Deneb Republic fleet arrives. Any other questions?"

There were none, and Fuller continued.

"Our battle plan is simple. We will confront and harass the Deneb Republic fleet, keeping them busy until reinforcements get here. That will be a period of as much as eight hours."

There were several groans.

"Yes, indeed. Twelve frigates against eight battle groups for up to eight hours. Our firing priorities have thus been carefully selected."

Fuller waved at the display and a large image of a Deneb Republic attack-ship carrier appeared in front of them.

"Our absolute top priority is their nuclear missiles. One of those can ruin your whole day. These will only be launched by an attack ship when they have an enemy in lock, and by enemy I mean one of us. We have to take them out.

"Our second priority is the launch rails of the attack-ship carriers, here and here, on both sides. We need to shut down their launch operations to minimize the proliferation of threat sources. If we can bottle up their attack ships and the missiles they carry, we're much better off."

The attack-ship carrier disappeared and an attack ship appeared.

"Our third priority is any attack ships they get off. They are hard to hit. The nice part is that if you hit them anywhere, they pretty much come apart. No shields. They each carry two of those damn missiles, so don't think they're innocuous after they fire just one of them."

The attack ship disappeared, and a battle cruiser appeared.

"Our fourth priority is the cruisers' guns. While the guns themselves have hard points in the shields to protect them, their targeting sensor arrays do not. They are blind, and the guns are in local control, if we take out their sensors, here, here, and here, on both sides."

The battle cruiser disappeared and a destroyer appeared.

"Our last priority – for when your guns don't have anything else to do – is the destroyers. These are mostly a nuisance. They can't hurt our ships, but they could be a lot of trouble if they could get in range of the planet. The primary target here is the engines. That's their strongest shield location, but they can't deflect our guns."

The destroyer disappeared.

"Now, the computer running this simulation – the Ariel DV engine – has been programmed with these target priorities. It can run your guns on automatic, and whenever it sees a target, it will take the shot, in priority order. I recommend you leave your guns on automatic during the engagement.

"We will try one battle simulation without, so we see how that works out, and then we will take the next one in automatic.

"Are there any questions?"

"Admiral?" Captain Bernard Horzen of *Lakshmi* asked.

"Go ahead, Captain."

"What about target assignment?"

"Excuse me, Captain?"

"Well, with multiple ships, the priorities should be resolved across the ships, Ma'am. No sense three ships firing on the same target just because they can all see it. With one computer running the show, can't we assign targets to the ships?"

"That, Captain, is an excellent idea, and one I should have thought of. I was writing them thinking in terms of one ship. I will modify the targeting to assign targets across ships.

"Anyone else?"

"One from me, Ma'am," Captain Donald Bach of *Minerva* said. "With routes from the flag, and the guns on automatic, do we even need to be on our ships?"

"That's another excellent question. Yes, Captain, for one simple reason. No plan survives contact with the enemy. You all know the mission. You all know the importance of the mission. We expect to take losses. We cannot guarantee that those losses do not include the flag. That something doesn't go wrong with the DV engine. That communications to Ariel aren't lost.

"Any of those circumstances leaves you, individually and together, to carry out the mission, and keep the Deneb Republic fleet a safe distance from the heavily populated Federation planet Meredith.

"We have all sworn oath, in our various positions, to protect and serve the people of the Federation. Sometimes that duty is more difficult, more dangerous, more cruel than others. Such as today. Yet we will fulfill our oaths, we will prevail, and the Deneb Republic will rue the day they decided to test our resolve."

Maneuvers

Their maneuvers were practiced in pure simulation. That is, the ships didn't actually move. The other thing is that the maneuvers were practiced at four-to-one in speed, on a fast clock.

One thing Sharp knew about space battles. They took a long time. Space was so vast, distances were so large, it took a long time to get anywhere. One could decide to intercept the enemy there, at that point, and set out for that intercept, but it might occur hours from now.

That was actually part of their advantage. Even with close-in fighting, eight hours to hold them off wasn't as long as it seemed.

So their first practice session, they ran on a four-times-faster clock. All the physics occurred four times faster, all the accelerations were four times faster, and so on.

For this first set of maneuvers, all the guns were on manual.

It did not go well. An hour and fifteen minutes into the simulation – five real-time hours – all the D Branch ships had been destroyed and the Deneb Republic fleet was spacing for Meredith, scores of Deneb Republic attack ships in the lead.

The after-action meeting was in the battle workspace on DV. Fuller walked everyone through the battle, then asked for comments.

What went wrong?

What went right?

What had they learned?

With a crew of people hand-selected for their ability to act independently, to make on-the-fly decisions with inadequate data, the initial conversation was not very productive. It took a while for things to settle down, for people to have some perspective, to get some distance from the events and view them dispassionately.

Once they had, they had broad agreement on a number of points. First was that people had often chosen not to accept the assigned route. Perhaps a third of the time. This left other people uncovered against attack, made it impossible for ships to support each other. It made them easy pickings.

Second was that, with the guns on manual, they had target-fixated on the thing they were aiming at, and missed opportunities to fire on other things along the way. For every target hit, four targets of opportunity were missed.

As more and more attack ships were launched with impunity by the enemy, the fight became almost purely against the attack ships and their missiles, and the attack-ship launch rails were virtually unscathed. Every Deneb Republic carrier had at least two surviving attack-ship launch rails at the end of the action.

One would have expected Sharp and Fuller to be disappointed in the results. They acted like it to their ship captains. But privately, they were elated.

The purpose of the first exercise was to get people to stop acting like hot dogs and start acting like a team, by showing them that hot-dogging was not a winning strategy.

Sharp held off the next exercises until Commander Matt Deckard in *Osiris* and Commander Alice Dobson in *Danaan* showed up. He knew they were close, based on the workspace battle display.

The next practice battle would be with almost the full

strength of Force DB.

They showed up within the hour. Fuller sent them both recordings of the training, the battle exercise, and the after-action discussion. Fresh from their time in the envelope, they viewed them all immediately.

Having done so, they signaled the flag they were ready.

"For this second exercise, I want you to humor me," Sharp said to Force DB's assembled captains. "The last exercise we ran completely manually. The guns were on manual fire, and you had the option to not accept routes. For this exercise, let's do the opposite. All guns on automatic, and accept all routes. Let's bracket our possibilities and see where we get with this one. Questions?"

There was silence.

"Very well. Dismissed."

The second exercise went much better. Ships usually attacked in pairs, following the routes Sharp laid in from his command bridge. Pairs operated in support of each other, close enough they could often cover the forward or after aspects of the other pair against threats in each other's guns' blind spots.

Ships' guns seemed to fire almost randomly, but they were reducing off-axis threats as they went. This group would fire on that attack ship over there, or that cruiser's targeting sensor array, or that missile, even as they bore in on their current target.

Threat sources disappeared as the Force DB ships penetrated the enemy battle groups, then turned around and came back through the injured enemy yet again.

Sharp was learning, too. Seeing what worked and what didn't, at least against the simulated enemy. Once *Baldr* and

Acala arrived, he would have three sets of four ships, two supporting pairs per set.

In the second exercise, Force DB lost six ships, but the four remaining were still an effective fighting force when they disengaged and fled the enemy fleet, even as the battle groups of the Federation Navy moved into the field.

More to the point, Force DB had immobilized the enemy fleet, forcing them to maintain full power to shields against their fast and dangerous enemy.

The Deneb Republic fleet had not been able to advance on Meredith.

"Well, that went better," Sharp said to Force DB's assembled captains. "We were successful at keeping them from the planet. Our losses were high, but they were mostly in the beginning stages, and I was also learning as we went. We'll do a couple more exercises once Berk and Ted arrive on *Baldr* and *Acala*. That will give me three divisions of four ships.

"What did you think?"

"I felt like a passenger, Sir," Captain Prudence Rialto said. "Not much to do when the routes and guns are on automatic."

"Yes, but the flag can't stand aside. Those groups of four are too effective. Which means we may get hit, and then you will need to carry on the battle without me."

"It seems to me we should assign those groups of four, or at least pairs, so they can carry on together if you're gone," Commander Clyde Matthews said.

"That's probably a good idea, Captain," Sharp said.

He turned to Fuller, who nodded.

"Got it. I'll take care of it, Admiral."

"Another part of that, Sir," Captain Donald Bach said. "We need to re-pair as we take losses. Not send two ships in individually, but pair up the survivors so we remain in pairs. The later losses were mostly of individual ships that had already lost their partner."

"Another good idea. We'll take care of that, Captain."

"Any other feedback?"

"Overall, we were much more effective with central organization, Sir," Commander Alice Dobson said. "It was more fun to watch, even though I was one of the casualties this time around."

Sharp nodded.

"Agreed, Commander, although the biggest thing for me is that we achieved our mission. We pinned them down until the reinforcements could arrive. That's our job. Keep them from advancing on the planet."

People nodded. They got it.

"All right, everybody. Get some sleep. Be well rested and well fed. When Berk and Ted get here, we'll just have time for another exercise or two before it's showtime.

"Dismissed."

"I've been analyzing enemy losses during that last exercise," Fuller said as they had dinner that night.

"Find anything interesting?"

"Yes. Enemy losses were higher when you had pairs jinking during their run through the enemy formation."

"That's a little counter-intuitive, Suzie. The jinking slows them down."

"Yes, D.K. But what it also does is bring other targets into sight of our guns. Our guns are blind fore and aft, but when a ship veers, it sees other targets. With the guns on automatic, DV takes the shot. It's got more chances when the ship's target window moves around."

"OK. That makes sense. Is there an optimum jink angle? A balance between jinking too hard, and slowing them down too much, and boring straight through, and missing the other targets?"

"I'm still refining that, D.K. It looks like it's a full ninety degrees rotation of the ship to bring the guns around and add as much side vector as we can to our high forward speed."

"All right, Suzie. Let me know if that changes."

"Yes, Sir."

Three days out from Meredith, it was time for the Deneb Republic fleet to start decelerating. Even as fast as deceleration occurred in the envelope, they had been accelerating a long time.

"Coming up on our turn, Sir."

"Very well," Deneb Vice Admiral Trent Hardesty said. "Fleet orders. Turn on the mark. Call it out, Mr. Garrity."

"Aye, Sir. Fleet orders sent. Mark is five minutes."

When time expired, the twenty-four envelopes of the Deneb Republic fleet began their turn.

When the Deneb Republic fleet started their one-hundred-eighty-degree turn – to bring their engines to the front and begin decelerating for dropping out of the envelope – *Baldr* and *Acala* bore on for more than a day, then began their own turns.

As they finished their own turns, they brought their ships up to war emergency power on the big engines.

They would drop out of the envelope more than a day earlier than the Deneb Republic fleet, and drop out of the envelope a little past the enemy's return to normal spacetime.

The D Branch ships would emerge into normal spacetime at the coordinates Deke Sharp had sent them over the envelope communications system.

"Admiral, you said you wanted to know if those reflections acted differently."

"Yes. What is it?"

"They've continued on straight, sir. They're not making the turn."

"Curious. Keep an eye on them."

"Yes, Sir."

More than a day later, the lieutenant commander at the flag tracking station spoke up again.

"Sir. Those reflections have started their turn."

"Let me see."

"Patching it to you, Sir."

As Hardesty watched, the two frigate-massed envelopes completed their turn and started decelerating very rapidly.

"There. You see that, Tracking?"

"Yes, Sir."

"Reflections, pure and simple. Nothing can decelerate that fast. They're reflections off our wake, but our wake changed angle to us as we made our turn."

"Yes, Sir. I see, Sir."

Baldr and *Acala* dropped out of the envelope near the other Force DB ships a couple of minutes apart. Sharp called the captains, Commander Theodore Lanham and Commander Larry Berkshire, as soon as both ships were in normal spacetime. They met in Sharp's battlespace simulation.

Sharp's avatar was wearing the grey shipsuit with three black stars on the collars.

"Vice admiral, Deke?" Berkshire asked.

"Yes. I'm currently commander of all Federation assets in

the Meredith system. As we are the first force on scene, it's the only way to avoid a change of command in the middle of the battle that's coming."

"Well, it's definitely coming. I think they're about thirty-six hours behind us," Lanham said.

"Yes. That was a great job tracking them, by the way. Hopefully, they just thought you were reflections."

"Well, they didn't try to interfere with us."

Lanham and Berkshire both looked into the display, at the Deneb Republic fleet and the various Federation Navy battle groups incoming.

"Looks like the Navy battle groups just started decelerating. It's going to be what? Two days before they arrive?"

"A little less," Sharp said. "We have to hold the fort for maybe eight hours until they get here."

"Oh, shit," Berkshire said.

"Yeah. Pretty much. We've been practicing, though, and I think we can hold them. I have some recordings for you to look at. Your command decks, like this one, in DV workspaces. Also a couple of exercises. I would ask you to view them quickly. Sort of scan them fast, and see where we're at."

Both pilots had shifted their avatars to shipsuits with commander's insignia.

"All right, Admiral. We're on it."

A couple of hours after *Baldr* and *Acala* arrived, Force DB held their third exercise. Again, it was with guns in automatic and all routes accepted.

This time, though, Sharp had three groups of four ships, arranged as pairs. The pairs' routes were set to support each other in each group, and to maximize the initial impact on the attack-ship launch rails on all eight attack-ship carriers of the opposing force.

The more they could do to lock up the attack ships, the better it would go. Some attack ships would get off, however. The enemy would start launching attack ships immediately upon hitting normal spacetime, and it would take some time for Force DB to get in among the enemy fleet.

It went better this time even than the second exercise. Sharp was learning, and the four-ship sets were better able to counter the enemy missiles. Jinking helped, too, and Sharp used it exclusively in their runs through the opposing force.

In the end, four D Branch ships were lost, but they held the enemy fleet in place for eight hours in the four-to-one fast time of the simulation. Sharp filled in his groupings as ships were lost. No single ship attempted the attack run, though sometimes a group of four – maneuvering as two pairs – became a group of three, maneuvering as a triplet.

During the break between exercises, Sharp set routes for all ships to move to the best position to face the incoming fleet. He had not been sure in which direction they would make their turn for deceleration, left, right, up, or down.

Both *Baldr* and *Acala* had seen them make a left turn, however, and Sharp moved Force DB to be better positioned for their eventual drop out of the envelope.

That would make their initial attack run hit the enemy sooner, and would hold down their losses to those damn attack-ship missiles.

The fourth exercise was held a couple hours after the third. Sharp was in his element now, and Fuller was impressed. He seemed to have ice-water in his veins as he called out adjustments to her, even as he set routes and oversaw the battle.

Sharp held losses to three D Branch ships, even while keeping the opposition force bottled up, all its power to shields and no movement to the planet. For eight hours they held, then fled the battle as Navy elements appeared.

That, though, was a simulation, and both Sharp and Fuller knew the real battle would present its own challenges.

There would be surprises, they knew.

How bad those surprises would be they did not know.

With the fourth exercise over, Sharp gave everybody twelve hours off for food and sleep. They would be in place two hours before the Deneb Republic fleet showed up in shiptime morning.

As Sharp and Fuller ate dinner – necessarily from tubes in the zero-gravity of their stationary position – they thought back over the exercises.

"So what are the surprises going to be, D.K?"

"Don't know. That's why they call them surprises. Are you ready to make changes on the fly?"

"Yes. I can modify the targeting solutions and the maneuvering solutions as we go if I have to."

"And that won't cause its own issues? Like dead time while something reloads or something?"

"Well, I have to be careful how I do it, but I can substitute pieces of the program in between when they run. This piece runs, and then the next time that piece runs, the new version runs."

"And they'll all change at once?"

"Oh, yes. They're all running the same program. One change, and all the instances change."

"OK. Then I guess we're as set as we're gonna be."

A SHARP EDGE

They didn't make love that night. They just held each other. They were together at the crux of it, but for how long they didn't know.

Confrontation

They woke, still enmeshed, and tethered to the zero-gravity nets.

"You sleep OK?" Sharp asked.

"Good. How about you?"

"Real good, actually."

"Excellent."

Breakfast was from tubes. Some sort of egg thing, and another of a bacon-flavored paste. Wonder of wonders, it actually had bacon bits in it. Sippy cups of orange juice and coffee, with a coffee cake – gooey, to prevent floating crumbs – rounded out the meal.

"That actually wasn't too bad," Fuller said.

Sharp nodded.

"Well, might as well log in and get people organized."

"Break a leg," Fuller said, then kissed him.

She floated over to the shuttle door.

"You, too."

Fuller nodded, then closed and dogged the airtight doors behind her. All airtight doors to be closed in combat.

Both strapped into their command chairs, fastening all the belts to keep them from flailing about under variable-gravity conditions.

Both logged into the battlespace display.

The Deneb Republic fleet was highlighted red now, meaning their exit from the envelope was imminent. In a couple of hours. Its position on return to normal spacetime was marked, and Force DB was pretty much right where Sharp wanted it. Out of range of their guns, with enough space to get some velocity up, but not so far as to be a long delay in getting to the enemy.

Of his own ships, about half showed green, meaning their pilots were in position in their command deck simulations. The other half were yellow, though two changed to green as he watched. Within five more minutes, all were green.

"OK, everybody," Sharp said over the all-ships channel. "Just another exercise. Let's not forget what we learned."

Then it was time to wait.

"Coming up on dropping from the envelope, Admiral."

On the Deneb Republic flagship, Vice Admiral Hardesty nodded.

"Let's keep our eyes about us, everybody. I don't like surprises. They can ruin your whole day."

That broke a little bit of the tension, and there were some chuckles. Hardesty smiled. Of such small things were successful commanders made.

They dropped out of the envelope. The scans settled quickly. There in front of them was the planet Meredith. Hardesty raised an eyebrow as he could see no heavy fleet elements in the display. There should be a couple battle groups at Meredith. On the other side of the planet, perhaps?

As the scans picked up smaller detail, Hardesty saw, between his fleet and Meredith, a clutch of a dozen frigates on his direct line of approach to the planet. They were close to him as well. Almost directly in front of him.

What was going on? Had they anticipated his arrival somehow? How were they positioned so precisely? A sensor ship in envelope space, perhaps? But they hadn't seen any. Just those two reflections. Had he been wrong?

If they anticipated his arrival so precisely, why were there no heavy ships present?

"CSP deploying, Admiral."

Hardesty nodded. Combat Space Patrol. Get a few attack ships out there to protect the fleet. The ready ships, one per launch rail on each of his eight attack-ship carriers. Thirty-two attack ships, mounting a total of sixty-four ship-to-ship missiles.

"Message coming in for the flag, Admiral."

A vice admiral, in shipsuit, appeared on his display. A good-looking guy – at least his avatar was – but with an edge to him. Young for a vice admiral.

"Deneb Republic commander. I am Federation Navy Vice Admiral David Sharp. You are in violation of Federation space. Surrender your vessels or you will be destroyed."

"Tracking. That's all we see are those twelve frigates?"

"Yes, Admiral. They are accelerating now. Frigate mass readings are correct. Energy readings show as attack-ship carriers. Accelerations are very high. Over twice what I would expect from a frigate."

So maybe he had been wrong about those reflections. They did have frigates with those energy readings that could accelerate that fast. Still, they were frigates, after all. Mass readings didn't lie.

"Open a channel. 'Vice Admiral Trent Hardesty here, Admiral Sharp. I seem to have you outnumbered. I will accept your surrender, however.'"

The message that came back was brief.

"On your head be it then, Admiral Hardesty."

Hardesty thought about launching additional attack ships, then reconsidered. Twelve frigates. Sixty-four nuclear weapons. This would be short.

Still, best to wait until it was over.

"Fleet orders. All power to shields."

Deke Sharp had sent the pre-recorded message while he got his command under way. Full acceleration – war emergency power – toward the Deneb Republic fleet. He laid in his routes from a library of them he had built up during the exercises, modifying them to fit the actual locations of the enemy ships.

"They're launching attack ships, Sir. Four per carrier," Fuller said.

"Understood."

Force DB was gathering speed toward the eight battle groups of the Deneb Republic fleet, but everything was happening now in real time, not at the four-to-one pace of the simulations. Sharp started working up his return routes while he waited.

"The attack ships are spacing in formations, Sir."

Sharp looked again. It was true. Oh, that would help. Leave it to the regimented discipline of a police state to fly combat fighters in four-ship formations.

Sharp modified his routes to take advantage.

This was going to be a turkey shoot.

Rather than pass through the enemy formation, he veered his four-ship supporting pairs across the enemy formation, going for the attack-ship launch rails once the attack-ships were chewed up.

"Don't forget the jinking, Admiral."

Sharp looked again at his routes, modifying several of them to increase jinking. They wouldn't get all of those attack ships right off, so he had to maintain his defensive posture.

"Understood."

Fuller saw Sharp modifying his routes and nodded. That was better.

Time dragged as the ships – the frigates on one side and the attack-ships on the other – inexorably closed with each other.

"No new launches, Sir. He may think that's enough to deal with us."

Another stroke of luck.

Well, this was going well.

So far.

As the attack ships approached missile range, Force DB jinked. The three groups of four jinked in different directions, building side vector and presenting their broadsides to the attack ships.

Forty-eight battle-cruiser guns fired on the thirty-two attack ships, which had come straight in, expecting little resistance. The computer spread its fire across all thirty-two ships, and all thirty-two disappeared in boils of fire.

Hardesty was seated in his command chair on the flag bridge of the Deneb fleet flagship looking at his display when his eight CSP attack-ship groups simply disappeared.

"Fuck! What the hell was *that*?"

"Energy readings are for battle-cruiser guns, Sir. Four per broadside."

"Launch all attack ships. We can't let them get in among our formations."

"Aye, sir. Fleet orders. Launch all attack ships."

"Order battle cruisers to open fire as available."

"Aye, Sir. Battle cruisers firing as available."

"New launches now, Sir."

Sharp nodded as he watched. It wasn't a simultaneous launch. Some of the launch crews were faster mounting attack ships on the launch rails than others.

Force DB was now moving into the front elements of the huge Deneb Republic fleet formation. Guns fired in rapid succession as the DV recognized targets of opportunity and took them. Each of the ships was a maelstrom of fire at the profusion of enemy ships.

They weren't the only ones firing. Cruisers opened up on the frigates as they came on target, but the cruisers' hits could not penetrate the frigates' diamond-hard shields. It made for a rough ride, but no one in the frigates – who were all logged into the battle on their virtual command decks – even noticed.

Force DB was running for the attack ships, following Sharp's routes to get at those launch rails. Attack ships now started after them, but the jinking of Force DB was working against them. They weren't spacing in formation anymore.

One fighter loosed a missile that overshot a Force DB ship that jinked at the right time, and it impacted a Deneb heavy cruiser and exploded. The cruiser started streaming air and debris from the jagged rent in its side.

Then the Force DB ships opened up on the attack-ship launch rails of the three leading Deneb Republic attack-ship carriers. Their shields' hard points were tough to penetrate with a single beam, but an entire broadside burned through and turned the launch rail, and usually an attack ship being mounted, into scrap metal.

As the ships jinked to bring their broadsides to bear on the launch rails on the other side of those carriers, *Ninhursag* exploded into a stream of debris.

"What happened there?" Sharp asked as he reorganized that pair of pairs into a single triplet.

Fuller shot a glance at the sensor logs from *Ninhursag* and had the answer quickly.

"She overheated a beam emitter and it flashed back. She basically shot herself."

"Modify targeting program to monitor emitter heating."

"Already working, Sir."

Fuller had the program open in front of her, added the check on emitter temperature, and taking a beam off-line until it cooled. She closed the program and updated it on the fly.

"Program modification in place."

A SHARP EDGE

Denouement

Deneb Vice Admiral Trent Hardesty watched from his command chair on the Deneb flag bridge.

"They're targeting our launch rails, Sir."

"Of course, they are. Continue to launch while we still can."

"Aye, Sir. Launches continuing."

"Are the battle cruisers firing on them?"

"Yes, Sir. Battle cruiser fire ineffective. Their shields are too strong."

Hardesty saw an errant missile hit his own battle cruiser.

"Comm. Tell those attack ship pilots to be careful."

"Aye, Sir. I'm monitoring. They're having a hard time locking up targets in among our own ships."

When *Ninhursag* exploded, Hardesty was pleased.

"Yes! We got one."

"No, Sir," the lieutenant commander at the flag tracking station said. "She blew up on her own. Looks like a beam emitter failure."

"Well, at least we know they're vulnerable to something."

"Yes, Sir."

Hardesty continued to watch, as cruiser-strength beams continued to ripple across his command. The amount of fire those frigates were pouring out was incredible. Three destroyers exploded as he watched, and his cruisers were being systematically blinded, even as they concentrated on his launch rails.

"How are they even aiming those guns that fast?"

"The guns appear to be under computer control, Sir. Any target of opportunity in their sight, they take it."

Another destroyer exploded.

"So I see."

Deke Sharp checked the time. At the slow pace everything happened in a space battle, just due to the distances involved, three hours had passed. He manipulated routes on his display.

Force DB made a broad turn and came back across the Deneb Republic formation, aiming for the five attack-ship carriers in Hardesty's thicker second rank. As they did, the attack ships chasing them were exposed to the frigates' broadsides, and another fifteen attack ships disappeared.

Some of the attack ships had made the turn, however, and were occluded by bigger ships in the way until they were behind the broadsides of the frigates.

They were learning.

The jinking of the Force DB groups was whittling away at the attack ships following even as they bore down on the carriers. Several more disappeared.

One attack ship got off both missiles, targeting one of Force DB's pair of pairs. The jinking took out one missile, but one got through, detonating in *Hachiman*'s engines. The frigate exploded when the engines let go, and Sharp reorganized the pair of pairs as a second triplet.

Then Force DB was streaming across the rear echelon carriers. Cruiser-strength broadsides targeted their launch rails as the frigates overspaced or underspaced their targets. One carrier after another came under Force DB's fire as they crossed the formation.

The attack-ship carriers weren't the only Deneb Republic ships to feel the frigates' fire. Attack ships continued to disappear. Another four destroyers exploded. Cruisers were rendered effectively blind to continued hits on their targeting sensor arrays.

When they were overflying the third carrier in the rear echelon, an attack ship caught up with *Lakshmi*. This was the same fellow who had taken out *Hachiman*, but he now had no missiles left. He rammed *Lakshmi* in her engines, and the engines failed. *Lakshmi* disappeared into a stream of debris.

"Add attack ships who've expended their missiles to the target list."

"Aye, Sir. Working on it."

It was minutes later that Fuller reported back.

"Targeting modification complete. On-line."

It was coming up on six hours into the battle as Force DB overflew the last two attack-ship carriers of the Deneb Republic fleet. These had had the most time to launch attack ships, and the frigates were firing nearly continuously keeping them and their missiles at bay.

Then, as they overflew the last carrier, an attack ship popped up from behind the cover of a cruiser beyond and loosed off two missiles. The angle was bad at that moment, and the missiles impacted on the noses of the frigates *Baldr* and *Baalham*.

In vacuum, the shields held, even against the ten megaton explosives, so there was no structural damage, but EMP and hard radiation sleeted through the ships, their systems, and their captains. Both pilots popped out of their virtual command decks when their virtual terminal processors failed.

"What's the status on *Baalham* and *Baldr*?"

"All systems non-functional, Sir. Hardened systems are rebooting. Engines, shields, weapons, and communications. All soft systems are reported permanently non-functional. Pilots are not in contact."

"Life signs?"

"Failing."

Sharp pounded the arm of his chair.

"Reboot complete. Contact re-established with *Baldr*, Sir. Voice only."

"Hi, Deke. Sorry. We missed that one."

"Ted, are you OK?"

"No, Deke. I'm already dead, I just haven't stopped breathin' yet. Worse shape than you were, buddy. I'm all shot through with radiation. Cabin dosimeter is off the scale."

"Fuck. I'm sorry, Ted."

"Luck of the draw, Deke. We sure got 'em, though, didn't we?"

"Yeah, we did, Ted."

"Do two things for me, Deke. Let my parents know I was thinkin' about 'em. I was always proud to be their son."

Lanham was wracked with coughing at this point. Sharp could hear blood hitting the deck aboard *Baldr*.

"I will, Ted."

"Second thing. Make it count for somethin', Deke. Make it count."

At that point, the other side went silent.

"On-board sensors now show no life signs aboard *Baldr* or *Baalham*, Sir," Fuller said in a breaking voice.

Sharp checked the status of the inbound Federation battle groups, then passed orders to the battle groups behind Meredith.

"Can we remote *Baldr* and *Baalham* to space formation with us?"

"Absolutely, Sir."

"Let's do that. Guns on automatic, all three ships. In the meantime, find me the flagship and the secondary flagship."

"Working on it, Sir."

Sharp hit the all-ships channel.

"Force DB. Withdraw to Meredith. The cavalry is just over the hill. All ships withdraw. Maximum acceleration."

"Flagships are carriers two and four in this rear line, Sir. Fleet flag is number two."

Sharp laid in his route to Meredith at maximum acceleration, swinging around and coming back across that last row of carriers. *Baldr* and *Baalham* made a coordinated turn with *Medea*, and the three ships spaced back through the Deneb Republic formation together, all rotating on their axis, all guns blazing.

As *Medea* was coming up on the fourth carrier in the line, Sharp took remote on *Baalham*, broke formation and steered her right into the side of the big attack carrier. He put all power into *Baalham*'s shields at the last second, and the diamond-hard shields of the frigate penetrated the shields of the attack-ship carrier. *Baalham* was almost completely inserted into the big ship.

"DV. Scuttling charge sequence FNS *Baalham*. Scuttling code Baalham 11092173841701."

"Code confirms. Confirm scuttling order."

"Confirm. Scuttle *Baalham*."

The ten-megaton explosion occurred *inside* the carrier's shields. She had no protection at all. Worse, the shields of the carrier channeled the explosion fore and aft along the hull of the big ship. It blew out the bows on the front, and, when it hit the engines aft, the engines let go, the shields failed, and the built-up pressure blew the ship apart.

There wasn't a remaining piece of the huge ship bigger than an outhouse.

Medea and *Baldr* were past her though, and out of the blast zone. They came close over the top of the third carrier and bore down on the second. Sharp took *Baldr*'s helm on remote and steered her right into the fleet flag carrier, diverting all power to shields at the last moment. Like *Baalham*, *Baldr* penetrated the big ship's shields and inserted herself into the hull of the big ship.

"DV. Scuttling charge sequence FNS *Baldr*. Scuttling code Baldr 23048152235712."

"Code confirms. Confirm scuttling order."

"Confirm. Scuttle *Baldr*."

Looking back at the blossoming debris field of Vice Admiral Hardesty and his flagship, Sharp muttered.

"There you go, Ted. You couldn't ask for more."

Medea flew past the first carrier in the line with a few attack ships in tow. Most that had been following *Medea* were a little too close to the explosions of the big carriers, and were no longer a problem. Three of them, however, were still chasing her.

"We've got company, Sir."

Sharp looked at the battle display and was considering tactics when *Osiris*, *Frigg*, and *Danaan* came boiling out from behind the Deneb Republic fleet, guns blazing. The attack ships disappeared in boiling balls of fire.

"We got 'em, Boss," Matt Deckard's voice came over the radio. "C'mon. Let's blow this joint."

Some straggler attack ships made after the fleeing frigates of Force DB as they accelerated toward Meredith, but jinking made following Force DB very hazardous and they broke off to stay with their fleet.

The attack ships had just broken off and Force DB was in the clear when Federation Navy battle groups started dropping out of the envelope behind the Deneb Republic fleet.

A SHARP EDGE

In front of Force DB, four more Federation Navy battle groups came out from behind the planet, accelerating hard toward the enemy fleet. They were joined by almost four hundred ground-based attack ships rising from the planet.

The twelve frigates of Force DB had held the massive Deneb Republic fleet helpless for nearly eight hours, until overwhelming force arrived.

The eight battle groups of the Deneb Republic fleet were a riven mess. Over a hundred attack ships destroyed. Half of the twenty-four destroyers destroyed. The battle cruisers blind, all their guns in local control. And two massive attack-ship carriers destroyed, the other six rendered ineffective, with ruined launch rails.

Total dead in the Deneb Republic fleet: over ten thousand.

Total Federation Navy losses: five frigates, and five crew dead. Captain Prudence Rialto on *Ninhursag*, Captain Ralph Mueller on *Hachiman*, Captain Bernard Horzen on *Lakshmi*, Commander Sean Furlan on *Baalham*, and Commander Theodore Lanham on *Baldr*.

Sharp keyed his communications to all Deneb Republic ship captains.

"Federation Navy Vice Admiral David Sharp to all Deneb Republic ships illegally in the Meredith system. Anybody else want to not surrender today?"

Planet Leave

As Force DB made its way to Meredith and Federation Navy battle groups made their way to the battle, Sharp called Vice Admiral Chester Matthews, the Federation Navy system commander for the Meredith system.

"Matthews."

"Deke Sharp, Admiral Matthews."

"Good afternoon, Admiral Sharp. I'm happy to see you survived the battle."

"Yes, Admiral. Thank you. I am now turning command over to you. We're pretty beat up now, and need to withdraw."

"Did you leave anything for us to do, Admiral?"

"Mostly take surrenders, I think."

Matthews nodded.

"You've done an incredible job, Admiral Sharp. Please pass my congratulations on to your battle group."

"Thank you, Admiral Matthews. Sharp out."

Sharp cut the channel, sat back and sighed.

"So we're done," Fuller said.

"Yeah. We're done."

"And we survived."

"Some of us did, anyway."

"Well, for the living, life goes on. Let's get some dinner. Under way, we can even eat real food."

"There's an idea."

They logged out of the battlespace display and were back aboard *Medea*.

Heading in to Meredith would take the best part of a day at

frigate accelerations, which they kept to for the remainder of their withdrawal from the battle. The remaining ships had all taken a pretty severe beating from the hits from beams of the Deneb Republic battle cruisers, impacts with debris, and close calls with nuclear missile explosions.

Just how severe became apparent as the captains of Force DB logged out of their command deck simulations. Bruises and sore muscles and joints from being slammed about in their safety harnesses were common, and items in the storage lockers – such as their food supplies – were pretty jumbled about.

Fuller made her way gingerly to the main cabin from the command chair in the shuttle where she had ridden out the battle.

"Oooh, that hurts."

"What hurts, Suzie?"

"Everything."

Sharp nodded.

"Pretty rough ride."

"I'm just as glad I wasn't there to experience it, but I feel pretty beat up."

"Well, let's have some dinner, then we can straighten things up a bit. Check on our supplies."

"Works for me, D.K. Breakfast was a long way back. I'm starving."

After dinner, Fuller straightened up their supplies cabinets while Sharp went into the other shuttle and checked on his special-purpose prosthetics and medical supplies. He also checked the dog suit. All had been packed pretty well and were undamaged.

They then fell into the bed in the main cabin, exhausted. Both took a mild pain-killer to tone down their aches from being so heavily jostled, to make sleep easier.

Both were out in minutes.

The next morning ship's time, after ten hours of sleep, they finally stirred.

"Oooh, I'm stiff," Fuller said.

"Let me service my prosthetics, then we can get some breakfast."

"OK. I'll help."

With his morning chores out of the way, and a real breakfast complete, Sharp got in the command chair and checked their status.

The seven surviving frigates of Force DB were spacing in formation toward Meredith, as they had left them last night while everyone recovered. They would arrive at the Navy's orbital Meredith Station Number Four in about four hours, around noon ship's time, as their trip time had been shortened by the hard push of acceleration they had made to get away from the Deneb Republic Fleet as they withdrew.

Sharp researched the hotels in Saratoga, the capital city of Meredith. There were a lot of cheap hotels in the night-life section of town, where Navy crews took planet leave, but that was not what Sharp was looking for.

Here we go. Saratoga Shores, a luxury beach resort outside the city. Sharp booked a cluster of seven cabins toward one end of the beach for a week. There was some nonsense about deposits and the like, but that disappeared when he gave his name as VADM David Sharp.

When his command status allowed him to see that everyone was up and about, he placed an all-ships call to Force DB. Everyone checked into the call within a couple minutes.

"Morning, everyone. Vice Admiral Matthews now has

command in Meredith, and we are all on R and R. So I've granted a week's planet leave to us all, and booked us into a beach resort on Meredith."

There were some cheers to that, and Sharp went on.

"When we get to Meredith Station Number Four, the small-ship station, we'll turn over our ships to the Navy for servicing and take our shuttles down to the Navy shuttleport. We'll all take a bus to the resort, so pack your planet duffles for the beach.

"See you all there."

Arriving in squadron strength at a Navy station, one could expect a few delays in getting everyone dock assignments and clearance, but there were no delays. The station commander himself came on the radio to grant Force DB immediate clearance to seven docks.

He would personally arrange the servicing and system checks of Force DB's surviving ships.

"It will be my honor to do so," he told Sharp.

When Sharp and Fuller landed the shuttle at the Navy shuttleport on the surface, he expected to have to arrange a shuttlebus to take them to the resort, but there was no need. A Navy VIP shuttle awaited them at their pad.

As they exited the shuttle, a Federation Navy lieutenant commander walked up to them with a petty officer second class. The lieutenant commander saluted.

"Admiral Sharp. Welcome to Meredith, Sir. This way, please."

The PO2 took their planet duffles and stowed them in the baggage locker of the VIP shuttlebus as they boarded. When everyone was seated, the lieutenant commander addressed

Sharp.

"We'll be picking up your ship captains and then taking you all to your hotel, Sir. Just sit back and enjoy the ride."

"Thank you, Commander Davis."

When all of the D Branch operatives of Force DB had been picked up, the shuttlebus headed out of the shuttleport and up the coast.

"Well, this is pretty comfy," Matt Deckard said as he settled back into the plush seating.

"It's very nice," Alice Dobson said.

Sharp nodded.

"It'll be nice to have some down time," he said.

When they got to the resort, they were already checked in. There was no fussing about payment methods or any of that. The Navy VIP shuttlebus delivered them directly to their cottages at the far end of the beach from the main buildings of the resort.

The shuttlebus dropped Sharp and Fuller off first, of course. The PO2 took their planet duffles into the cottage, placing them inside the door.

"I hope you enjoy your stay on Meredith, Admiral Sharp."

"Thank you, Commander Davis."

The lieutenant commander saluted and he and the PO2 reboarded the shuttle for the short trips to the other cottages.

"Well, that was the VIP treatment, for sure," Fuller said as they carried their planet duffles into the bedroom.

"Yeah. I didn't even have to deal with the typical payment arrangements. Somebody took care of it all."

"Otto?"

"Probably."

They went out into the living room, and Fuller checked out the room service menu.

"Hey, D.K. They have Dufort *Esprit* on the drinks menu."

"By the bottle?"

"Umm, actually, yes. At five thousand credits a bottle."

"Order two, and ten snifters."

"You're serious?"

"Sure. Why not?"

"Why ten snifters?"

Sharp shrugged.

"In case some get broken?"

"OK, I guess. You're the guy with the expense account."

"Oh, and get a box of good cigars."

Fuller looked through the cigar list, and saw a brand she recognized from Dominic Trask's humidor. She ordered, and then they went out on the lanai.

"Beautiful," Fuller said.

"Very nice. Kind of disorienting, though. It's like, what? Five, six o'clock ship's time?"

"Yeah, and it looks like it's coming up on noon here."

Sharp chuckled.

"Gonna be a long evening."

While they waited for room service, Sharp called in to Otto Pasha on Ariel. It was the beginning of the day there.

"Pasha."

"Hi, Otto. It's Deke."

"Deke! I'm glad to see you're OK. I watched the battle as it happened, and I can't believe anybody survived all that."

"Five of us didn't, Otto."

"I know, Deke. I was sorry to see that. I recruited all those people, you know. Only to have them die in service. But you did the job. Against incredible odds, you held them until the Navy could get there."

Sharp nodded. There wasn't much to say to that.

"With losing Prudence, Ralph, and Bernie, we're low on senior field operatives now. I was going to put Matt and Alice up for senior."

Pasha nodded.

"That makes sense, Deke. I'll put the paperwork through on this end."

"And thanks for taking care of the resort for planet leave on Meredith, Otto."

"Wasn't me, Deke. The Navy must have done that. They're pretty happy with you fellows over there right now."

"Ah."

Sharp was quiet a moment.

"Otto, can you and Claude hold down the fort there for a couple of months? I was thinking of stopping through Elizabeth on the way home."

"Sure, Deke. After an assignment like that, take what time you need."

"Thanks, Otto. Be talkin' to you."

"Take care, Deke."

Room service showed up in a little electric cart, and brought in two bottles of the Dufort *Esprit*, ten snifters, and a box of Cartagena *Magnifico* cigars, along with a cutter and a butane torch lighter.

Sharp invited the other six Force DB captains – all D Branch field operatives – over for cigars, cognac, and, at some point, dinner.

Matt Deckard was the first to arrive. He saw the Dufort *Esprit* on the table.

"Oh, Deke. You shouldn't have."

Sharp laughed and covered the bottom of two snifters. They toasted each other in silence and sipped.

"Ah. I'd almost forgotten just how good it was."

The others drifted in to the lanai of the center cottage of the seven at this end of the beach.

Alice Dobson eyed the cognac dubiously.

"I've never been much for cognac," she said.

"Have you ever had Dufort *Esprit*?" Deckard asked.

"Well, no."

"Then you don't know whether you like cognac or not. You just know that you don't like the lesser cognacs."

Deckard poured enough to cover the bottom of a snifter and handed it to her. She smelled and then sipped.

"Oooh. That's nice."

"Congratulations," Deckard said. "You now have a very expensive vice."

"Work hard, play hard," Sharp said.

The assembled operatives toasted to that.

"One other reason we're celebrating," Sharp announced. "We lost three senior field operatives yesterday, and Matt Deckard and Alice Dobson have been up for senior for a while. So, effective today, Matt and Alice have both been promoted to senior field operative."

There were cheers and toasts and claps on the back, but no jealousy. Deckard and Dobson both had good reputations with the other field operatives, and everybody knew they were next in line for promotion.

They were starting on the second bottle of the Dufort *Esprit* when Admiral Kurt Jurgens showed up from his office, in full uniform. He heard the party going on and walked around the back of Sharp's cottage to the lanai.

"Admiral on the deck," Deckard announced.

Everyone stood, but Jurgens waved them back down.

"At ease, everybody. At ease. I just wanted to stop by and say thank you."

Deckard offered him a cognac – *How did Deke know to get extra glasses?* Fuller wondered – and he accepted it. He also took a cigar and tucked it into a pocket for later.

"I don't want to crash your party, but I wanted to tell you what's going on. All of the Deneb Republic ships surrendered to Admiral Matthews. We're now trying to figure out what to do with the fifty thousand surviving spacers."

"Offer them citizenship here," Sharp said.

"Really, Deke?"

"Sure. Oh, probationary period and all that. Seven years or something. But how many of those people do you think really want to go back? And think of the intelligence coup."

"Well, that's something to think about. We'll hold them for a while – prisoners of war – because we don't know what the High Commissioner and the Federation Council will want to do about the Deneb Republic over this."

"Annex them," Clyde Matthews said. "The rest of their navy can't be much anymore. They went for all the marbles and lost."

"Another interesting thought."

Jurgens considered while he sipped his cognac.

"Anyway, as I say, I wanted to stop by and say thank you to you all, in person. I have been, man and boy, in the service for over thirty years, and I have never seen anything so brave as what you did. Facing down eight battle groups with a dozen frigates will go down as one of the great naval battles of all time."

"We had our losses, too, Kurt," Sharp said.

"And they will not be forgotten, Deke. Their names have been added to the honors list. Captains Rialto, Mueller, and Horzen, and Commanders Furlan and Lanham, will have ships named after them in the future."

Hearing their names from Jurgens, knowing that he knew them all off the top of his head, made a big difference to Sharp, and his throat was husky when he replied.

"Thank you, Admiral."

Jurgens nodded, then finished his cognac.

"Party hardy, my friends. You deserve it."

Jurgens got up and, with a little wave, was gone.

"Nice fellow," Deckard said.

"Sometimes the best rise to the top," Sharp said.

The resort's menu specialized in seafood items, and their quality was legendary. They ordered dinner, and the lanai was soon filled with the aromas of fresh seafood. Snapper, roughie, ahi, mahi-mahi, lobster, shrimp. Accompanying wines were chosen without regard for the price, or perhaps with a negative regard. Unfiltered cabernets, private reserve pinot noirs, premium chardonnays, ordered by the bottle.

After dinner, it was back to cigars and cognac – even to a third bottle of the Dufort *Esprit* – before fatigue finally caught up with the survivors of Force DB. They wandered off to their own cottages before they fell asleep where they were.

The rest of the week at the resort was one long party. Swimming and sunning during the day, eating and drinking, smoking and talking, into the night. Nothing matched that first epic night, but, by the end of the week, all were happy to have survived, and had put the nightmare of that epic battle behind them. The space to decompress had been necessary. Now they all just wanted to go home.

The resort had transportation duties back to their shuttles, as they did not all leave at once. They drifted off in ones and twos over the last two days.

Sharp and Fuller were the last to leave. The resort's limousine dropped them off at *Medea*'s shuttle at the Navy shuttleport.

Back To Elizabeth

High Admiral Mitt Prendergast was meeting with John Robertson, the Chairman of the Central Committee of the Deneb Republic. He was new to the position, his former boss, High Admiral Hugo Biarritz having disappeared.

It was only a week since the Disaster of Meredith.

"What I want to know," Robertson shouted, "is how the hell twelve frigates can defeat our entire fleet, eight battle groups."

"We've analyzed the video and sensor readings the fleet was sending back in real time, sir, and we don't know for sure. We do know that the enemy ships were frigates in mass readings only. Energy levels read as more those of an attack-ship carrier, while the guns were the strength of those of a battle cruiser."

"How can they even do that, Admiral? You can't fit all that into a frigate's mass."

"Actually, sir, you might be able to, if you had a minimal crew. One person. Maybe two. What life-sign readings we could pick up were very low, but it could have been as little one or two people per ship. When the two ships got close enough to ram our carriers, we picked up no life-sign readings at all."

"Did we know they had these new ships when the Navy proposed this idiotic attack, Admiral?"

Robertson had actually pushed the attack, because the population of the Deneb Republic was getting restless against Robertson's heavy-handed rule. A war was always a good way to get the public behind you. But it was decidedly not in Prendergast's best interests to correct the chairman on the point.

"No, sir. We had heard nothing about them, which is alarming in itself. But, without seeing them in action, it probably wouldn't have changed the calculus."

Robertson nodded. He was calming down now, Prendergast noted, but not by much.

"How many of those new ships do you think they have?"

"Not many, sir. That may even have been all of them."

Robertson raised an eyebrow, and Prendergast continued.

"Consider, sir. We hadn't heard of them at all. That doesn't sound like a large-scale construction program. They were kept very secret. That also doesn't sound like a major program. Finally, when the major fleet elements did show up, they were all conventional ships. Not one of these frigates among the forty-eight ships."

"All right. That makes sense. And what are our remaining fleet elements?"

"Twelve battle groups, sir."

"And are those sufficient to defend the Republic?"

"Yes, sir."

"Even against these super-capable frigates, Admiral?"

"Well, we did destroy five of them, sir. If I'm right, they may only have seven left."

Once aboard *Medea*, Sharp and Fuller went through the inventory list, checking that all necessary items had been refreshed by Navy maintenance and supplies staff during the past week. Sharp also checked the ship's log, the reaction-mass tanks, and the status on the guns.

One did not go into space without checking, personally, every item. It only took the smallest of omissions to cause potentially deadly consequences. Space was unforgiving of the careless.

A SHARP EDGE

Sharp noted that *Medea*'s port-side beam emitters had been replaced, and the ship taken out and the port beam emitters tested. He thought he had leaned on them pretty hard during the battle, so he was glad to see maintenance had been on top of it.

Sharp got a call request from the station commander while they were checking everything.

"Good afternoon, Admiral Sharp."

"Good afternoon, Captain Pomeroy."

"Is everything satisfactory, Sir?"

"Yes, Captain. We haven't found any discrepancy so far. One always checks, of course. Space is intolerant of error."

"Absolutely, Sir. I'm glad that we are up to your standards."

"Yes, Captain. Well done."

"Thank you, Sir. You just let us know when you're ready to leave, and we'll have departure clearance for you."

When they were ready to depart, Sharp strapped into the command chair, and Fuller strapped into a drop seat. No need to sit in the command chair of the shuttle now, for normal – that is, non-battle – spacing.

"Elizabeth first?" she asked.

"Elizabeth first," Sharp said. "It's on the way home, anyway, and there's someone I need to thank."

Medea dropped away from Meredith Station Number Four on thrusters, then headed for the envelope at her normal cruising speed, about double what one would have expected of a frigate. That cat was out of the bag now, and there was no sense wasting time loping along.

They passed within sight of the Deneb Republic fleet, still buzzing with shuttles removing captured Deneb personnel a week after the battle. The ships themselves would probably be cut up for raw materials to make new Federation Navy ships.

Sharp had heard that the Navy was considering a large number of the Medea-class frigates in new fleet deployments.

Sharp called Dominic Trask while they were en route to the envelope.

"Trask."

"Hi, Dominic. Deke Sharp."

"Deke! You survived. And Suzie?"

"Also survived. We got a bit roughed up, but we survived."

"I've heard what all went on, of course. My sympathies on your losses."

"Thank you. Dominic, we were wondering if we were still welcome as houseguests at your beach house."

"Absolutely, Deke. That would be wonderful. And you can tell me your story. The news reporting is absolutely bloodless on some things, and they're usually wrong anyway."

"We have some stories for you, Dominic. No doubt about it."

"Wonderful. You're leaving Meredith now?"

"Yes. We're on our way to the envelope. Figure about ten, eleven days."

"Will do, Deke. See you then."

Sharp cut the connection.

"Well, we're still welcome."

"That will be fun. To see them all again."

They went to bed that night in normal space. When they woke up, *Medea* was in the envelope, and on course for Elizabeth.

Fuller remarked on it over breakfast.

"Talk about space travel becoming ho-hum boring. We made the transition into the envelope and didn't even stay up for it."

"Mostly it's a non-event, Suzie. The ship knows what it's

doing. Anything one does to interfere with that is more dangerous than the ship handling it."

"I suppose. It's just being pretty jaded, is all."

"Oh, that it is. That it is."

Ten days in the envelope was ten days in the envelope. Being mostly bored and restless.

For Deke Sharp, though, it was very calming. Even at the beach resort, he had still been partying and relaxing among his direct reports. People he might have to send into harm's way. People he might have to overrule in their performance of their jobs and duties.

In the envelope on the way to Elizabeth was the first time since leaving Elizabeth that he had been totally at ease. Left to his own devices. Nothing to plan, no one to play an act for. Off-stage, as it were.

There was nothing he could do, no messages he could send, no news or reports he could read. No one to supervise, no one to report to.

At the same time, at two-hundred-thousand-plus gravities, he was moving as fast as he could.

Medea dropped out of the envelope in the Elizabeth system. Sharp and Fuller still had twelve hours to the navy's orbital Elizabeth Station, even at her cruise acceleration.

They had adjusted ship's time during the trip so they were in sync with local time when they arrived. It was four in the morning on a Thursday, Gotham time, when they dropped out of the envelope.

They didn't wake for the transition.

Over breakfast, Sharp looked over to the display as Elizabeth grew closer.

"It'll be good to see Dominic again," Sharp said.

"You seem very close to Trask, for what little time we've actually spent together, D.K. It was only weeks on Elizabeth before, and with Trask only on the weekends at that."

Sharp thought about it and nodded.

"I don't have many opportunities to make friends, Suzie. Paul and Lydia on Humphreys. Tim and Daphne on Ariel. That's about it. Everyone else is someone I report to, or who reports to me. And some of them are people I will have to send into danger. Anyone else I know, I can't really talk about work, or anything important."

Fuller nodded. Most people had friends at work, but Sharp and she didn't. For Fuller it was because anybody at work was potentially a subject of investigation.

"And he seems close to you as well, D.K. That seems even more unlikely."

Sharp shrugged.

"Not really, Suzie. He's a multi-decabillionaire. All of his contacts are business contacts. Opportunities for profit. Potential competitors. As far as friends, if you have that kind of money, how do you know if someone wants to get close to you to be real friends or only because they're gold-digging?"

"And you?"

"Dominic knows I don't give a shit about his money. I have power. I don't have to care about money."

"So you're both safe for each other as friends."

"Yes, and that's why we can be close. Neither of us has many opportunities to have friends."

"I wonder what it is you most value in each other as friends."

"That's an easy one, Suzie."

"What's that?"

"He's honest and he's competent."

Fuller nodded.

"And you as well. Makes sense."

Medea's shuttle put down on the helipad of Trask's beach house in the fading light of dusk. Robert came out with staff, who took their planet duffles to the guest suite Sharp and Fuller had used before. Robert led them after.

"I hope that your trip was satisfactory, sir, ma'am."

"More than that, Robert, it was excellent."

"Very good, sir. I am pleased for you."

He led them into the room.

"Dinner is at seven. I assume you prefer it on your patio?"

"Yes, thank you, Robert."

The butler nodded.

"If there is anything else you need, do not hesitate to ring."

Robert left, and Fuller headed for the bar.

"Let's see if there's any of that cognac left. I miss alcohol during transits, D.K. The complete abstinence."

"Space and alcohol don't mix, Suzie. You never know if or when things are going to go sideways."

"Oh, I know. I wasn't militating to change it. But I'm happy to have feet back on the ground."

She checked the cabinet at the bar.

"Oh, look at this, D.K. A new bottle."

"Dominic must buy it by the case."

"Cognac and cigars on the patio, then? We have an hour until dinner."

"Sounds good."

Life at the beach house fell into the pattern they had established before. Dinner on the patio, sleep – and sex – on the big luxurious bed. Breakfast and lunch on the patio.

Fuller ran the raft out into the calm sea behind the breakwater and swam hard laps around it, both in the morning and the afternoon. Getting back the muscle tone that had been lost in the forced inaction of space travel. The 'rubber-band machine' could alleviate some of that, but not all.

After the afternoon swim, she came back to Sharp on the patio, peeled out of the wet bikini bottoms, and lay out naked to sun and dry off.

"I really like that raft, D.K. Can we do one of those at home?"

"Not sure, Suzie. The breakwater here is what makes it work. In the surf back home, probably not."

"Well, shoot. I wouldn't want to give up the surf, though. It's too much fun to bodysurf the breakers."

Sharp nodded, eyes closed, and sighed.

It was good to be back at Trask's beach house.

It would be even better to get home.

The Trasks arrived Friday night before six. Dominic Trask, being anxious to get out to the beach house and greet his guests, had left the office earlier than normal, even for a Friday.

Trask greeted them in the salon when they appeared for drinks before dinner.

"Deke!"

Trask strode across the room and threw his arms around Sharp. Sharp returned the hug, then Trask held him out at arm's length.

"You're looking good. I'm so pleased."

Fuller got a hug as well, if a more perfunctory one.

"We were so worried about you two. We knew you took losses, but the Navy hasn't released any names or details of the battle. Just that large Navy forces engaged and stopped the Deneb fleet. Took their surrender. So we won?"

"Yes, Dominic. We won. And, as you say, we took our losses. All of them my people."

"Ouch. Well, you must tell me all about it later."

Janine and Marie arrived, and there were hugs all around. They both expressed their relief as well.

"Dominic told us you were going into danger, but wasn't specific," Janine said. "When we saw the news, we feared the worst. Until Dominic heard from you, that is."

"I'm so happy you're both OK," Marie said. "And that you were successful."

Robert announced dinner, and they all moved to the dining room.

Dinner this evening was shrimp scampi tossed with pasta. The soup was French onion, while the sides were blanched young asparagus spears and a garden salad. Dessert was chocolate mousse with a coffee-flavored whipped cream, while the wine was an excellent estate-bottled sauvignon blanc.

Conversation perforce stopped during dinner.

After dinner, Trask, Sharp, and Fuller retired to the patio for cigars and cognac. Fuller didn't smoke, but she enjoyed the aroma of the cigars.

"And now, Deke, you must tell me the story."

Fuller was surprised that Sharp did not hold much back. He told Trask of Fuller's virtual command decks, including Sharp's flag deck. Of the demolition of the first wave of attack ships. Of their sweeps first left to right across the forward three carriers and then back, right to left, across the rear five carriers. Of their escape.

Along the way he mentioned the loss of Prudence Rialto,

and Fuller's on-the-fly modification of the program. The loss of Ralph Mueller and Bernard Horzen, and another on-the-fly program change from Fuller. And the loss of Sean Furlan and Ted Lanham to the pop-up attack of a single attack ship.

Sharp also told how he had used Furlan's and Lanham's ships to spear the enemy flagships, then destroyed them with the frigates' scuttling charges.

"And then the Navy showed up, we ran away, and they surrendered."

"Because you had gutted them. Yes, I see. Still, a remarkable story."

"With many thanks to you, Dominic Trask," Sharp said. "Without your warning, the outcome would have been very different."

"Even so, it was a close thing, Deke. Twelve frigates up against eight battle groups of much larger ships? I'm surprised any of you survived."

"They are very special frigates, Dominic."

"Yes. Yes, of course. More of an envelope-capable attack ship, I would think. I wonder if one might also mount missiles on them."

"They aren't considered offensive ships, really, Dominic."

"Perhaps they should be, Deke. Imagine if you had faced their thirty-two ships with even thirty-two of those frigates, also armed with ship-to-ship missiles. The tonnage ratio would still be terribly lopsided. Why, you could field a hundred such ships against a fleet that size. They would be helpless against them."

Fuller was surprised at Trask's understanding of the ship designs, then remembered that he had had significant investments in military contractors for years.

"Then why is the Navy almost exclusively made up of those

big, helpless ships, Dominic?" Fuller asked.

"Inertia, Suzie, and privilege. Consider. Deke was acting as what? Vice admiral? And he had twelve reports. Twelve ships. That's it. No staff. No thousands of people under his command, at least until the Navy showed up in force.

"In contrast, the vice admiral he turned command over to when he left had twelve battle groups under his command. Call it ninety *thousand* officers and spacers. And that's just aboard ship. The supply and maintenance and support tail on a command that big is immense.

"Who will make the decision to give up all of that for a hundred or so people in small ships?

"Even more to the point, Deke was essentially flying and shooting all twelve ships throughout the battle. Did I get that wrong, Deke?"

"No, that's essentially right, Dominic."

"And there you are, Suzie. Who would make a decision to deploy such ships, and give up all that privilege and status?"

"Kurt Jurgens might," Sharp said.

Trask considered.

"You're right. He might. I will have to bring it up to him."

Fuller raised an eyebrow.

"When one has amassed enough resources, Suzie, one gets to meet and know many people in high positions within the Federation. Kurt and I have met several times, and were table companions at an event a few years back. I am certain he would be willing to entertain my thoughts on this matter.

"Perhaps he would authorize some small project to field and test a design intended to make the best of what we have learned."

"I would be interested in that, Dominic," Sharp said.

"Oh, I'm sure that as the fleet commander in the recent

fracas, you would be consulted, Deke."

The conversation wound down, the cigars burned down, and the cognac ran out. Sharp and Fuller took their leave of Trask and headed to the guest suite.

Dominic Trask continued to stare out to sea for half an hour before retiring.

The weekend with the Trasks was as the earlier ones had been. Happy times, with Fuller and Marie horseback riding and swimming, Sharp mostly sunning and watching the young women, and meals from Trask's excellent kitchen. Breakfast buffet and lunch sandwiches on the patio of the main house, with exquisite dinners in the dining room, its window wall open to the sea.

After Sunday afternoon dinner, they all took their leave of each other. The Trasks headed back to the city, while Sharp and Fuller headed back to space.

It was time to go home.

The Big Question

Aboard *Medea* and headed for the envelope, Sharp got a call from Trask at eight o'clock the next morning.

"You're on the way to the envelope, Deke?"

"Yes, Dominic. We're almost there."

"I wonder if you could do me a favor. There should be a virtual builder's plate in your ship's maintenance files. Could you tell me the manufacturer and the build number, please?"

"Sure, Dominick. Hang on."

Sharp checked the ship's maintenance files. Ah. There it was.

"It's General Ship & Fitting, Dominic. Build number is shown as 73079."

"Excellent. Thanks, Deke. Good spacing, and let us know when you get home."

"Will do, Dominic. You take care."

They were in the envelope, spacing for Ariel – twelve days in the envelope away – and eating lunch. As they had gravity, they were eating normal food, not prepared foods from tubes. This lunch had been packed for them by Trask's kitchen, and was excellent. Cold roast beef on rye, with Swiss cheese and mayo.

"One thing I don't understand, D.K. You told Dominic a lot about the battle. A lot of non-public information. Are you not concerned about that?"

"Not with Dominic."

"Why not?"

"You heard Janine, Suzie. She said Dominic had not told them much other than that we were heading into danger. Her knowledge of what happened was purely from the news."

"And?"

"We told Dominic that a Deneb Republic fleet was on the way to Meredith, and we were going to intercept it. All his wife knew was that we were heading into danger."

"Ah, so he didn't even tell his wife anything confidential of what he knew."

"Correct."

Fuller nodded.

"OK, that makes sense, I guess. But he might act on his knowledge from a business point of view, D.K."

"But he won't be public about his moves. He won't say, 'Here's why I'm doing this.' He'll just move some investments around, without disclosing anything."

"And make more money."

"Think of where the Federation would be right now if he hadn't called me, Suzie."

"Forget I said anything, D.K."

"What about you, Suzie? We've been gone, what? Three months or something by the time we get home?"

"More like four. Then again, D.K. How many officials who were agents for the Deneb Republic got arrested? Navy, police, D Branch?"

"Maybe a thousand."

"I think that's the biggest official corruption ring ever busted."

"Well, yeah. There's that."

"So I'm good. Hank will understand."

Sharp nodded. Hank Gammon, Ariel Attorney General and Principal Investigator Suzanne Fuller's immediate boss.

"Good. I worried about that."

"Nah. Not a problem."

A SHARP EDGE

Gabriel Artino was the CEO of General Ship & Fitting, but he still didn't feel comfortable in the position. It had been about two years since Carmine Lonzi and his lieutenants had been executed by D Branch – with an explosion in the conference room just down the hall from this office! – for funding piracy in the Federation. Artino had been appointed Lonzi's successor CEO by the board.

The revelation had shocked Artino. Carmine Lonzi had been a legend. Someone to look up to. That he had been so involved in such a heinous business was a surprise to everyone, but personally shocking to Artino. There were some things one just did not do. How had Lonzi not known that?

But it also meant that Artino still had something of a probationary status with GS&F's shareholders and board of directors. Could he perform? Would GS&F be profitable under his management?

His thoughts were interrupted by a message from his secretary.

"You have an incoming call request from Dominic Trask, Mr. Artino."

His secretary didn't tell him who Dominic Trask was, nor did she need to. Most people were at least passingly familiar with the wealthiest man in the Federation, as was Artino.

More to the point, Dominic Trask was a big shareholder in GS&F. Not a majority shareholder. There were no majority shareholders. Trask owned four or five percent of GS&F, which made him one of – if not the – largest shareholders of the company.

Nevertheless, Artino had never had any personal dealings with Trask.

Artino accepted the call request, and a familiar face appeared on his display.

"Gabriel Artino."

"Good morning, Gabe. Dominic Trask here."

"Yes, Mr. Trask. What can I do for you today?"

"Well, call me Dominic, for one."

"Yes, Dominic."

"For the second, I have some information for you. I have heard that the Navy may be looking into purchasing additional ships based on your build number 73079."

Artino looked up the build number in a side panel, and it was marked Top Secret. Artino had such a clearance, and he approved the access. A frigate-sized one-man ship, with huge engines and guns. All built from standard parts – attack-ship carrier engines, battle cruiser guns – to control cost.

"That design is classified Top Secret, Dominic."

"I understand, Gabe, so let's not talk details. I will just say that my understanding is that the Navy may be looking at a bid request on a two-man version of such a ship. You know. Bunk beds, two of those comfortable command chairs, more food storage – that sort of thing."

"Interesting if true, Dominic."

"Oh, I believe this will happen, Gabe. My thoughts, though, were if you were to have one of your teams design such a version – and given your previous construction of 73079 and perhaps its sisters – you would be well-placed to give the Navy a well thought-out design, likely winning the bidding process."

"Sort of a what-if project, Dominic?"

"Exactly, Gabe. We just happened to have such a design handy. Know what I mean? Oh, and if this two-man version were to mount ship-to-ship missiles, like an attack ship, that would probably be a nice addition as well."

"How many missiles were you thinking, Dominic?"

"An attack ship mounts what? Two missiles, I think?"

"Yes, that's right."

"Then I think more than that would be good. Four, perhaps. Or, if you work up a rack for the missiles, and five or six fit, I would go with that. Whatever works, but I think at least four would be a nice number."

"All right, Dominic. Thank you for the heads up."

"No problem, Gabe. You have a nice day."

Trask cut the connection and Artino pulled up the design layout on build number 73079. The bunk beds would be no problem. There was a bed already. A second bunk above was no problem. Perhaps some privacy curtains. Extra food storage, sure.

The double command chairs was an interesting wrinkle. There was room. If there were a bit of space between them, they could duplicate the displays and controls rather than share them.

Artino – who came up within GS&F through the ship engineering department – made a copy of the design layout drawings and marked up the copy.

He sent it down to engineering – everyone there had a Top Secret clearance – and asked them to work up a proposal.

If the Navy did come out with a bid request, GS&F would be well-placed to get the bid. And that could help a lot with Artino's little probation problem with his shareholders and board.

It was over a week into their trip when Fuller brought up the battle.

"Hey, D.K?"

"Yes?"

"I've been thinking about the battle."

Sharp nodded. After something like that, it came back to you occasionally. When you were otherwise unoccupied. In the envelope, they were both 'otherwise unoccupied' a lot.

"Why does the Navy always use such big ships if something like *Medea* and her consorts can give them such trouble?"

"I think Dominic had it right, Suzie. Inertia and privilege. 'This is always the way we've done it. Besides, I like it this way.' No more than that."

Fuller shook her head.

"It seems silly. With twelve ships and thirteen people, we boxed up a fleet of thirty-two such big ships with sixty-thousand spacers."

"Actually twelve ships and two people, Suzie. The other pilots didn't have to do anything. They were a safety play in case the comm or computer went down."

"Yes. That's right. The two of us and twelve little ships. About the equivalent of what? Four destroyers in mass?"

"Yeah, something like that. More like three, I think."

"And in space, mass is cost."

"Yup."

Fuller shook her head again.

"Silly. More, it's stupid."

"Not my decision, Suzie."

"Oh, I know, D.K. It's still stupid."

When it had been three weeks since what wags were calling the Battle of Meredith, Dominic Trask sent another call request. He did not expect this one to be accepted immediately.

Admiral Kurt Jurgens scanned down his outstanding calls list. The Chief of Naval Operations of the Federation Navy had had a busy month, but now, three weeks after the Battle of Meredith, things were calming down.

One item jumped out at him. A call request from Dominic Trask. Of course, Jurgens knew that Dominic Trask was the richest man in the Federation.

More to the point, however, Jurgens had met Dominic Trask perhaps five years before, when Jurgens had been the system commander in the important Elizabeth system. Trask had been then, and likely still was, a sponsor of the annual Navy Veterans Gala in Gotham, a fund raiser for Navy veterans, widows, and children.

As system commander, Jurgens had sat at the main table and found, to his surprise, that he liked Dominic Trask. An interesting man, well read, well informed, and insightful.

His curiosity piqued, Jurgens accepted the call request. To his surprise, Trask appeared almost instantly.

"Trask."

"Hello, Dominic. Kurt Jurgens here."

"Hi, Kurt. Been a long time."

"Indeed, indeed. What can I do for you, Dominic?"

"I must tell you first, Kurt, that Deke Sharp is a personal friend of mine."

"Really."

"Oh, yes. In fact, he and Suzie Fuller left for what people are calling the Battle of Meredith from here – from my beach house – and they returned here on their way home to Ariel."

"That's interesting, Dominic."

"I believe they returned here to thank me, because it was my call to Sharp about some financial oddities I was seeing that allowed him and Suzie to turn up the Deneb invasion."

"I had heard something along those lines, Dominic."

Trask nodded.

"In a similar vein, I heard some of the inside story about what happened during the Battle of Meredith."

"That's disturbing."

"It was in the context of our existing confidential relationship, Kurt, and I hold a secret clearance based on some of my more government-related companies. Nothing to worry about."

"Ah."

"I do have one question to ask you as an outgrowth of that battle, however."

"Sure, Dominic. Go ahead."

"Why the hell are we still fielding big ships when they're sitting ducks for properly designed small ships?"

That was putting it pretty baldly, though one should never expect Dominic Trask to hedge his words.

"That's a question I can't answer, Dominic."

"Ah. So you see it, too."

"Of course. I think it's mostly a matter of how we've always done things. That, and some feeling on the part of flag officers that they should have a large span of command."

"Yes, well, all spacing into battle as a flag officer on one of those big antiques is going to do in the future is ensure you die with a lot of company. The Deneb fleet flag and assistant flag both went to hell with an honor guard of four thousand or so, isn't that right?"

Jurgens winced at Trask's use of the word antiques to describe most of the Navy vessels under his command, but Jurgens couldn't fault Trask's characterization.

"Yes, Dominic. That's right."

Trask nodded once, sharply.

"Right. Twelve ships. Thirteen people, but eleven of those were supernumerary, Kurt. Deke and Suzie controlled all the ships from his flagship. The others were only there in case communications was lost. So I have another question and a proposal for you."

"Go ahead, Dominic."

"Why don't you stop the acquisition of further big ships and buy a couple hundred of these small ships? Some mods, maybe. A two-man version, to allow a pair of non-married personnel to man them. Maybe some ship-to-ship missiles."

"And your proposal, Dominic?"

"Kurt, if you make that move, I will back you. A word here, a word there. About what a smart move it is. About how much better prepared we would be for future encounters. About what it would do for our fleet strength. You make the move, I will publicly back you."

"Don't you have investments in ship-building companies, Dominic? Military contractors?"

"Of course, Kurt. I have significant positions in most of them. But, whatever kind of ships you buy, I make money. It makes no difference to me financially. It makes one hell of a difference to me in how well prepared the Navy is to protect me and my family, however."

Jurgens nodded.

"Very well, Dominic. I will consider your input carefully."

"I can't ask for more than that, Kurt."

Medea dropped out of the envelope into normal spacetime.

"Well, there it is. Ariel," Sharp said.

"Oh, I can hardly wait to get home."

"Still about twelve hours."

"I know, I know. Still."

Home

A Navy staff car picked them up from their pad at the New Destin Navy Shuttleport and drove them home.

"The base commander insisted, Admiral Sharp," the driver explained.

When Sharp gave him a questioning look, he responded simply.

"Everybody in the Navy knows about Meredith, Sir. We drivers drew straws for the honor. I won."

Sharp looked to Fuller, who shrugged.

"Word travels fast in the Navy, D.K."

"Yes, Ma'am," the driver said.

They had signaled ahead to Daphne and Tim. Sharp and Fuller had left Elizabeth on Sunday evening and, with twelve days in the envelope and a half-day getting to or from the envelope on each end, they landed on Ariel Saturday afternoon.

When the Navy staff car pulled up, the driver got out of the car and came around to open the rear passenger door. He saluted Sharp and Fuller as they got out of the car.

Tim Hansen and Daphne Duplay came out of the door of Sharp's and Fuller's house to greet them. Duplay held Thomas Hansen, now almost five months old. He had been a newborn when they left.

The driver put their planet duffles inside the door, then saluted them again before getting into the car and driving off.

"What's all that about, Deke?" Hansen asked.

"Long story, Tim."

Fuller walked up and gave Duplay a hug, then turned her attention to the baby.

"Oh, look at you. You're such a big boy."

Thomas laughed and held his arms out to her. She took him from Duplay.

"My, he's gotten big."

"Yes, and he's a very happy boy. A joy, really. He just smiles and laughs all the time. Unless he needs some titty."

"Well, I understand that, Daphne. Food is food."

"Speaking of which," Hansen said, "we were just waiting for you two to fire up the grill."

"Well, let's go, then," Sharp said.

They walked across the beamed vault of the living room, around the big stone fireplace to the right, down the short passage to the gourmet kitchen, across the eating area, and out onto the patio, only stopping to pick up beers along the way.

Fuller gave Thomas back to Duplay, then walked over to her chaise, plopped down, lay back and sighed.

"What's with you, Suzanne?" Duplay asked. "You act like you just ran a marathon. When you travel in space, don't you just sit there?"

"Yes, Daphne, you just sit there, with the engines running continuously. You're moving constantly, even when you're just sitting still. It's exhausting. The only times the engines aren't running, you're weightless and want to barf. This is the first time I've been stationary, on a planet, in two weeks."

Thomas was nuzzling her chest, so Duplay pulled her bikini top off a breast and started tanking him up while the guys fussed the grill.

"Well, you're back home now, Suzanne. Time to lay back and relax."

Fuller lay back in the sun, her eyes closed.

"Oh, it feels so good. Daphne, you have no idea."

"Like the first time I slept through the night after weeks of this one getting up every two hours?"

"Yeah. Like that."

After dinner, Hansen and Duplay wanted the whole story of what went on during their trip. They told the public version, though from their own point of view. Sharp was nowhere near as forthcoming as he had been with Trask. Fuller noticed, and followed his lead.

"Well, that's a hell of a story, Deke," Hansen said.

"Yeah, D.K. Wow. You're lucky to have survived."

"Yes. Yes, we are."

"It was a chance thing," Fuller said. "Some did, some didn't. We did. Luck of the draw."

"What about you guys?" Sharp asked. "What went on while we were gone?"

"Do you remember Stephanie Borden, the real estate agent?"

"Sure," Fuller said. "Steph was great."

"Well, I asked Stephanie to check on the houses either side of you. We can't go on being your weekend guests forever."

"Anything come of it?"

"Oh, yes. Your neighbor in, uh, that direction, is willing to sell. He's been thinking about it. He wants a lot more money than you paid, however."

"Is it a nice house?"

"Oh, yes. Same builder, as a matter of fact."

"A lot more money, though?" Sharp asked.

"Oh, yes. Prices have gone up quite a bit since the commuter trains started running out this far."

"The commuter trains run to West Coast Village now?" Fuller asked.

184

"Oh, yes. That happened while you were gone. Couple months ago."

"They're early. Earlier than they thought, anyway."

"Well, the station's not built yet, but people were complaining. Why wait? You don't need a station for a commuter railroad to get started anyway. So they sell tickets in a booth for now while they build the station. Tickets and monthly passes."

"Is the price out of line, then?" Sharp asked.

"Not really," Hansen said. "And we can afford it anyway. If he puts it on the market now, it may even get bid up."

"Well, it'll be fun to have you next door," Fuller said. "We'll have to put a path in."

"When's the closing?" Sharp asked.

"Couple more weeks," Hansen said. "You'll still have us hanging around for a couple more weekends."

"Oh, good," Fuller said.

It was easy to fall back into the customs and patterns of being home. On Sunday, they swam in the ocean, walking down the stair from the headland behind the house.

"Not quite as convenient as Trask's beach. And no swim raft," Fuller said.

"Yeah, but you have the surf."

"Indeed," Fuller called back as she ran for the water.

The morning spent swimming, lunch with Hansen and Duplay on the patio. Hansen and Sharp grilled lunch meat sandwiches with melted cheese.

After the fresh-air poisoning of the morning's beach fun, Sharp and Fuller both napped on the chaises on the patio in the afternoon.

Sharp was awake when Fuller stirred.

"It's good to be home, D.K.," she said dreamily.

"Oh, yes. How about another day of weekend before work?"

"Deal."

Hansen went in to work on Monday. Duplay, Sharp, and Fuller stayed at the West Coast Village beach house. It wasn't until Tuesday morning that they took a self-drive cab into the village to catch the morning train in to work.

Duplay went along, Thomas in a baby carrier on her back.

Sharp and Fuller bought monthly passes at the booth next to the construction site of the passenger station. As West Coast Village was the first station on the new service, the train was waiting for departure when they arrived, and they went directly aboard.

The train started out at the posted departure time, made three additional stops, then ran express the rest of the way into the city.

"I thought this was going to be slow at first. Those other stops," Fuller said.

"Those are the four new stops," Duplay said. "West Coast Village to start, then the three on the way. From there it's express. That way they didn't have to change the existing train schedules."

"It's faster than I thought."

When they arrived at the downtown station, they headed in three different directions. Duplay and Thomas, to her and Hansen's condo downtown, Fuller, to her office downtown, and Sharp, to the cab stand for a self-drive cab to D Branch's corporate headquarters campus two miles northwest of downtown.

Sharp went to his office, the office next door to Otto Pasha's, and found it emptied out.

Well, that was disconcerting.

Sharp walked next door to Otto's office, the one he maintained here as head of operations. He also had an office next to Claude Allard's for his understudy role to the director of D Branch, on the other side of this, the top floor of the main building.

Pasha was in the office, but sitting in one of the guest chairs. The desk furnishings and paraphernalia in the office were Sharp's.

"Good morning, Admiral," Pasha said, and waved Sharp to the chair behind the desk.

Sharp went behind the desk and sat in his normal task chair there.

"You been waiting long, Otto?"

"No. I had a notification set on your pass-entry to the building. I just ran over here to beat you."

"So what's going on?" Sharp asked, waving around the office.

"Claude decided, if we could pull off an operation like the Battle of Meredith, we didn't need him around anymore. A week ago Friday was his last day. He's off to his cabin in the mountains, and couldn't be happier. Marie, too, for that matter. You missed out on cake."

"So you're now the head of D Branch?"

"Yes, Admiral. And you're head of operations."

Sharp waved off the title.

"That admiral business was just for the battle, Otto."

"No, Deke. Actually, it wasn't. Admiral Jurgens made all your commissions official. You, Fuller, the eleven operatives with you at the Battle of Meredith, and all the other field operatives in D Branch."

"Our status, then, Otto?"

"TDY to D Branch. To the Justice Department for Fuller."

"Why did he do that?"

"Because otherwise you wouldn't qualify for the Federation Cross. It's a military decoration, and he put in for it for all thirteen of you. Said your actions at the Battle of Meredith were the bravest damn thing he'd ever seen – his words – and he wouldn't let it go unnoted."

"He didn't have to do that."

"You didn't have to take twelve frigates up against the weight of steel you faced at Meredith, either, Deke. No one would have faulted you for calling that just a bit much."

"But we did have to, Otto. The Federation casualties otherwise would have been horrific."

"I think that's exactly the sort of calculation that ends up with the Federation Cross, Deke. That whole jumping-on-the-grenade thing. Don't knock it. It gives you tremendous clout with the Navy. You and Fuller and the others. We have a mission here, and that sort of thing is an advantage in carrying out our mission."

Sharp nodded. Pasha was right about that. His Navy avatar would no longer be bereft of decorations. The Federation Cross was all he needed.

And it wouldn't be stolen valor.

"What else is going on, Otto?"

"Admiral Jurgens asked my permission to build a new class of Navy ship based on the D Branch ships. Couple modifications. Two-man ships. Bunk beds. Two command chairs, but now with extra padding while the crew is in your virtual battlespace. Oh, and ship-to-ship missiles. Four or five of them. What with the Federation Cross and all, I was gracious and said, 'Sure.'"

"What does he do for the virtual battlespace, Otto? Does the Navy have a DV engine like we have?"

"No, but we're speccing out what the computer facility has to be to make it work. For testing, they'll use our machine here. Once the design is approved, they'll build a facility on Meredith."

"And their backup facility, Otto? They almost lost Meredith this time."

"For that, they can use ours, Deke. For a while, anyway. Probably won't need a backup facility, but if it comes to that, they can use ours. Ultimately, they won't be happy with that and will build another, but it spreads out the expenditure."

Sharp nodded.

"Lots going on."

"Yes. And Friday we have a memorial service. We'll unveil five more stars on the honor wall in the lobby. We've been waiting until you came back."

"Suzie will want to be there."

"Yes, I figured Admiral Fuller would want to attend."

"Anything else, Otto?"

"How about Maxine's for lunch, Deke? It's been months."

Sharp laughed.

"Sure, Otto. Maxine's for lunch."

Pasha got up and headed for the door.

"See you downstairs at eleven-thirty, Deke."

Many of the headquarters staff of D Branch was in the lobby. All of operations. All the department heads. A pair of operations people stood by five covered stars. There were dozens of existing stars on the wall, but they had never added five new ones at once.

As director of D Branch, Octavius Pasha stood in the front of the crowd and read off the names, one by one. Sharp and Fuller stood to one side. They and all the field operatives of D Branch were in Navy dress uniforms, acquired for this ceremony.

As Pasha read each name, the pair of operations people standing by the new stars removed the cover of one star at a time.

"Prudence Rialto.

"Ralph Mueller

"Bernard Horzen.

"Sean Furlan.

"Theodore Lanham."

With five new stars now uncovered, a bugler lifted his horn and blew Taps. Pasha and everyone in the audience covered their hearts with their right hand, except Sharp, Fuller, and the field operatives in the crowd, now all Federation Navy officers on TDY to D Branch.

They saluted their fallen fellow officers.

Prototypes

Admiral Jurgens brought up Dominic Trask's proposal with his boss, Bret Fender, the Defense Commissioner of the Directorate of the Federation of Human Planets. It had been nibbling at him since Trask brought it up.

The Defense Commissioner was not Jurgens' superior because Jurgens was a full admiral, but because Jurgens was currently the Chief of Naval Operations, and the Navy was the only real military the Federation had. Ground troops were generally the responsibility of the individual planets of the Federation, and the Marines reported through the Navy.

Of course, Jurgens did not mention Dominic Trask. He had received similar input from the surviving D Branch operatives after the Battle of Meredith.

They talked about the prisoners of war and the captured ships first.

"What's the status of your Deneb Republic prisoners, Kurt?" Fender asked.

"We've gotten them all removed from their ships and transported to Meredith. They're in a camp on the coast. Officers in bunk rooms, enlisted in barracks tents."

"How many are there?"

"A battle group is normally seventy-five hundred or so. Almost four thousand on an attack-ship carrier, about three thousand on a battle cruiser, and three hundred or so on each of two destroyers. Figure sixty thousand on eight battle groups.

"We have about forty-eight thousand survivors of the battle in custody. Eight thousand were lost on the two carriers, thirty-five hundred on the twelve destroyers, and another five hundred or so spread about, especially on the attack ships."

"Security problems?"

"Non-existent so far, sir. They're pretty happy at the moment. They like the weather, and they say our prisoner camp food is better than what people can manage for home-cooked food back home. By a lot, actually. We've had a lot of inquiries about immigrating."

"Officers or enlisted?"

"Both, actually. If I were a rear admiral in command of a battle group that surrendered, I don't think I would want to go home to the Deneb Republic."

Fender nodded. That wouldn't be pleasant.

"And the captured ships. Have we evaluated them for our use?"

"Yes, sir, and it won't work. First, there's a lot of damage, and tracking that all down and making sure it's repaired will be a big effort. Second, all the systems are different. Another big effort to bring them up to our standards. Third, they complicate maintenance and service, because they will always be different from our ships."

"What's your plan, Kurt?"

"We'll send them to the breakers, Bret. We have all that steel, refined and already in orbit."

"Just grind them up?"

"Yes, sir. That steel, already out of the gravity well of a planet, is a great resource. That's the fourth reason not to re-use them as they are. They're already worth a lot just by being high-quality steel in space."

Fender nodded. Made sense.

"All right, Kurt. Thanks for the report. Keep me informed please."

"Of course, sir. Has the Deneb Republic had anything to say

about their personnel and ships?"

"Oh, yes. You may find this amusing, Kurt. They complained about our firing on their 'visiting ships.'"

"Visiting ships?"

"Yes. You know. They were out on maneuvers, and just popped in for a visit, and we fired on them. They're most outraged about it, I understand."

"Did our people tell them to fold their outrage until it was all sharp corners and shove it up their collective ass?"

"Something along those lines, I understand, but with more flowery language. Diplomats, you know."

Jurgens snorted.

"One last item this time, Bret."

"Go ahead, Kurt."

"Yes, sir. I've been thinking about what happened at the Battle of Meredith that started all this. Twelve frigate-sized ships basically maimed eight battle groups to the point their ships couldn't be fought effectively."

"The D Branch ships, right?"

"Yes, sir. Not something we considered for the Navy, they were designed for D Branch's special case. A lone field operative. One-man ship, but it has to be fast, and oh, let's put some guns on there.

"As I say, sir. We never considered those for the Navy, but I'm not sure now that eschewing such ships was the right move."

"Given their performance at Meredith."

"Yes, sir. We did take our losses, but with one-man ships, it was five persons total. Further, if they had had more ships, they could have taken greater risks, and not even manned most of them. They were basically all being fought by a single ship with a two-man crew. Make it thirty such ships being fought in groups of six or eight, and you have maybe ten total personnel on the battlefield."

Fender nodded.

"What do you suggest, Kurt?"

"I'd like to order prototypes – maybe sixteen or twenty of them – and game them out. Make sure we get the same results within our command structure."

"Identical ships?"

Jurgens shrugged.

"Couple of mods, maybe. Bunks and chairs for the two-man crew. Add some missiles. Nothing fancy."

"Was the two-man crew at Meredith hot-bunking?"

"Married couple."

"Ah. Can't count on availability there."

Fender nodded.

"And supplier?"

"We'll just get them from the same outfit, sir. They already have all the plans and fittings and the like."

"All right, Kurt. I can sign up for that. Go ahead and do it, and I'll talk to Frank. Or you can."

"I'll talk to Frank, Bret. If I hit any snags, I'll let you know."

"Gorski."

"Hi, Frank. Kurt Jurgens."

"Oh, hi, Kurt. What can I buy for you today?"

It was sort of a running joke between Gorski, head of procurement and logistics, and Jurgens, head of operations. Procurement used to create problems for logistics, but that had ended when they had been combined under one command. Now, procurement didn't buy things that logistics couldn't support.

"Twenty new ships."

Gorski raised an eyebrow.

"You're not kidding?"

"Not at all, Frank. Did you look at the videos of the Battle of Meredith I sent over?"

"Ah. You want twenty of those little frigates. Whatever they are."

"Exactly. Frank, those ships would do the same to our battle groups as they did to the Deneb Republic's. At least I think they would, and now the Deneb Republic knows about them."

"From real-time transmissions from their fleet during the battle. Right. So we could end up against ships like that ourselves."

"You bet we could. So I need some ships like that, so we can work up doctrine against them, if nothing else."

"What about the ones we already have, Kurt?"

"Oh, those weren't ours. Not the Navy's, anyway. Those were a semi-custom job for D Branch. I need some of my own to work on tactics against them."

"But...?"

"Yeah, it's likely I'll want more of them. With Deneb getting feisty, the pols may decide to go out there and punch out some of their stuff, and I would rather do it with those ships than with our battle groups."

Gorski nodded.

"Makes sense to me, Frank. Who built the D Branch ships?"

"General Ship and Fitting. And I'm happy with them running twenty prototypes on a cost-plus no-bid contract. They'll be cheapest anyway, because they have the designs already."

"Sounds good. Any mods?"

"Yeah. Let me send you this short write-up."

Jurgens sent it, and Gorski looked it over.

"Those don't look hard, Kurt. What about that weak after aspect? You lost two ships to a missile or ship up the ass. I think we can deal with that."

"Really?"

"Oh, yeah. If you got one coming in, the computer can kill the engines and close up the shields, then open them and quick restart the engines once it's detonated. It's just a matter of shutting off the reaction mass and turning it back on before things overheat."

"Nice. Anything for the cabin?"

"We may be able to tighten up the radiation protections in the front, Kurt, but the crew is always going to be vulnerable to a hit in the forward aspect. How about an anti-missile gun aimed forward instead? A point-defense gun. Those are pretty small."

"I like it. Let's do it, Frank."

"All right, Kurt. Let me work on this. I'll be in touch."

"Thanks, Frank."

Gorski cut the connection.

"Mr. Artino, you have a call request from a Captain Merrill Forester."

Gabriel Artino, CEO of General Ship & Fitting, checked his action list. There it was. He accepted the call. The avatar of a Federation Navy captain appeared on his display.

"This is Gabriel Artino."

"Mr. Artino, I am Captain Merrill Forester. I am with the Federation Navy's procurement department."

"Yes, Captain Forester. How can I help you today?"

"I have a cost-plus no-bid contract for GS&F to produce twenty ships similar to your previous construction of your build number 73079. I would not bring this directly to you, but

I understand that build number 73079 is a secret design, and I don't know who else might have clearance to discuss it."

"I understand, Captain. Contacting me directly is fine. You say you have a contract awarded already?"

"Yes, sir. Let me send you the details."

Forester sent the document, and Artino scanned it quickly.

"I see, Captain Forester. Very well."

"Will you have any problems fulfilling this contract, Mr. Artino? I bring to your specific attention the modifications to the previous design, and the delivery schedule specified."

"We actually have a design with most of these modifications already on the boards, Captain. I think the point-defense gun is the only thing new to me, and that is a standard module used in our other construction. We will have no problems there, and we can probably beat the specified delivery schedule."

"Excellent, Mr. Artino. This is being pushed by higher, and expedited performance is desired."

"I see also that staged delivery is preferred, Captain. To start working up the early ones, I suppose."

"Yes, sir. Exactly correct."

"Very well, Captain. And you are my contact for delivery dates and such other details that may arise."

"That is correct, Mr. Artino."

"Excellent. We will get right on this, Captain, and advise of deliveries as soon as we have our project schedule together."

"Thank you, sir."

Artino cut the connection and sat back in his chair.

Well, Dominic Trask had been right. The only wrinkle was the point-defense gun, and that was easy. The missile rack was well above the cabin because of the size of the engines, so there was plenty of room there without impacting the missile rack design already completed.

Four missiles. Good enough. The current rack design held five, but they didn't have to fill them all.

Artino leaned forward to contact his contracts and project management groups.

"And thank you, Dominic Trask," he muttered as he punched in the connections.

Deke Sharp was working in his office in D Branch headquarters when he received a call request from Admiral Jurgens. He accepted the call and Jurgens appeared on his display in virtual terminal.

"Deke Sharp."

"Hello, Admiral Sharp. Admiral Jurgens here."

"Good afternoon, Kurt. What can I do for you?"

"Deke, I've ordered twenty new ships like the ones you had at the Battle of Meredith. Couple of mods. Two-man crew, so bunk beds and two command chairs. Some ship-to-ship missiles. And a forward-facing point-defense gun for those troublesome frontal hits from missiles."

"Really?"

"Oh, yes. The Deneb Republic knows about those ships now, and we have to have some response to them if they field something similar. More to the point, I think the Navy needs ships like that in its deployment mix."

Sharp nodded. The politicos may decide to send some people to visit the Deneb Republic and convince them of the error of their ways.

"I understand, Kurt."

"Good. What I was wondering, Deke, is if you and Admiral Fuller could take some time out from your other duties – maybe a day or two, total – to bring a couple of people up to speed on just what you did to fight these ships so effectively.

We would send you a couple of our best candidates. Once you trained them, they could develop the doctrine and train everyone else."

"Of course, Kurt. We'd be happy to. You don't need to actually send them here, though. We'll train them in our virtual battlespace. They just need to have virtual terminal capability."

"Of course, Deke. Just a figure of speech."

"Ah. Very good."

"I'll be back in touch when the first delivery of ships come in and we can get started."

"But there's no need to wait for that either, Kurt. We don't need the ships to train in the virtual battlespace. You could have all your pilots trained by the time ships come in."

Jurgens started, and then smiled sheepishly.

"Of course, we could. What was I thinking?"

Jurgens shook his head and Deke chuckled.

"One more thing, Deke. I'll send you the specs. These new ships have missiles and a forward point-defense gun, so you should build that into your considerations."

"Understood, Kurt. Just have your training candidates get in touch with me."

"All right. Thanks, Deke."

Jurgens sent the design specs for the new ships, then cut the connection. He didn't worry about sending those to Sharp.

As head of field operations for D Branch, Deke Sharp probably had a secret clearance higher than Jurgens' own.

Training

Sharp and Fuller were sitting in the living room of Sharp's condo that evening.

"The Navy is building twenty more ships like *Medea* to try them out for themselves," Sharp said.

"Really?" Fuller asked.

"Yes. Admiral Jurgens says he wants to build doctrine against them in case the Deneb Republic shows up with them next time. He also wants to test them to see if the Navy wants a lot more of them for itself."

"I would think they would, D.K."

"Yeah. I would, too. But he's gonna have a couple guys get in touch for training. Asked if you and I could train his best two guys so they could go back and train everybody else."

"You said 'Yes,' I hope."

"Of course."

"Good. Sounds like fun, actually."

"There's a couple new wrinkles with these new ships, too, so we should probably talk about those."

An hour later, they broke for the night.

Fuller then went into the DV engine and made some mods to her battlespace simulation.

It was the beginning of the next week that Sharp got a call request from a Captain Rodgers.

"Deke Sharp."

"Good morning, Admiral Sharp. My name is Darrell Rodgers. Admiral Jurgens asked me to contact you, Sir."

"Yes, Captain. Are you one of the trainees?"

"Yes, Sir. I and Commander Terry McGrath."

"When are you available, Captain?"

"We are at your convenience, Sir."

"Very well, Captain. I will discuss it with Admiral Fuller and send you time and login credentials."

"Yes, Sir. Thank you, Sir."

Sharp cut the connection and called Fuller.

"I heard from Jurgens' trainees. They're good to go any time."

"Let's not keep the Admiral waiting. How about first thing tomorrow?"

"That will be about noon for them. Assuming they're on Meredith time, that is. Should be good."

Fuller nodded and cut the connection.

Sharp sent the date, time – eight in the morning New Destin time on Ariel – and the login credentials to Fuller's battlespace display to Captain Rodgers. He told them to be fed and serviced, and either lying down or seated in a comfortable chair. 'We'll be at this a while.'

He got a 'Wilco' in reply.

At eight the next morning, Sharp and Fuller logged into the battlespace display, each from their own office. Rodgers and McGrath's avatars were standing at ease in the display waiting for them. All four of them were in uniform.

The trainees saluted, and Sharp and Fuller returned their salutes.

"All right, gentlemen," Sharp said. "We got all the formal stuff out of the way. We'll be here a while, we might as well be comfortable. Switch to shipsuits."

All four switched their avatars to shipsuits.

"All right. First thing on the agenda is that you need to view the training video we already have. So take your seats."

Sharp slapped his hand on one of the two command chairs present in the simulation, and the two trainees sat down.

"This runs about an hour. We'll see you when it concludes."

Sharp started the first recording of Fuller teaching the D Branch operatives and he and Sharp left the simulation.

When they returned, the video had just concluded.

"Any questions, gentlemen?" Fuller asked

Rodgers and McGrath looked at each other, then back to Fuller.

"Yes, Ma'am," Rodgers said. "These ships are frigates?"

"That's right, Captain. One-man frigates, except for the command ship. That was a two-man frigate, with Admiral Sharp and I aboard."

"I don't understand, Ma'am."

"What was your last posting, Captain?"

"Executive Officer on an attack-ship carrier, Ma'am."

"And you, Commander?"

"Attack Group Commander, Ma'am."

"I understand. You're wondering why Admiral Jurgens would assign the two of you – used to commanding large groups of spacers – to learn how to space a two-man frigate."

"Well, yes, Ma'am," Rodgers said.

"Very well, Captain. Let me explain it to you. Admiral Sharp and I, in one of these ships, with eleven auxiliaries of the same class, defeated eight battle groups of the Deneb Republic Navy at the Battle of Meredith."

"We'd heard about you and Admiral Sharp, Ma'am, but that was in *these* ships?"

"Yes, it was, Captain. And we're going to teach you what we learned, and then you are going to go back to the Navy and teach everyone else. Is Admiral Jurgens' purpose clear now, why he would send you two gentlemen to learn what we can teach you?"

"Yes, Ma'am."

"Good. So let's get started. We'll need two more command chairs, so Admiral Sharp and I can observe."

Fuller made an adjustment to the battlespace in a sidebar of her display, and two more command chairs appeared, one on each side of the original two.

"Be seated, gentlemen."

All four took seats, then Fuller explained the first exercise.

"Admiral Jurgens has two full squadrons of these frigates plus spares coming in. In this exercise, one squadron will be operated as a unit against four battle groups. The time scale has been sped up by four-to-one so we can simulate an eight-hour battle in two hours."

"Eight frigates against four battle groups, Ma'am? Sixteen ships?"

"At the Battle of Meredith, Admiral Sharp and I spaced twelve frigates against eight battle groups, comprising thirty-two ships. We've made this exercise a bit simpler, at better odds."

"Yes. Ma'am."

"When the enemy battle groups appear, you will initiate hostilities. Your goal is to immobilize the invading fleet while awaiting reinforcements. The exercise will conclude in eight normal hours, or when all of the enemy or all of your ships are disabled or destroyed. Are you ready to begin?"

"Yes, Ma'am."

Fuller looked across to Sharp, who nodded. He had remained silent through Fuller's responses to their questions, but he spoke up now.

"You may begin, Admiral Fuller."

Four battle groups – four attack-ship carriers, four heavy cruisers, and eight destroyers – dropped out of the envelope in front of them.

Captain Rodgers spaced all eight frigates to the attack.

He got handed his head. The frigates barely lasted two hours against the invading fleet. Thirty minutes in the simulator.

"You were unsuccessful, Captain."

"Yes, Ma'am. It's very difficult."

"Yet you were learning toward the end, Captain. Among other things, you were relying on the Commander more. There's no sense you being overworked while he watches."

"Yes, Ma'am."

"We'll go again before we change it up for you."

Rodgers didn't do as poorly the second time. His squadron lasted four hours – one hour in the simulator – against the invading fleet.

"Better, Captain. Much better."

"Thank you, Ma'am."

"Now we're going to change chairs, Captain."

Sharp and Fuller got up, and Rodgers and McGrath switched to the observer seats.

"I am going to play for you the actual bridge recording of the Battle of Meredith, gentleman. You will observe, from the bridge of *Medea*, what actually happened."

"Oh, this I gotta see," McGrath said.

"Indeed, Commander. I think you will find it instructive. Note that we were also learning as we went along."

Fuller adjusted the simulation in a sidebar of her display, and avatars of her and Sharp appeared in the recording in the central two command chairs. Then the eight battle groups of the Deneb Republic fleet dropped out of the envelope in front of them.

"Oh, shit."

The real-time Sharp and Fuller were standing off to one side.

"Indeed, Captain. Enjoy the show. We will see you in a couple of hours."

The real-time Sharp and Fuller disappeared from the simulation, and the recording began running.

When Sharp and Fuller returned to the battlespace simulation, the recording was just ending, with Deke Sharp turning over command to Vice Admiral Matthews as four Federation Navy battle groups and four hundred ground-based attack ships spaced from Meredith to the enemy fleet. Eight Federation Navy battle groups had them pinned against the planet from the back side.

Rodgers and McGrath both jumped to their feet and gave Academy-crisp salutes to Sharp and Fuller and held them until Sharp and Fuller returned their salutes. Not just admirals, who had said all the right things and kissed all the right rings for an entire career, Sharp and Fuller had been at the pointy end of the stick and prevailed against insane odds.

"Reactions, gentlemen?" Fuller asked.

"That was inspiring to watch, Ma'am," Rodgers said.

"Good, Captain. Because you're going to watch it again. I have given you access to the controls of this simulation. You can't leave it and get into the rest of this system's resources, but the controls of this envelope are now available to you.

"You are to analyze the battle, look into the command program I was running, analyze the targeting selection and the gunnery controls, the maneuvering – the whole thing. You have two days. You will retain login privileges to this simulator during that period.

"On Friday, you will space your squadron once more against four enemy battle groups."

"Yes, Ma'am. Thank you, Ma'am."

"Dismissed," Sharp said.

Sharp and Fuller dropped out of the battlespace display.

Rodgers and McGrath did not.

On Friday morning at eight New Destin time, all four were back in the battlespace display.

"How did your last two days go, gentlemen?" Fuller asked.

"Busy, Ma'am."

"Good. Get some practice in, did you?"

"Yes, Ma'am."

"And in your analysis, what did you notice?"

"Several things, Ma'am," Rodgers said. "One is the pair-of-pairs organization of your forces, allowing ships to support each other with their anti-missile and anti-attack-ship fire. Another was the constant jinking to bring guns around and scramble your vectors against incoming fire. Oh, and rotating the ships to cover the upper and lower aspects. That made the jinking at ninety degrees to the maneuvering thrusters, due to the gyroscopic effect, which took some getting used to, but it was effective."

"Another was the guns being on automatic, Ma'am," McGrath said. "That worked really well, though it is not standard Navy practice. And your target priorities were well-chosen."

"One thing we noticed, Ma'am," Rodgers said, "was that you did not use the forward point-defense gun or the ship-to-ship missiles."

"Or closing the shields over the after aspect of the ships when missiles got through," McGrath added.

"Our ships didn't have those little enhancements, gentlemen. They were added after the Battle of Meredith. Your ships will have them, though, as does this simulation."

"Really, Ma'am?"

Rodgers and McGrath exchanged glances.

"That's very impressive, Ma'am," McGrath said.

"We did what we could with what we had, gentlemen. The Navy used our experience to upgrade our little ships for their new purpose. And how did you do against the enemy force? You did practice, right?"

"Oh, yes, Ma'am. And you were right. Making better use of Commander McGrath helped a lot. He's made some changes to the program that have proven effective."

"Excellent, Commander."

"I'm a bit of a computer jock, too, Ma'am," McGrath said.

Fuller nodded. That was likely why Jurgens had chosen him.

"All right. How about you show us what you've learned?"

"Yes, Ma'am."

Everyone got into their command and observer chairs. Sharp gave the word, and Fuller started the simulation with four battle groups dropping out of the envelope.

After two hours, with seven intact frigates fleeing the enemy fleet, Fuller was complimentary.

"Excellent work, gentlemen. You accomplished the mission, delaying the enemy, with the loss of a single ship."

"The timing on closing off the after aspect of that one ship was a little delayed, Ma'am."

"Yes. The computer got a little surprised by that one. Nonetheless, nice job."

"Thank you, Ma'am."

"You see now," Sharp said, "why you have the upgrades you do on the Navy version. We lost one ship to beam emitter overheating, which Admiral Fuller corrected in the programming of the targeting software. We lost two ships to after-aspect hits, which you mostly avoided with the new ability to close off the after aspect with the shields. And we lost two ships to a pop-up attack, which you can now counter with the forward point-defense gun."

"Yes, Sir," Rodgers said. "But you didn't actually lose those two ships to the pop-up attack. The pilots were killed by the radiation, but the ships remained combat-capable, so you only lost three ships. As our ships will not be manned, that would be a non-event in our case."

Sharp nodded.

"Correct, Captain."

Having Sharp's concurrence with his opinion clearly pleased Rodgers.

"All right, gentlemen," Fuller said. "Man your stations. Let's try something a little harder."

As they took their seats, *eight* enemy battle groups dropped out of the envelope.

"Oh, boy," McGrath said.

"Here we go," Rodgers said.

Two hours later, all eight intact frigates spaced away from a disheveled and effectively disarmed enemy fleet.

"Outstanding, gentlemen," Fuller said. "You accomplished your mission without the loss of any ships."

"The change Commander McGrath made to the program was effective in stopping leakage through the after aspect, Ma'am. That limited our losses."

"Understood, Captain. Bear in mind, however, that a real battle will result in surprises. Unpleasant surprises."

"Like what, Ma'am?"

"Consider if the enemy took life-sign readings on your ships, and decided to concentrate all their fire on the one manned ship, Captain. If they knock you out, the other ships are without human control. They'll do the best they can under computer control, but there's a reason we don't use computer control on attack ships."

"Yes, Ma'am. Enemy computers can characterize and then predict their responses."

"So the enemy might decide to pour all his fire onto the command ship."

"Ouch," McGrath said.

"Indeed, Commander. Let's not tell them that little wrinkle."

Sharp cleared his throat, and Rodgers and McGrath turned to him.

"Having observed this exercise, I consider your training complete, gentlemen, and I will so inform Admiral Jurgens."

"Thank you, Sir."

Sharp and Fuller shook their hands and congratulated them.

"Dismissed," Sharp said with a nod.

Rodgers and McGrath saluted and dropped from the battlespace display.

Working Up

"They're ready to go in your opinion, Deke?" Jurgens asked.

"Yes, Kurt. They did really well in the final simulations. I'll send you the recording."

"I'd appreciate it. Did your simulations include the new ship capabilities?"

"Yes. All of it. The missiles, the forward gun, and the rear-aspect closure. Commander McGrath actually made a program modification to clean up the rear-aspect closure process. It was leaking under certain circumstances, and he closed it up."

"Well, that's good news. So they're ready to train others?"

"Yes. I'll have to arrange logins to the simulation for them and their students, but we can handle that."

Jurgens nodded.

"I'd appreciate that as well, Deke. We're working on getting our computer center up and operating, but I was a little surprised at just how big a computer capability D Branch has."

"No sense collecting intelligence if you can't analyze it, Kurt."

"Of course, but two hundred thousand blades? That caught me flat-footed."

Sharp chuckled.

"Don't forget the high-bandwidth QE radios, Kurt."

"No, we have it all specced now, and we'll be installing that on an expedited basis. Just surprised me is all."

Jurgens shrugged, then continued.

"All right, Admiral Sharp. Thank you for all that, and we'll be in touch."

"Any time, Admiral Jurgens."

Jurgens nodded and cut the connection.

Chairman of the Central Committee of the Deneb Republic John Robertson was meeting once more with High Admiral Mitt Prendergast, the successor to the ill-fated Hugo Biarritz.

"Have you got any better idea of what those frigates really were, Admiral?" Robertson asked.

"Yes, sir. We think they mounted the power system and engines of an attack-ship carrier and the guns of a battle cruiser on a reinforced frigate-sized frame. From our estimates, the cabin could only hold supplies and environmental for a one- or two-man crew."

"How were the guns able to fire so fast and accurately? I saw the battle videos, and they were firing nearly continuously."

"We believe the guns were under computer control, sir. If they saw a designated target, they took the shot."

"These ships have that much computer power aboard?"

"No, sir. We don't think so. We think the computer was elsewhere. The fire was centrally controlled, as two ships never fired on the same target."

Robertson nodded.

"Yes, I noticed that. Why were they mostly immune to our fire, Admiral?"

"It has to do with the energy density of the shields, sir. The shields are generated by the engines. If you take the shields of an attack-ship carrier and shrink them down to the size of a frigate, the energy density of the shields increases by a lot. A factor of ten or twenty. We simply couldn't penetrate them."

"OK. That makes sense. So can we do the same thing? Build ships like this? Have the fire computer-controlled remotely?"

"We think so, sir. I'd certainly like to try."

"All right. Go ahead, Admiral. A dozen, say. Like they did.

Let's see how far we get."

"Yes, sir. Thank you, sir."

When the recording ended, Admiral Jurgens exited his virtual terminal display and rotated his desk chair toward the window of his office. It looked out over the plaza where Deke Sharp had executed Vice Admiral Kent Corcoran and Rear Admiral Thomas Greenacre, almost three years ago now.

A lot of water under the bridge since then. The pirates gone. Their supporters executed. Their financiers executed. An invading fleet of the Deneb Republic detected and then stopped dead in its tracks.

All Deke Sharp's doing.

And now this. Eight frigates, with two men as their total crew, destroying the combat effectiveness of *eight* battle groups. Half of the destroyers crippled, the other eight destroyed. All eight cruisers blinded, their guns in local control. All eight attack-ship carriers rendered toothless, their launch rails tangled masses of crumpled metal.

It was a simulation, sure. But that simulation tracked what Deke Sharp – who was not, after all, a naval officer trained for space combat – had managed to do to the real Deneb fleet. Jurgens had watched that recording, too. More than once.

They did come along once in a while. Revolutions in naval warfare. People and organizations who failed to adapt usually did poorly. That was the big lesson of history.

More subtly, they often came about in the same way. The existing perspective would proceed to its end game. This was often more – of everything. Bigger, more expensive, more powerful, more armored, more armed.

Then something new – a new perspective – would come along. It was often smaller, speedier, more difficult to confront.

A SHARP EDGE

It had happened to the Spanish Armada, when Philip II's fleet ran up against the more-maneuverable ships and faster-loading cannon of Elizabeth's navy. It had happened to the Imperial Japanese Navy, when the Emperor's battleships ran up against the stand-off offense of the American carrier-based fleets.

Now it was happening again, and Jurgens didn't intend to get caught with his pants down. The Deneb Republic had recordings of the Battle of Meredith, too, and it never paid to assume your opponent was too stupid to see the obvious.

The current paradigm of naval combat – and therefore of naval construction – had played out.

It was also clear now that his selection of Captain Rodgers and Commander McGrath had been well considered. The frigates against battle groups scenario was the clash of perspectives, the vanguard of maneuverable small ship against the end game of big-ship technology.

But attack ship pilots were already steeped in small ship tactics against big ships. They already thought in those terms.

His particular choices – Rodgers and McGrath – could have been hidebound in Navy doctrine for small ships, but Sharp and Fuller had handled that. They let them go on their own first, and they had lost. Badly.

Only after Sharp and Fuller had rubbed their noses in it – had proven that attack-ship tactics wouldn't succeed – had Sharp and Fuller shown Rodgers and McGrath how to fight the new ships.

Give credit where it was due. Rodgers and McGrath had jumped in with both feet and changed their tactics – had actually improved on Sharp and Fuller's tactics by using the new ship capabilities – and achieved superlative results.

Jurgens could field four – or even eight – squadrons of the new frigates against a whole navy, and never have more than a dozen or so spacers in harm's way.

Jurgens' thoughts jerked to a halt. No. Wait. That was wrong.

He need have no crew in harm's way at all.

Rodgers and McGrath had fought the simulated battles from within the computer battlespace display. They hadn't needed to be on board the ship at all.

For that matter, Sharp and Fuller had fought the Battle of Meredith totally from within the battlespace display. Yes, they had been on-board *Medea*, but they hadn't needed to be.

Hell, they could have fought the battle from here on the planet. Or from their living room on Ariel, for that matter.

The more he looked at the whole thing, the better he liked it.

Jurgens nodded. Time to kick this thing into high gear.

Captain Darrell Rodgers was in his office on Fleet Base Meredith writing up, for his own use, his impressions of the training he had just received from Admirals Sharp and Fuller.

As he was finishing up, new orders came through.

FROM: ADM Kurt Jurgens, CNO
TO: RADM Darrell Rodgers
SUBJECT: Orders

You have been promoted to Rear Admiral. The permanent status of this promotion is pending action by the Federation Commission, which is expected. Captain Terry McGrath is your chief of staff.

You will command Attack Force 101. Your table of organization consists of eight squadrons of attack frigates. Delivery of the first two and a half squadrons is imminent.

A SHARP EDGE

You will select and forward to me requests for personnel, comprising eight captains and eight commanders you consider prime candidates for operations per your recent operational training.

You will train these personnel along the lines of the training you recently completed, aiming for similar results as achieved by you and Captain Terry McGrath.

Consider support personnel that will be required in your table of organization as you train.

Congratulations, Admiral.

Rodgers simply stared at the screen for several moments, then read it through again slowly.

'Attack Force' was new. The attack ships of an attack-ship carrier were organized as 'Attack-Ship Wings.' Since it was a new force designator, it was numbered, per Navy practice, as '101'. To any Navy guy anywhere, that meant '1'.

But *eight squadrons*? When a single squadron could immobilize and render combat incapable eight battle groups, who would they even attack with a force of eight squadrons?

Anybody Admiral Jurgens wanted, apparently.

Then again, Admirals Sharp and Fuller had had to scramble to get their three divisions into place to meet the Deneb Fleet, and almost hadn't made it. Something like thirty-six hours of slack. When transits took weeks, that wasn't much.

Sounded like a deployed force, then, not a reaction force.

His thoughts were running down that line of thinking when a familiar voice came from the open door.

"Mornin', Admiral," Terry McGrath said.

"And good morning to you, Captain. Some news, huh?"

"I guess we done good."

"Looks like."

McGrath had just sat down in front of Rodgers' desk when there was a knock at the door.

"Come in, Lieutenant."

The lieutenant came in, saluted, and held out a box to Rodgers.

"I'm Admiral Jurgens' aide. With his regards, Sir."

Rodgers opened the box. It was a set of rear admiral's collar stars. They weren't new. They might even have been Jurgens' once upon a time.

Oh, my.

"Thank Admiral Jurgens very much for me, Lieutenant."

"Aye, Sir."

The lieutenant saluted and left.

"Wow. That's special," McGrath said. "Nice to know somebody up there likes us."

"Probably the only one. The big-ship boys are gonna feel threatened."

"Reasonable. I would if I were them."

"Yes, but what this means is that Jurgens knows that and doesn't much give a damn. This is the future of the Navy. Oh, not for force projection and carryin' Marines around and stuff. But if you're going to face another fleet in battle, we're it."

"Wow. You know, you really talk purty, Admiral."

McGrath gave him a crooked grin and Rodgers laughed.

Rodgers took off his collar tabs and tossed them on the desk.

"You might as well take these, Terry."

"Thank you, Sir."

McGrath swapped out his collar tabs. Rodgers fixed his own new collar tabs, then mugged for McGrath.

"How do I look?"

"Actually, those look really good on you, Darrell."

There was another knock on the door. A chief petty officer, with a work gang and a large four-wheeled cart. Rodgers looked over and the chief saluted.

"Yes, Chief?"

"We're here to move you to your new office, Admiral."

"New office?"

"Yes, Sir."

"And where is that, Chief?"

"Building 19A, Sir. The tenth floor. Office 10-01."

"Huh. Imagine that."

"Let's grab some lunch, Admiral," McGrath said. "We can check out the new digs after chow."

Rodgers nodded and got up from his desk.

"Do you have orders to move Captain McGrath, too, Chief?"

"Yes, Sir. Right after you."

"And what's his office?"

"Same building, same floor, Sir. Office 10-02."

"Very well, Chief. Carry on."

"Yes, Sir."

Rodgers and McGrath left. They headed down the hallway to the exit for the walk across to the officer's mess, leaving the chief petty officer to shake his head at admirals and captains who didn't even know where their own offices were.

Rodgers and McGrath didn't talk about their new assignment in the mess hall. Too many ears, and it was obvious this was not a public effort.

A couple of people they knew, however, came over when they saw their new collar insignia.

"Hey, congratulations, you guys."

"Thanks," Rodgers said.

"What's your new assignment?"

"We don't know yet," Rodgers said.

"We're still trying to make sense out of our orders," McGrath said.

"Yeah, well, good luck with that."

They all laughed.

"Thanks."

After lunch, they went to their new offices. Rodgers was moved in, and they were working on McGrath's, so they settled down in Rodgers' office.

"So all I know is I'm your chief of staff in something called Attack Force 101. What the hell is that?"

"You know that the battle groups are numbered from one, right? Battle Group 1, Battle Group 2, Battle Group 3. Like that, right?"

"Yeah," McGrath said.

"Well, Attack Force is a new group designation, and the Navy, for whatever reason, decided to start with 101."

"So we're the first one of whatever it is?"

"Yeah," Rodgers said.

"And what is it?"

"Eight squadrons of those frigates."

"The frigates we trained on with Admiral Fuller?" McGrath asked. "Eight *squadrons*? Sixty-four of those ships?"

"Yeah."

"No shit."

"No shit," Rodgers said. "I think Admiral Jurgens has decided the Navy needs to change, and he's not afraid to do it. Deneb is still out there, and they know about the new ships."

"And could make some of their own."

"Probably so."

"So what's our first order of business, Admiral?"

Rodgers shrugged.

"Get sixteen of the right people in here and get them trained up."

"That's not going to be easy. They have to be willing to set aside their learned responses to use those ships effectively."

"Like we did?" Rodgers asked.

"Well, yeah, actually. But I like to think of us as not quite so beholden to doctrine as, maybe, Luntz and Takagi, say."

Rodgers nodded.

"That's a fair point. Maybe we should start with twenty or twenty-four, and figure on washing out some of them."

"Or have backup crews. For when someone gets taken out, or goes on leave, or something."

"And what, Captain McGrath, do you think is going to take out a crew?"

"Well, if their ship gets taken out...."

"Who says they're aboard ship?"

McGrath opened his mouth and stopped, then closed it with a click.

"You're right. We fought those simulations from here."

Rodgers nodded.

"Exactly. Now, we might have crew sick or on leave or something, like you said. So spares is good. I'm all for that. But I think we all stay right here."

"Do the ships stay here, too, Sir?"

"No. The three divisions Admiral Sharp had at the Battle of Meredith were completely dominant over the Deneb battle groups, but they almost didn't get here in time. Thirty-six hours is not a lot of leeway. I think we deploy the squadrons around the Federation. Be closer to the action."

McGrath nodded.

"You know, another thing we could do is have them out in

space. Get them up to some speed and just let them orbit the star. But getting them up to the envelope would be a lot quicker if they were moving already. We should be able to cut the time-to-envelope in half, maybe more."

"I like it, Terry. They come in from wherever, get serviced at the Navy station there, then go out and accelerate up to half or two-thirds of envelope speed."

"Then cut the engines and let them orbit, or let them drift across the planetary system. Once in a while, you turn them around and head them back the other way."

"That would work. Well, we have a bunch of stuff like that we need to think through. We also need to make some accommodations here for action rooms. Some place where people can get comfortable for long periods in virtual terminal."

"And services, Sir. You drop out, grab a sandwich and a drink, hit the head, and are back in virtual terminal. The two guys on a crew take turns."

Rodgers nodded. That was a solid idea. There was a lot of time when nothing was going on, but you did have to be on top of things for when the situation changed.

"All right. Let's start working some things up. And we need to talk about specific personnel. If I don't have some specific personnel requests to Jurgens in the next two days, I think he'll be disappointed."

Shifting Gears

While Kurt Jurgens was considering a new organization for the Federation Navy, Suzie Fuller was considering a new organization for their household.

On the weekend after the memorial service at D Branch headquarters, she brought it up with Sharp. They were out on the patio sunning. Hansen and Duplay had not come out to the country this weekend, there being some event in town they wanted to attend.

"D.K?"

"Yes?"

"You're head of operations now, right? Not assistant head."

"Yes, Suzie, that's right. Claude retired, and Otto moved upstairs. Well, down the hall, anyway."

"Right. So no more field operations, right?"

"Right."

"Uh-huh. You know what that means."

Sharp opened one eye to look sideways at her.

"You think it's time?"

"I'm not getting any younger, D.K."

"Well, that's true enough. Neither am I."

"Yeah, but it's more important for me. Your part of the job is simpler. Already done, in fact."

Sharp nodded.

"Sounds right."

Fuller kicked his calf, and regretted it. The prosthetic was harder than human. He felt it, though.

"D.K! When?"

"Now if you want, Suzie. Whenever you're ready."

"You seem so nonchalant about it."

"Well, the decision was already made, right? It was part of buying the house. As far as timing, it had to be after I was out of operations, and we're there. So whenever you're ready is good for me, Suzie."

"Oh. OK. Well, I could stand to lose ten pounds first. Get in my best shape. And quit drinking. Get my implant removed. Then one full cycle without it. How about in a couple months we go see the docs?"

"Sure. Whenever you're ready, I'm good."

"You could at least be excited about it, D.K."

"I am excited, Suzie. And, laying out here in the sun, I'm relaxed. I'm *relaxed* excited."

"You're maddening, is what you are."

Sharp chuckled and rolled over.

Time for some sun on the other side.

Life was good.

Fuller brought it up with Lydia Thompsen when they next talked.

"He just doesn't seem excited, Lydia."

"Suzie, you're talking about a man who spent the best part of the last twenty years being knifed, shot at, and blown up. D.K. being excited is not happy-making."

"I know, but..."

"Suzie, is he happy?"

"Oh, yes. He's *suffused* with happiness. It's silly. It's like he glows."

"Then that's as good as it gets, honey. When Deke Sharp gets excited, bad things happen. You know that as much as I do. You've been there."

"Yeah, I suppose you're right. Thanks, Lydia. That helps a

lot."

"Just count your blessings, Suzie. You have a real man to be an involved and caring father to your children. It doesn't get any better than that. And may God have mercy on the man who tries to hurt you or the kids, because D.K. won't."

Fuller nodded. She thought of Gary, her fuck-friend, across the garden from her house on Humphreys. She had never considered him husband material, just convenient when her persistent needs drove her to call *somebody*.

Deke Sharp, though, was different. Had been, since he had been her brother's friend when she was just a child.

"Yeah, you're right there, Lydia. I guess I'm spoiled."

"You just couldn't see the forest for the trees, Suzie. You've got everything important a gal could possibly want. Don't ruin it worrying about trivia."

As Fuller worked up to her best shape, a question occurred to her.

"D.K?"

"Mmf. Yeah?"

"Sorry to wake you, but I had a question. IVF, or artificial insemination?"

"IVF."

Fuller nodded.

"That's what I was thinking, too, but why? It's more involved."

"You have eggs stashed by, Suzie. You gave one to Daphne, after all. But, since then, there's been a lot of time in space. From here to Elizabeth, to Meredith, to Elizabeth, to here. And throw in a battle with nukes going off all over the place. IVF is genetically safer, I think."

"OK. That makes sense. I guess I didn't think about the

battle in there, because there was a bunch of spacing earlier. Humphreys to Elizabeth and back, then to here."

"Three legs. This last was four more legs, and a battle. It's the battle I worry about most. That was pretty crazy."

"Yeah, it was, wasn't it? You'd better let them know, then. Maybe a month. Maybe less."

"I'll take care of it. They've got some prep to do, and you need to be on meds, I think."

"Yeah. I'll check with Daphne. She did the whole thing. And they'll probably want to check me out before we even start meds and stuff."

"Oh, I'm sure of that. I'll have them work up a schedule."

By this time, in-vitro fertilization had advanced a lot from its early days, and it was a pretty standard procedure. It was still two months of hormones and preparation before they made the first implantation attempt.

The next weekend, they were out at the country house with Tim, Daphne, and Thomas, now eight months old. He could flip himself over now, and was rocking back and forth on his hands and knees, getting ready to crawl.

They had come over from next door, the house they had closed on while Fuller was working up to the IVF. Hansen and Sharp had arranged for a gravel path between the houses so they didn't have to walk out the long driveway, down the road, and back up the other long driveway.

"Do you think you took?" Daphne asked.

"Don't know yet. It's too early for testing. Another week, I think. But I spotted this week, and that's a good sign."

Duplay nodded.

"That sounds good, Suzanne. I did, too. The first time. And it took. Resulting in this little guy."

"Not so little anymore."

"No. He'll be crawling soon. That will be the first time you can't put him down and find him there later. Give him five minutes and he could be anywhere."

"They'll be what?" Sharp asked. "A year and a half apart?"

"Something like that. Did you try for a specific sex?" Duplay asked.

"Yes," Fuller answered. "It's not a hundred percent, but we tried for a girl."

"Oh, that will be fun," Duplay said.

"Have to make sure they know they're genetic half-siblings from the get-go, or there could be some trouble there," Hansen said. "Girl next door and all that."

"Gosh, I hadn't even thought of that," Fuller said, "but you're right."

"Well, we're not even sure you've taken yet," Sharp said. "We'll just have to see. Even with modern methods, it's not a hundred percent. Maybe more like two-thirds."

"You should know in another week or two," Duplay said.

Two weeks later, Fuller was positive.

"I had a positive EPT this morning."

"Great," Duplay said. "Oh, this will be fun."

"I knew it was going to be positive, though. My boobs have been itching like crazy. There's things going on in there."

Duplay turned a critical eye to Fuller's bare chest.

"Yeah, I think your nipples are darkening a little already. Mine turned several shades darker by the time he was born."

"Figure eight months from now if all goes well," Fuller said.

"I can hardly wait," Duplay said. "Babies are so much fun."

Attack Force 101

Construction crews were working on one of the two big conference rooms on the tenth floor of Building 19A on Meredith Fleet Base. The single attached half bath was being expanded into the neighboring offices to provide a total of five full baths.

They were also building a snack and meals center on the other side of the room. The existing furniture in the room and its stepped floor had been removed, and twenty-six reclining chairs were being mounted to the now-flat floor.

The Operations Center should be complete in another couple of weeks.

The other large conference room was being left as-is, with the exception of an upgraded main display on the front wall.

This morning, two dozen officers – half a dozen each of captains and commanders, the rest lieutenant commanders – stood about munching on the snacks and breakfast munchies that had been set out on the sidebar, along with coffee and juices.

Admiral Darrell Rodgers and Captain Terry McGrath came into the room and sat in loose chairs in the speaker's well facing the stepped, fixed chairs of the audience portion.

"All right, everyone," McGrath announced. "Let's get started. Grab some last snacks and drinks and take your seats."

The assembled officers added a snack or two to their plates, refreshed their coffee, and took their seats. Rodgers and McGrath were content to wait several minutes, chatting with each other as the process played out.

When everyone was seated, Rodgers stood up. He walked

about as he spoke to them, catching people's eyes individually as he moved about.

"Welcome to Attack Force 101, ladies and gentlemen. My name is Rear Admiral Darrell Rodgers. Captain Terry McGrath here is my chief of staff.

"Some of you know Captain McGrath and I, some of you don't. Trust that we know each and every one of you, by reputation if nothing else. You were hand-selected by us for this assignment. Admiral Jurgens gave us carte blanche to select the personnel for this unit, and we went for the best of the best.

"We have been necessarily somewhat secretive about Attack Force 101. Everything you will hear today is classified. No one else, inside or outside the Navy, needs to know what we will talk about today. It's so important to keep this quiet that we shanghaied all of you into this unit without even telling you what it is.

"Attack Force 101 is the new combat arm of the Navy. Not 'A' new combat arm; 'THE' new combat arm. If combat is likely, it is we who will carry it out."

There was some murmuring and conversation about that in the audience.

Rodgers nodded.

"That is a pretty remarkable statement, I will admit. Yet it is amply justified by the action known as the Battle of Meredith several months back."

The display lit up, and Rodgers gestured to it. It showed an icon representation of eight battle groups.

"You have likely heard of the Battle of Meredith, but you haven't heard the whole story. It has been covered up by the Navy, and for very good reasons.

"The Battle of Meredith was an incursion in force by the

Deneb Republic into Federation space, with eight battle groups dropping out of the envelope in the Meredith system. With just three battle groups at Meredith, the Navy was badly outnumbered. Further, Deneb agents within the Navy's officer corps had moved to ensure that reinforcements could not arrive in a timely way.

"Vice Admiral Sharp and Rear Admiral Fuller took on that Deneb Republic force with twelve frigates, which they operated via computer controls.

"Yes, my friends. Twelve frigates against eight battle groups.

"With those twelve frigates, those two officers were able to hold that massive incursion force in place for eight hours, until reinforcements arrived. Seven frigates spaced away from that battle, leaving the Deneb force combat-incapable behind them.

"The Deneb force surrendered to arriving Navy battle groups. Eight ships destroyed, twenty-four captured. Ten thousand Deneb spacers killed, fifty thousand captured.

"By twelve frigates, ladies and gentlemen.

"What had been a massive incursion into Federation space became nothing more than a salvage operation."

That caused quite a buzz of conversation. Everyone had heard of the Battle of Meredith. Everyone knew that no fewer than twelve battle groups of the Navy had been involved, as well as hundreds of ground-based attack ships. Most of them had flown one of those attack ships in the final attack.

But none of them had known how the battle had been waged before their own arrival on the scene.

Rodgers waited for the conversation to die down. Then he switched the display to a cutaway diagram of one of the new, modified frigates.

"Now those frigates were very special ships. They have a frigate's mass, but the applicability of the appellation ends there. The engines of an attack-ship carrier. The guns of a battle cruiser. The attack-ship-carrier shield strength shrunk down to frigate size, which makes them almost impervious to enemy fire. A crew of just two.

"Further, we learned some things from the Battle of Meredith, and the current generation of these ships includes modifications that make them both more survivable and more deadly. Attack-ship missiles. A forward anti-missile gun. A rear shield closure.

"Attack Force 101 will consist of *eight squadrons* of these ships, where it took but three divisions to disable or destroy eight battle groups at the Battle of Meredith.

"In fact, in simulations, with a single squadron of the improved version of these ships – which Admirals Sharp and Fuller did not have at Meredith – Captain McGrath and I were able to repeat their performance at the Battle of Meredith with a single squadron, and we did not lose a single ship."

Rodgers let the reaction to that go on for quite a while, content to eat a breakfast roll and pour himself a cup of coffee before he walked back out to the center of the speaker's well.

They quieted as he took up his position.

"You, ladies and gentlemen, will fight these ships. Two of you per squadron, the commander and assistant commander. You have been hand-selected for this role, on the basis of your proven abilities to operate independently, your skills flying attack ships, your ability to think outside the box, your computer skills.

"You may have some doubts about your ability to take on such a role, but I don't. If you're going to fail, you're going to have to do it by yourself. I won't help you. I have tremendous faith in each and every one of you. To fail, you're going to have to surprise me.

"I will mention one more thing. I was an attack-ship pilot. Space wing commander. Spacing these things is unbelievable. The power. The speed. The firepower. All the things you like about attack ships is here, and much, much more."

Rodgers looked around the room, then nodded.

"Captain McGrath will send you study materials. Training in earnest begins tomorrow. Dismissed."

The pilots of Attack Force 101 were sitting in the conference room, eating supper off the writing arms of the chairs. They had worked individually all day on the study materials and were still at it.

For supper, they had sent a couple guys out to the mess, and they had returned with a tray of lasagna, a tray of salad, and a sheet of apple cobbler, with all the plates and utensils needed. There were still drinks from this morning.

And there was coffee, of course. It was the Navy, after all.

"So what do you guys think?" Lieutenant Commander Monroe 'Lefty' Crockett asked.

"I wasn't real happy about it at first," Lieutenant Commander Digby 'Dogbone' Sturgeon said. "Give up attack ships? But then you look at those performance numbers. And eight of them for each pair of us? Thirty-two missiles and sixty-four cruiser's guns? That's some serious hell-raisin' right there."

"Yeah," Captain Morris 'Blondie' Stevenson said. "I watched some of the combat recordings of Captain Sharp when he cleaned out the pirates. He took two destroyers and a space station apart with those guns. Just sliced 'em up. Like baloney. One ship."

"You seen the Operations Center?" Lieutenant Commander Timothy 'Slick' Roberts asked. "Buncha comfy chairs. We don't even leave this building. We pilot those ships from here, in virtual terminal."

"That's gonna be weird," Dogbone said.

Commander Lewis 'Billy Bob' Thomas looked toward the three women – a commander and two lieutenant commanders – sitting together down front.

"What about you gals?" he asked. "You gonna feel safe lyin' there in virtual terminal with all us horny guys around?"

"You buncha faggots?" Commander Lee Ann 'Hot Bitch' Crosby asked. "Ha! You need to worry about each other. We three are the least at risk here."

A bunch of guys who knew Hot Bitch – and her mouth – from prior assignments laughed.

"Besides," she went on, "I know Mad Man McGrath. The guy who pulls any shit in this outfit is gonna wish he hadn't. 'Cause he's fucked."

"Yeah," Captain Gerald 'The Scotsman' MacPherson said. "And Shooter Rodgers is good people, too. More than that, he's good. Real good."

"Great ships, no long trips in the envelope, and Shooter and Mad Man as commanding officers," Lieutenant Commander Gary 'Sunshine' Sonnenfeld said. "What's not to like?"

"How are we doing this morning?" Rodgers asked.

"Good," McGrath said. "I do have a couple ideas, though, now that everyone is here."

"Shoot."

"Well, people were pretty excited yesterday. They sent a couple guys down to the mess to pick up food for everyone so they could keep working. I think we ought to have a mess here, on the floor."

"Do we have a space big enough, Terry?"

"Not really. But we could demolish the walls between some unused offices at the other end of the hall. Just put a door across the hallway, and we have a big open area."

"And we put a kitchen there?"

"No, Sir. Just have the support staff bring stuff in from the mess hall. Need a cart is all. Tables and chairs in the room. A buffet counter."

"Do it. Get dishes and utensils, too. Put in a dishwasher. No sense lugging that stuff back and forth. And get a couple of food-service types on support staff. Probably need three or four of them."

"Aye, Sir."

"What else?"

"People were working late on the study materials, then dragged themselves back to quarters. They all have their own offices on this floor. How about a real comfy couch for sleeping on? One in each office. They could crash here. Oh, and a 'Do Not Disturb' flag they can set on their office door."

"That's a great idea, Terry. There may be some relief-crew action depending on how things work out in actual engagements. So that's a big positive for that, too."

"So do it?"

"Yeah, but ask them what they want. Some may want a recliner instead. Some may have good ideas of what to get. Ask around, make the call, then do it."

"Got it."

McGrath gave a sloppy salute and let himself out of Rodgers' office.

Rodgers went back to preparing his "Eyes Only" status report for Admiral Jurgens.

"Good morning, everyone. Let's take our seats," McGrath

said.

The assembled pilots and co-pilots grabbed some last breakfast items and moved to their seats. It was just before the eight o'clock official start time.

"Thank you. We don't have our operations room yet, so we'll have to use the ready room here for a while longer. Make yourself comfortable for some serious virtual terminal time today."

Lieutenant Commander Richard 'Big Dick' Clemens got up out of his chair and sat on one of the steps up the side of the room. McGrath raised an eyebrow.

"Sorry, Sir. I always fall outta the fuckin' chair."

Everybody laughed, including McGrath.

"OK, if anybody else needs the floor, that's OK."

Two other people took up positions on the floor.

"All right. This morning we are going to view a training simulation given by Admiral Fuller. Your login credentials were in your training materials yesterday. When you login, you and your co-pilot will get your own simulation.

"After that initial training, which is mostly about where the controls and all are, each team will face a real combat situation in the battlespace simulator. Your squadron against four battle groups. Your goal is to delay the battle groups from advancing for eight hours.

"This is similar to the Battle of Meredith situation, except you have better odds: eight of your frigates against sixteen enemy vessels. The Battle of Meredith was twelve frigates against thirty-two enemy vessels.

"The battle simulation is run at four to one, so you have to delay the enemy for two hours. Your vessels and theirs will all be four times faster than reality.

"These training and exercise simulations are queued up for

you in your logins. When you have been defeated – trust me, you will be – drop out of virtual terminal and there will be lunch here in the ready room. We'll pick up again as a group after lunch.

"All right, everybody. Have at it."

When lunch came in, McGrath grabbed lunch for himself and Rodgers and went to Rodgers' office. They ate together, and let the pilots have the ready room to themselves.

"So how'd they do?" Rodgers said.

"They all got defeated. Couple teams did better than us, most did worse."

"Which teams did better than us?"

"Hot Bitch and Slick, and the Scotsman and Dogbone," McGrath said.

Rodgers nodded.

"That makes sense."

"Yeah, but they're all pretty upset about being defeated. You should hear 'em."

Rodgers chuckled.

"Did you tell them Shooter and Mad Man got defeated the first time, too?"

"Yeah, that mollified them a bit, but they want another go."

"Well, let's see how they do the second time."

After they all got defeated the second time, in mid-afternoon it was time to change things up.

"All right, everybody. Now you know why we're having training. These ships are so new, we have to space them in a new way to be effective. I think you all see that now.

"So the next thing on my schedule is to unlock the recordings of how Admirals Sharp and Fuller prepared for the

Battle of Meredith, and the battle itself. Up till now, you've just had the recordings of Captain Sharp against the pirates.

"So let's all sit in on the Battle of Meredith first, then we can talk about it. You all can view their prep recordings later by yourselves.

"So, Battle of Meredith now. See you in a couple hours."

They all logged out of virtual terminal at the same time, and there were instant conversations going on about the battle.

"Oh, shit," Hot Bitch said. "That was fuckin' great. I think I came twice."

She cooled herself off by fanning her face with a sheaf of papers. There was a lot of laughter at that.

"Spinning the ships was a big deal," Lieutenant Commander Holly 'Holiday' McAllister said. "It gave the guns access to everything."

"Having the guns on computer control was a big deal," Captain Fred 'Toll Booth' Tolliver said. "That's against Navy doctrine generally, but it sure works with these ships."

"Yeah, in such a target-rich environment, it works," Billy Bob said. "We were hittin' people all over the place without hardly tryin'."

"It was the 'pair of pairs' strategy that impressed me," the Scotsman said. "The ships were able to protect each other. Kind of a wingman strategy, but two layers deep."

"Yeah, that really worked," Slick said.

Terry McGrath walked into the room then, and everybody quieted down.

"Ah. You're all back. Good.

"There's one more thing you need to know about that battle. Those ships were manned. While Admirals Sharp and Fuller fought the battle in virtual terminal, as you saw, they were physically present in their ship.

"The other ships were manned as well. Everyone arrived in Meredith space with just days to spare. There was no time to debark people, and they were afraid a loss of communications would render them ineffective. No strategy had yet been developed. So all twelve ships were manned.

"Those five lost ships were five lost spacers, including to radiation exposure, which is a nasty way to go.

"All thirteen people in those ships received the Federation Cross for Valor for taking on eight battle groups with twelve frigates. Admiral Jurgens called it the bravest damn thing he ever saw.

"We will not be doing that. We will be back here, all safe and snug in our command chairs, piloting our ships remotely. But let's never forget the people who threw themselves into the breach to save this planet."

"To the honored dead," Blondie said.

"To the honored dead," everyone repeated.

McGrath nodded.

"OK. That's it for today. You have several days to yourselves now, with the assignment to watch Admirals Sharp and Fuller develop their strategy for the battle. You can also rewatch the battle yourselves.

"Now, their ships did not have the forward gun, they did not have missiles, they did not have the ability to close the rear aspect. You do.

"So I want you to practice. See if you can repeat this exercise more effectively. Stop the enemy fleet and hold it for eight hours. You still have better odds than they did, and you have better ships.

"But you're going to have to set aside some of what you know to make it work. You were all selected for your independence and ability to think outside the box. You're going to need all of that now.

"Time for some announcements. Meals will be served here three times a day for the time being. The construction that just started down the hall is to wall off a big enough room for a private mess on this floor. In the meantime, you'll have to continue using the writing arms in this room if you eat here.

"Second, we'll be mounting a 'Do Not Disturb' flag on every office door frame, so you can crash here if you want, and not drag yourself back to quarters every night. I just sent you all a question as to whether you want a couch or a recliner in your office for that purpose. I'm also looking for recommendations for really comfy stuff to buy.

"OK, that's it. We will reconvene in four days, on Monday morning. Good shooting, everybody."

Ships

On Gloucester, in the Deneb Republic, Michael 'Red' Tucker drew a beer and took it down to the chief petty officer sitting at the bar.

"Thanks, Red."

"Why so glum, Chief?"

"Oh, it's just some shit at work"

"Yeah, there's always some guy, right? Assholes are everywhere."

"Nah, it ain't that."

The chief thought about it. Tucker was about to think that was it when he continued.

"We got our asses kicked a couple months back. Federation captured eight battle groups."

"No shit."

"Yeah. There's nothin' official, but word gets around."

"Sure does."

"Yeah. So what are we doin'? We're buildin' frigates."

"Frigates?"

"Yeah. Somebody got a bug up his ass to build frigates. Some new hot-shot design or somethin', but they're still frigates."

"Wow."

"Yeah. Hot-shot design or not, they're still frigates. But that's what we're doin', Red. Probably designed by some desk jockey."

"Well, of course, Chief. If you had a real Navy guy do it, they'd build something a little more substantial, wouldn't you think?"

"Yeah. Anyway, not my problem. But I worry about our guys."

"Good thing you're not ship-based anymore, Chief."

"Yeah, but I still worry. I got friends. Ya know?"

Once he got home, Tucker turned on his coffee machine and made himself a cup of coffee. While it was on, he sent a message over its concealed QE radio.

That message went directly to D Branch intelligence division at D Branch headquarters, where it eventually ended up on the desk of Octavius Pasha.

"Jurgens."

"Hi, Kurt. Otto Pasha."

"Hi, Otto. What's going on?"

"We got some intelligence that came in that I think you should know. From Deneb."

"From Deneb?"

"Yes. We have some people there. One of them heard about some new construction their Navy is working on. Something about some hot-shot new frigates. New design."

"Shit."

"Yeah. No numbers or anything like that. Our guys don't ever push for information, lest they blow their covers. Not in the Deneb Republic, anyway. But that's what we heard."

"All right, Otto. Thanks for the heads-up."

"No problem, Kurt. You take care."

"Hot-shot new frigates, from a new design?" Federation Defense Commissioner Bret Fender asked. "Are you sure, Kurt?"

"That's what Octavius Pasha told me, Bret. Those exact words."

Fender nodded. Pasha was now the head of D Branch, and D Branch didn't tell you anything unless it was solid. Most times, they didn't tell you anything at all. But Pasha had worked with Claude Allard a long time, and Fender didn't expect D Branch's intelligence to suffer under the new regime.

"And they have all the sensor data on our frigates from Meredith?"

"Yes, sir. Engine power levels, beam weapon power levels, acceleration. They can figure them out. They don't have anything on the modifications, just the frigates as they were at the time of Meredith, but still."

Fender nodded.

"Not good news. If they build enough of them, they could come out here and clean our clock. And your proposal is what, Kurt?"

"Eight squadrons of the frigates, sir. Including the twenty already ordered."

"Eight squadrons?"

"Yes, and eight spare ships. Deneb apparently isn't backing down, and I think we're going to have to do something about it at some point. As it is, eight squadrons of these small ships is about the same expenditure as just two battle groups."

Fender nodded. Yeah, it made a lot of sense. And he had the funding for an additional two battle groups already.

"All right, Kurt. I'll talk to Frank about it. Get him to extend that order. A total of seventy-two?"

"That's right. Thanks, Bret. I don't think we'll be sorry."

Gabriel Artino was on an inspection trip to the big General Ship & Fitting central shipyard on the planet Merry. Here, major subassemblies of Navy warships were manufactured, to be lifted to space individually, then assembled in orbit.

Warships were just too big to be built on the ground.

Except for one.

In the giant expanse of Secure Assembly Building No. 3, eight frigates lay in cradles, side by side down the long building. They were nearing completion, their main components having been assembled. They were being fitted out now.

Artino stood on the balcony at one end of the building, outside the fourth floor offices, and looked out across the ships. Frigates by mass, but much, much more.

"This is the second squadron, Mr. Artino. The first squadron is in orbit now, on their space trials. We have four more to build under this contract."

Artino nodded.

"There is a new contract coming, Mr. Baldwin. You have seven more squadrons to build."

"Seven more squadrons, sir?"

"Yes. A total of seventy-two ships."

"Nine squadrons?"

"Well, eight squadrons and eight spares, Mr. Baldwin. That contract will be coming soon."

"So when we lift these to space...?"

"Lay down eight more."

"And if the contract doesn't come through, sir?"

"Then we'll have spares."

"Yes, sir. Nine squadrons. Wow."

Artino nodded. Wow, indeed. But Captain Forester had told him the contract was coming. They were just waiting on the paperwork. And Captain Forester had mentioned bonuses for expedited delivery.

"Thank you for the tour, Mr. Baldwin. I am most impressed with your speed on this contract."

"Yes, sir. Thank you, sir. We did have almost all the fixtures already, so we weren't exactly starting from scratch."

"Excellent work nonetheless. Keep it up."

"Yes, sir."

Baldwin led Artino out to his limo, and Artino headed back to his offices in Hartford, the planetary capital.

"That's been D Branch's secret all this time, Deke."

"Yes, Otto. In peacetime. It's not peacetime anymore. We've been attacked, in a big way, by the Deneb Republic, and even now they're trying to match our capabilities with their new-design frigates. I think the Navy needs this capability to prosecute this war with the best possible outcome. We have other secrets, and we'll make more."

Pasha thought about it for several seconds, then nodded.

"All right, Deke. You have authorization to proceed as you've outlined."

"Thanks, Otto. This is a war we don't want to lose."

When he got off the call with Pasha, Sharp contacted Admiral Jurgens.

"Jurgens."

"Hi, Kurt. Deke Sharp."

"Yes, Deke. What's going on?"

"D Branch has a capability we haven't shared, until now. Facing war with the Deneb Republic, we've decided now's the time."

"I'll take any advantage I can get, Deke. Whatcha got?"

"We can communicate with ships in the envelope."

"No shit. I didn't think that was possible."

"It's not, in the normal way. But if you modulate your engines just right, other ships in the envelope can see it."

Jurgens thought about it and slowly nodded.

242

"And this is a mature technology?"

"We've had it for years, Kurt. In peacetime, we kept it secret, but now is not the time to hold back anything you can use in a war."

"How do we implement it, Deke?"

"It's mostly software, Kurt. There is one hardware module involved, and we'll make you up enough units to equip your new frigates and ship them to Meredith so your people can install them."

"Has Otto agreed with this, Deke? I don't want to step on any toes over there."

"I just got off a call with him, Kurt. I have authorization."

"Then I'll take it. And thanks for keeping me on your gift list, Deke."

Sharp chuckled.

"No problem, Kurt. We're already working up the modules you need. Then we'll send them on to Meredith."

"Good morning, everybody," McGrath said to the pilots. "An announcement first. Our first squadron of ships has completed their space trials. They'll be released to us at eight in the morning Hartford time on the planet Merry, which is two in the afternoon here. They're docked to Merry station.

"We'll space those ships to Meredith in pairs, so you get some easy practice piloting multiple ships at a time. The top four teams on the scoreboard will take this squadron to the envelope. They will also bring it in to Meredith Station once they drop out of the envelope.

"So Hot Bitch and Slick, Scotsman and Dogbone, Giraffe and Sparky, and Derrick and Holiday, report to the operations room at one o'clock."

"Fuckin' A," Hot Bitch said.

"Nice," Captain Alex 'Giraffe' Johnson said.

Giraffe was right at the height limit to fit into an attack-ship cockpit, hence his call sign. Commander Russ 'Derrick' Hemler had arms like a gorilla, and could lift almost anything. Lieutenant Commander Jeff 'Sparky' Combs had an unfortunate history with electronics and power systems, prompting his transfer from maintenance to pilot early in his Navy career.

"Remember, you guys. This isn't a simulation anymore. You'll be piloting these ships within the battlespace simulator, but those ships are each thousands of tons of steel, electronics, and reaction mass. They're real, and a screw-up puts the lives of real spacers at risk on those stations and other ships in the traffic pattern. Unlike our exercises here, it's button-down time. No hotdogging. Let's show everybody just how good we really are.

"On to business, this morning we'll continue analyzing the Battle of Meredith and your adaptation of Admiral Sharp's tactics to our new ships."

The four pilot/co-pilot crews were in the Operations Room at one o'clock. There was a briefing of the mission, as always, even for a ferry job like this. They would take possession of the ships when General Ship & Fitting turned over the logins to the Navy's systems, depart from Merry Station per traffic control, and take them to the envelope.

When they hit the envelope, communications with the ships would be lost. They would space the trip under the instructions their pilots left them with at the time of transition, however, so those had to be loaded before they hit the envelope. Both the route and the braking maneuver when the ships got into Meredith space.

Each crew would space two ships simultaneously, linking them together in the battlespace simulator so the ships spaced in formation. That linking would be done only when both ships had left the traffic control space, so they had to depart sequentially before being linked.

At a bit after two o'clock, the Navy computers verified that the ships had been turned over. The crews took their command chairs and logged into the battlespace simulator.

When Hot Bitch got into the simulator, seated in the virtual command chair, she looked to her right. Slick was there.

"Well, we both got into the same simulation. First hurdle taken care of. Let's start pre-flight, Timothy. By the book."

"All right, Lee Ann."

Slick – Lieutenant Commander Timothy Roberts – knew something about Hot Bitch nobody else did. As her long-time wingman, he knew the whole impulsive and profane Hot Bitch persona was an act.

Commander Lee Ann Crosby was, above all things, a pilot. An excellent pilot. Her 'by the book' was a superfluous instruction. She always did everything by the book. It was the big reason they were both still alive.

He was very lucky to have been assigned to her.

It had started out sort of weird, though.

Lee Ann Crosby was very attractive, in an expensive and overpowered sports car kind of way. Not pretty in the girl-next-door way so much as sexy and dangerous in the designed-for-performance way. He supposed he was sort of the male equivalent. Darkly handsome, with an edge to him some women found irresistible.

Neither was the sort of person one took home to meet the parents. Not without getting warnings afterwards.

When they had met, the evening before his assignment as her wingman had become effective, they had gone to dinner together. She had looked him up and down. He had done the same with her.

"Shit," she had said. "The sexual tension between us is going to get in the way. When do your orders become effective?"

"Tomorrow morning at eight o'clock."

"Well, then, let's fuck tonight and get it over with. Then you and I can be ex-lovers who are still very fond of each other. That'll work better."

So they had. And what a night it had been. But, well before eight o'clock, he was out of her quarters. They had been nothing but professional since.

The only remnant of that night was that they did not call each other Hot Bitch and Slick on their private comm channel. Sure, in public, with the squadron, or on the squadron channel.

But on their own channel, they were Lee Ann and Timothy. They made a great team, sexual attraction and jealousy never got in the way, and they had been together, by now, for years.

They were coming up on the end of the pre-flight checklist.

"Yaw thrusters, left," Slick said.

Hot Bitch tested the thrusters – left forward and right rear – at five percent.

"Check," she said.

"Yaw thrusters, right."

Right forward and left rear.

"Check."

"Pitch thrusters, up."

Forward up and aft down.

"Check."

"Pitch thrusters, down."

Forward down and aft up.

"Check."

"Roll thrusters, right."

Right down and left up.

"Check."

"Roll thrusters, left."

Left down and right up.

"Check."

Slick closed the pre-flight checklist display.

"Checklist complete, Lee Ann."

"All right, Timothy. I guess we just sit and wait for our departure clearance."

"Coming up in fifteen minutes."

Hot Bitch nodded. She looked around her in the battlespace display. Not a simulator now, it was showing her reality. That really was the planet Merry below, Merry Station above, and a real ship in which she sat.

Their two command chairs, their panels, and the floor they sat on seemed suspended in space. All the rest of the volume around them was the display.

Below, the planet was huge. Almost half the sphere about them. The low orbit of Merry Station meant the planet was only a few hundred miles away.

Above them, the station was almost as big, obscuring most of the rest of their view of the space around them.

A tone sounded.

"There it is," Slick said.

"Release clamps."

Slick sent the command to the docking port and there was an audible 'clunk' as the station's clamps released.

"Clamps released."

Hot Bitch applied down thrusters at five percent to move

them slowly away from the station. She edged the front down thrusters up to ten percent to generate down pitch, aiming the nose of the ship away from the station.

When they were a hundred feet clear of the station, Slick announced it.

"Required clearance achieved."

"Roger clearance achieved."

Hot Bitch edged the main engines from idle up to five percent, and the ship began to accelerate in its departure run away from the station.

Within half an hour, the engines were at fifty percent, and the ship was out of traffic control. The station and the planet were slowly receding behind them in the display.

"OK, Timothy. I guess we go back and start pre-flight on bird number two."

"Roger that, Ma'am. Switching view to bird two."

The view shifted abruptly, and they were once more in a ship docked to the station, the planet below, the station above.

"All right, Timothy. Let's start pre-flight. By the book."

Once ship two had departed the station and cleared traffic control, Hot Bitch brought the engines up to one hundred percent. Ship two accelerated hard after her earlier-departed sister.

The trick was not to catch the other ship, but to catch it and hit the same velocity at the same time. Catching it and going zooming past it wasn't the goal.

The computers helped with that, as, when Slick paired the ships as spacing together, the computer automatically brought up the first ship's engines as ship two approached.

Soon, both ships were spacing together for the envelope, accelerating hard at the full capability of their engines. There was no need to hide their capabilities, as Sharp had usually done with *Medea*, because the enemy already knew their capabilities. Had been shown their capabilities up close and personal.

"All right," Hot Bitch said. "Formation established. We still have ten, eleven hours to the envelope. Time for a break. You first or me first?"

"Go ahead, Lee Ann. I'm good."

"All right, Timothy. You have the conn."

"Aye, Ma'am. I have the conn."

Hot Bitch dropped out of the battlespace simulator and was back in the Operations Room on Meredith. With crews in space, there was hot food on the sidebar, tended by a staffer.

Hot Bitch hit the head, then came back and got food. She sat in one of the dining chairs to eat. As she ate, a couple of other people got up out of their command chairs. They hit the head, got food, and sat with her.

"In formation, headed for the envelope?" the Scotsman asked.

"Yeah," Hot Bitch said. "Piece o' fuckin' cake. Log in, space the ships, then log out and have supper. What's not to like?"

The Scotsman shook his head at her, and she laughed.

He and Dogbone, in contrast, always did things by the book.

Deliveries

Every month for the next eight months, General Ship & Fitting turned over another squadron of the special frigates to Attack Force 101.

Captain McGrath assigned the second and third group of four pilot crews to the second and third deliveries. For the fourth through ninth deliveries, McGrath assigned just two crews to pick up each squadron. They spaced those squadrons in fours – a pair of pairs – as McGrath built up the experience of the crews in handling multiple ships at a time.

The ships were serviced at Meredith Station Number Four, then spaced out to a solar orbit well past the traffic pattern of the planet. Minimal station-keeping was handled by the computers.

When the ninth squadron arrived, and all the crews had experience spacing pairs and pairs-of-pairs of the ships together, they all took a big personnel shuttle from the Meredith Fleet base up to Meredith Station Number Four. Captain McGrath went along.

They were all clustered around an observation window in the zero-gravity portion of the station, looking out at one of the frigates docked to the station.

"I thought they looked a bunch different than the ships Admiral Sharp sailed against the Deneb fleet," Holiday said.

"Well, there's the missiles," Slick said.

"And the anti-missile gun on the cabin," Billy Bob said.

"Yeah, but the cabin looks a lot smaller," Holliday said.

"The cabin is the same size," McGrath said. "What you're noticing is that there are no shuttles docked to the ship.

Shuttles are pretty big. They have to be, to land on a planet and return without any servicing. Admiral Sharp's frigates all had two shuttles docked, because those frigates were manned. That made the cabin itself look a lot bigger."

"OK, that makes sense," Toll Booth said. "Why no shuttles on these?"

"With nobody on board, there's no need," Hot Bitch said. "Those shuttles are basically escape pods. If something goes wrong with the ship, you have a way to the planet."

"That's right," McGrath said. "And there's two of them for redundancy. With shuttles along, you always have a way home. But not putting shuttles on these frigates when they're unmanned means a lower moment of inertia, which means faster response to roll, pitch, and yaw thrusters."

"More maneuverable," Lefty said, nodding.

"What if we man the ships?" Sunshine asked.

"Well, then, you bring along shuttles," McGrath said. "They mount the Navy's standard one-man shuttle."

"And in the meantime, we don't have to drag that shit around with us," Hot Bitch said. "Nice."

They toured the cabin in groups of six, it not being big enough to accommodate more. The zero-gravity nets were deployed, allowing them to maneuver in the cabin as they floated about.

"Same controls as in the simulation," Slick noted. "If we had to space these in person, we would be able to do that."

"Yeah, it would be a pain in the ass – zero-g and all that shit – but we could do it," Hot Bitch said.

When all the crews had taken turns viewing the cabin, they reassembled at the observation window.

"Well, this was worth doing," Giraffe said. "Nice to actually see the ship. May give us some more ideas."

"That was the whole point," McGrath said. "Be kinda weird to be fighting these things and not actually ever seen one, wouldn't it?"

"Yeah, well, weird shit is what we do," Hot Bitch said. "Still, it was interesting."

They made their way back to the big personnel shuttle for the trip down to Meredith Fleet Base.

That trip was the first time any of them had been in space for almost a year.

When the fourth squadron had arrived, Admiral Rodgers and Captain McGrath encouraged the crews who had handled a whole division – a pair of pairs – on the ferry run to take a squadron out on maneuvers for practice. They made attack runs on a convenient group of asteroids in orbit farther out from Meredith.

Hot Bitch and Slick, and the Scotsman and Dogbone, were first up, those two crews having brought the fourth squadron to Meredith in divisions.

Of course, it was Hot Bitch and Slick who had an incident. Hot Bitch tried a particularly violent evasive maneuver, and the ship she was piloting ran into its sister. They bumped while going in the same direction, and the shields held, so there was no damage. The computer software for flying in formation simply couldn't keep up with her maneuver.

Slick made a modification to the formation flying software – anticipating the movement of the other ship from its control inputs instead of waiting for sensor readings of its actual change in position – and cleared up the problem.

Before restoring the squadron to its parking solar orbit, the crew that took it out would take it in to Meredith Station Number Four for service and refilling of reaction mass.

During those stopovers, station personnel added a hardware module, newly arrived from D Branch, to the communications stack in the electronics bay.

The Scotsman brought up his concerns about Hot Bitch with McGrath one time when they were alone in the Operations Room. Everybody else in the room was in virtual terminal spacing their ships, including Dogbone, and the Scotsman was on a head and food break when McGrath stopped through.

After all, if their squadrons were given a shared assignment, he would have to deal with her and her impulsive nature.

"I have to tell you, Sir, I have some concerns about Hot Bitch and her attitude. If we were given a shared assignment. You know. Dogbone and I do things by the book, Sir, and, well, that seems alien to her."

McGrath chuckled, and the Scotsman looked nonplussed.

"Sorry. I shouldn't laugh. You don't need to have any worries about her, Captain."

"But I do, Sir."

McGrath sighed.

"Captain MacPherson. Years ago, when I was deputy attack group commander, Commander Crosby was assigned to my attack group. I worried about her. A lot. But as deputy attack group commander, I had access to all the cockpit recordings. Video and audio. I reviewed those recordings and stopped worrying.

"Her attitude, her apparent impulsiveness, her profanity? It's all an act, Captain. The protective disguise of a capable woman in what is largely a man's profession.

"In the cockpit, Commander Crosby is the most professional, most capable, and most by-the-book pilot in this unit, yourself not excluded. She is also a fantastic pilot. She's a natural, and has only gotten better with experience.

"So if you get a shared assignment with Commander Crosby, you should consider yourself lucky, Captain, and just try to hold up your end of the bargain, because she will definitely hold up hers."

"Truly, Sir?"

"Absolutely, Captain."

'Then I'll take your word for it, Sir. There had to be a reason she was selected for this outfit, given you already knew her so well. And I'll hope my shared assignments are with her."

"There you go. Except for one thing, Captain. If Admiral Rodgers and I give a shared assignment to the two best pilots in Attack Force 101, you know it will be the toughest assignment you've ever faced. For normal assignments, we would normally split you two up."

The next time the Scotsman, Hot Bitch, and several other crew were in the Operations Room taking a meal break, Hot Bitch told some absurdly profane joke, and the guys laughed.

The Scotsman did not, however. Instead he caught her eye, and he winked at her. She winked back.

The Scotsman knew now, as Mad Man McGrath did, who and what Hot Bitch really was.

And she knew that he knew.

The navy of the Deneb Republic was also getting deliveries. Their defense sector was not as efficient or quick as that of the Federation, however. Also, they did not have an existing design and all the fixturing in place for their new ships. They had to start from scratch.

As a result, nine months after making the decision, they finally received the three squadrons of new-design frigates they had ordered. Space testing revealed some issues that needed to be cleaned up.

It would be another three months before their ships were cleared for operations.

When they were, they found they could very nearly reproduce the performance of the Federation frigates as shown in the videos they had received of the Battle of Meredith before the Deneb Republic fleet had surrendered.

High Admiral Mitt Prendergast declared the experiment successful, and asked the Chairman of the Central Committee, John Robertson, for additional ships of the type.

The Chairman took it under advisement.

Almost nine months along, Suzanne Fuller was more than ready for her baby girl to get tired of uterine living and come out and join the rest of the world.

This Saturday afternoon, Fuller lay out nude on the chaise on the patio, shaded by an umbrella from the semi-tropical sun. She was too hot all the time now, and sunning was out of the question. The cool on-shore breeze today was all that made being out on the patio bearable.

"Ugh. I am so tired of this. I look like some child's drawing of a mountain range. Bump, bump, BUMP."

Sharp chuckled. With her swollen breasts and massively distended abdomen, the description was apt.

"It shouldn't be long now," Duplay said.

Duplay was also nude, but sitting up, breastfeeding eighteen-month-old Thomas.

"You've had, what? Two false starts so far?" she asked.

"Yeah. A few small contractions, then nothing. Twice."

"But that means you're close, Suzanne."

"Close doesn't count. I want the baby, not the belly. Oof! It would also be nice if she stopped kicking me."

"Sounds like she's impatient, too, Suzie," Hansen said.

"I suppose," Fuller said. "At least we're in agreement."

"You know, once the baby comes and you officially go back to work, you'll have to go into the office," Sharp said.

"Some of the time, at least," Fuller said. "Working at home these last two months has been nice, but I feel out of touch with what's going on. I really need to get back in to the office once in a while."

Jacqueline Sharp Fuller was born nine days later, two days before Fuller's due date. Sharp and Duplay were both present, in the small hospital in West Coast Village. The doctors had seen no reason in Fuller's history or prognosis to prefer the big trauma center in downtown New Destin.

Little Jackie was born early in the morning. Mother and baby both being fine, they went home to the sprawling house on the coast the next afternoon.

Twelve days later, on Saturday, the four friends were all out on the patio again, with their babies. Fuller was pretty well recovered from the childbirth itself, though there was still weight to lose and muscle to get back into shape. Jackie was still in the sleep-and-eat phase, her only two major activities this early.

Fuller was lying out in the sun now, though she kept the baby covered.

"Oh, that feels so good," Fuller said.

"Yeah, it's nice when they're finally out," Duplay said. "You stop being hot all the time."

"And the sun feels so good now."

Jackie was asleep at her breast, but would wake up once in a while to suck a bit, then fall back asleep. Fuller jostled her a bit, and she started sucking again.

"C'mon, you. I need you to fill up so you'll go down for a while. No sleeping on the titty."

When Jackie was finished tanking up, Fuller burped her. Sharp then took his daughter over to her bassinet, in the shade under the eave of the house, and lay her down for her nap.

Thomas was already down for his nap on the sofa under the eave.

"When are you going back to work?" Hansen asked.

"Oh, I've already started some stuff. Checking mail, taking the occasional video call, reviewing some filings. I'll ramp up over the next couple months, then start going in several days a week."

"That soon?"

"Yeah. I don't want to. I'd rather stay home with Jackie. But I also don't want to lose my job. It's a great job."

"She already has a double breast pump," Sharp said.

Fuller nodded.

"I think I'm gonna have to pump these puppies twice a day, or they'll explode. And doing two at once saves time."

"How do you even do two at once?" Hansen asked.

"Oh, it's a machine. Like you put on a cow or something."

"Wow."

"Then I'll put it in a fridge in my office and bring it home for the next day for Daphne to feed Jackie."

"Don't worry if you don't get enough, Suzanne," Duplay said. "I'll still be wet then. Thomas is taking his time, and I'm letting him set the pace. I'm not pushing him, and we both enjoy the together time anyway. I'll have plenty for Jackie if it comes to that."

"I can't believe you just volunteered to babysit for Suzie, Daphne," Sharp said.

"For the first year anyway, D.K. I like babies, and I like being busy. After that, we'll see. Besides, it means Timothy and I have a babysitter for the evening sometimes. Hard to get, out here on the coast."

"So they'll grow up together," Fuller said. "That's nice."

"And I think I'm going to change languages every day, Suzanne. No reason they can't grow up knowing multiple languages. Much easier when they're babies."

"Oh, that would be fantastic, Daphne."

Political Questions

Rear Admiral Rodgers received a call request from Admiral Jurgens within hours of filing his most recent status report on Attack Force 101. He accepted the call.

"Rodgers."

"Hello, Admiral. Admiral Jurgens here."

"Yes, Sir. How may I help you today?"

"I've read your status report with interest, Admiral. I asked the Federation Defense Commissioner to give me a year to be in a position to respond to the Deneb attack, and my clock is running out. I therefore expect to hear from the Defense Commissioner soon."

"I understand, Sir."

"From your report, I take it you are in a position to commence operations if that is the will of the Council?"

"Yes, Sir. We have completed staffing and training, and are now engaging in readiness exercises on an ongoing basis."

"Excellent. That's an answer I'll be happy to give the Defense Commissioner. You've beaten my timeframe after all. Given the scope of your task, that's excellent work, Admiral Rodgers."

"Thank you, Sir. You've been very forthcoming with anything we needed."

Jurgens nodded.

"Now let's hope your boys and girls are ready over there."

"Oh, we're ready, Sir. You can bet on that."

Jurgens forwarded Rodgers' status report on to Bret Fender, the Federation Defense Commissioner. As expected, he got a call request later that day.

"Jurgens."

"Hi, Kurt. Bret here."

"Yes, sir. How are you?"

"Doing very well, if I read this status report correctly."

"Yes, sir. We're ready."

"You beat the year you asked for by almost a month. And you're sure you're ready?"

"Yes. Probably readier than we ever will be, Bret. They're at a high state of training and readiness now. That's hard to maintain. That edge. But we're there now."

"That's excellent news. I have a call with the High Commissioner tomorrow, and I know it's going to come up. We can't let the Deneb Republic's incursion go unanswered. But he's worried about reports that they're now working on ships like yours."

"Ships like Admiral Sharp's, you mean, sir. Our ships now are much improved versions. We don't think Deneb has an answer for them."

Fender nodded.

"That sounds good to me, Kurt. But you're sure?"

"Absolutely, sir."

"Excellent. Good work, Kurt. We'll see what the High Commissioner and the Council want to do."

"All right, Bret. Just let us know. We're ready."

The Federation High Commissioner, Geoffrey Dunleavy, considered, once again, his options. The decision was coming up quickly, as the year Bret Fender, the Defense Commissioner, had requested was coming to an end. Even considering the normal overruns, it would soon be his decision to make.

What was to be done about the Deneb Republic?

There were myriad possibilities, of course. Only a moron considered life to be made of either-or decisions, and Dunleavy was no moron.

First, of course, he could do nothing. He found this solution unsatisfactory, however. If an incursion of that magnitude went unanswered, it encouraged the Deneb Republic to simply try again. They might not be so lucky the next time.

And luck it had been. Dunleavy knew the whole story, and one couldn't rely on someone like Dominic Trask to see an attack coming in such a timely way as a matter of policy. Or for D Branch to be prepared to throw themselves into the breach to hold the line until the Navy showed up, either.

Not a slight against either Trask or D Branch. Quite the contrary. But one couldn't fashion policy around such fortuitous occurrences either.

Leaving such an incursion unanswered also encouraged others to try their hand. The Deneb Republic was not the only reprobate regime in human space. Far from it. The Federation was a welcome exception to the rule in that regard.

At the other end of the spectrum, Dunleavy could send the Federation Navy to the Deneb Republic, all guns blazing, to destroy the Deneb Republic Navy and topple the government. They could then install a better government – a representative government – and nurse it to health.

That alternative was also a disaster in the making. Without a heritage of democratic institutions and a popular culture that appreciated them, the whole thing would come crashing down.

It would be akin to planting mature plants in an unprepared field. They would all be dead within the week. Such things had to grow from seeds.

So, too, democracies.

The need to do something about the Deneb Republic was

pressing. The intelligence that they had begun building their own super-frigates placed even more urgency on a solution. If Dunleavy dallied, the Federation might well find its Navy shot out from under them.

Then the jackals would be on the herd for sure. All the other rapacious dictatorships would rush in to claim spoils amid the carnage. The Federation would be dismembered.

What middle options were there, then?

One, Dunleavy supposed, was to go out there and give the Deneb Republic Navy a black eye. Damage it enough that it would have a hard time coming at the Federation again. If they could do that while not leaving the Deneb Republic so weak as to be easy pickings for its neighbors, who would be as liable to jump on it as on the Federation, that could work.

It would leave John Robertson in power, though, and he was surely the problem. Their navy just did as it was told. It was Robertson who made all the decisions.

Surely getting Robertson out of power would be of benefit. To the Federation, at least.

Another would be to hit the Deneb Republic Navy hard – perhaps end its combat effectiveness altogether – which might lead to Robertson's ouster. It would probably also trigger a series of wars over the Deneb Republic's planets as its neighbors swept in on the remains.

Not a good outcome. War is bad for the neighborhood. And usually the worst of the dictators would prevail.

Dunleavy sighed, and shelved his considerations once again.

It was not yet time to decide.

The call request came in on schedule.

"Fender."

"Please hold for the High Commissioner."

"Of course."

There was a click, then a pause for a few seconds.

"Hello, Bret? You there?" Dunleavy asked.

"Yes, sir."

"Thanks for taking my call. I know most people send all kinds of documents around all the time, but I like to check in with people personally once in a while to get a better feel for what's going on."

"Of course, sir."

"So what's your status these days? What's new in Defense?"

"I'm happy to report that our new ships – the so-called super-frigates – are in place, and the crews are trained and ready for operations."

"Truly?" Dunleavy asked.

"Yes, sir."

"So if I were to order an attack on the Deneb Republic today, you would be able to space there and prevail over their navy?"

"Yes, sir. No question."

"You're a month early then. From what you promised me."

"Almost, sir," Fender said. "Perhaps three weeks early."

"You've done a tremendous job, Bret. You and your people. I never expect anyone to come in early anymore. Or even on time. Thank your people for me for doing such a fine job."

"I will, sir."

"And now I have a decision to make. One question before I let you go. If you were to space this new force to the Deneb Republic, how long would it be where I could still withdraw it without any ships penetrating the border?"

"About three weeks, sir. Perhaps a bit longer."

"And they would receive that recall message? And be able to stop before the border?" Dunleavy asked.

"Yes, sir."

"They would be in the envelope, right? How would you even do that?"

"I don't know, sir," Fender said. "I'm told we know how to do that, but I haven't been told the mechanism. It's a huge secret D Branch shared with the Navy."

"Remarkable. And as for their orders once they arrive?"

"The actual pilots remain here on Meredith, sir. We can give them orders at any time."

"All right, Bret. I guess now the ball is in my court. It looks like I have some homework to do."

"We're here for you, sir. And we're ready."

The High Commissioner nodded, gave a little wave, and cut the connection.

Dunleavy sighed. Time to get the politics seriously under way. He placed a call request with his Foreign Commissioner, Jean-Marc Lacombe. Lacombe took it right away.

"Lacombe."

"Hello, Jean-Marc. Geoffrey here."

"Yes, sir. How are you?"

"Well, it looks like I finally have to make a decision on the Deneb Republic."

Dunleavy brought Lacombe up to date on the Navy's state of readiness.

"So we finally have to decide. And your options are the same as before, Geoffrey?"

"Yes. I won't leave them alone, painting us as weak. I won't completely demolish them, leaving them to the dogs. It has to be one of the middle two. I would love to be able to blacken their eye a bit, and bring down Robertson, but that probably won't be enough to do it. And he's the real problem."

"Yes. Many adjectives can be applied to John Robertson, but

subtle and nuanced aren't among them."

Dunleavy chuckled.

"No, they're not. We also need to figure out what the Federation Council is likely to approve. Many of the actions we can take will precipitate a war."

"I think all of them will, Geoffrey. What the Council approves will, in some part, depend on what we ask for. For myself, I would prefer a war in which the Federation is not a belligerent over one in which it is."

Dunleavy nodded.

"Which is why we can't let the Deneb Republic off the hook. If we do, we will still be a belligerent, because we'll invite attack as being weak."

"That's my read as well. But we don't need to have this all decided to get things under way. If we know we're not going to let the Deneb Republic off scot-free, we can get our forces under way. We still have three weeks to work on the Council."

"That's an interesting point, Jean-Marc. You think I should give the go order?"

"Yes. Get them under way, Geoffrey, then you and I can work on the Council. They may be able to sharpen our thinking on the specific actions we take once our people get there."

"Fair enough. I'll give the word."

It was mid-morning only two days after Admiral Jurgens' last conversation with the Defense Commissioner that Fender called him back.

"Jurgens."

"Good morning, Admiral Jurgens. Bret Fender here."

"Yes, sir. How are you?"

"Good, Kurt. I have orders for you."

"Already?"

"Yes. Surprised me, too. You are to muster your forces and make for the Deneb Republic."

"The mission, sir?"

"That's the part we don't know yet. It could be up to and including taking down the entire Deneb Republic Navy."

"They haven't decided yet."

"No, not completely. They've decided we're going to do something, they just don't have particulars yet. But they're decided enough to get you under way."

"Understood, sir."

"I'll have written orders to you within the hour. In the meantime, get yourselves organized."

"Yes, sir."

Admiral Rodgers called an Attack Force 101 general meeting for that afternoon. All twelve two-man crews assembled in the ready room, though Rodgers suspected that there were two or three squadrons being used for maneuvers that were currently on autopilot.

As always, there were snacks and beverages.

Captain McGrath called the meeting.

"All right, everybody. Take your seats, please."

When everybody had taken a seat, Admiral Rodgers came in. Everyone stood.

"At ease. Be seated," Rodgers said.

"The powers that be have decided that it is time to teach Deneb a little lesson for the incursion that resulted in the Battle of Meredith. They have decided we will be Deneb's teachers."

"Hot damn," Hot Bitch said. "We get to go shoot at shit."

"Yes, Commander Crosby. We get to go shoot at shit."

There were some cheers and a few high fives in the crowd at that, then Rodgers reclaimed the floor.

"Now exactly how big of a lesson they haven't decided yet. Do we go to the Deneb Republic and bloody their nose a bit? Do we go out there and render their fleet toothless. Or do we go out there and turn it all into scrap steel and bodies. They're still thinking about it.

"But, since it's five weeks or so to get there, they don't have to decide yet.

"We, however, have been instructed to get under way. Now, there's a bunch of stuff we don't know yet. Like, what the mission is. Where the Deneb fleet is. You know, minor stuff like that."

Chuckles drifted across the crews.

"But we need to get ready and then leave. So any ships currently on maneuvers have to work their way through Meredith Station Number Four and top off. One squadron stays behind, as spares and home guard. The other eight will space when ready.

"When we have eight squadrons ready, we space for Deneb.

"Any questions?"

"Shouldn't we take the spares squadron, Sir? Rather than leave it here?" Giraffe asked.

"The concern is that if some portion of the Deneb Republic Navy spaces against the Federation while we engage the other portion, that the Federation not be uncovered, Captain Johnson. Our eight squadrons should be able to reduce the Deneb fleet."

"What about support, Sir?" Holiday asked. "That's a long way from home to be without reaction mass."

"Admiral Jurgens anticipated our orders, Commander McAllister. Or that those orders might be coming, anyway. Two Federation Navy battle groups, with logistic support ships for long-term deployment, left yesterday for Deneb. They have a lot of extra missiles and reaction mass for us. We'll pass them on the way, but we'll time our arrival to have them when we need them."

"What about practice against other frigates, Sir? Do we know if Deneb has built ships like ours?"

"We believe they have built ships like Admiral Sharp had at the Battle of Meredith. My understanding is that Admiral Jurgens is preparing exercises for us on that subject. We'll see what he has for us to practice on while our ships are on the way."

Rodgers looked around the room.

"Anything else?"

There were no other questions.

"All right, everyone. Let's check all our ships for readiness status and cycle the ones that need anything freshened up through Meredith Station Number Four. Keep Captain McGrath advised of your progress.

"Dismissed."

Reactivated

The Deneb Republic still had intelligence assets in the Federation of Human Planets, if nowhere near as many or at as high a level as they did before the Federation had swept up many of their agents.

Those intelligence assets saw unusual things going on, and they sent that information on to Deneb Republic Navy Intelligence on Gloucester.

Deneb Republic High Admiral Mitt Prendergast was meeting with his intelligence chief, Admiral Kelsey Donahue, at Donahue's request.

"It's your meeting, Kelsey. Go ahead."

"Yes, Sir. We're seeing some intelligence out of the Federation that's getting worrisome. No one thing, but a number of things taken together. Our ability to draw conclusions from what we are seeing is further degraded by the losses we took in our intelligence assets last year."

"I understand, Kelsey. What are you seeing?"

"First, two battle groups spaced for parts unknown. We normally can find out where they're going, but not this time. Their destination is more secret than normal."

"That's not that big a deal. Two battle groups is a small force, after all, and we did lose all those assets."

"Understood, Mitt. But the other thing we learned is that they spaced with support ships normally only used for long trips. Reaction mass tankers and the like. Those normally aren't used within the Federation because every planet has a navy station."

"OK. Now you have my attention."

"Right. And the other thing we've seen is at least three squadrons of those small frigates. It may have been four. They were prepping for a deployment."

"Oh, shit."

The two battle groups with supply ships could be escort for the frigates. R&R and the like. The little ships weren't that comfortable, and the Federation thought about things like that.

Plus they didn't have very long legs. Not Meredith to Gloucester and back, anyway.

Three squadrons of the frigates would be a hell of a handful.

Deneb had three divisions of the small frigates. Twelve ships. That was what the Federation had showed at Meredith, and only seven had survived.

Prendergast had pushed for more, and another twelve were in the works now, but they weren't finished. Maybe if he leaned on the shipyard a bit, they could be.

Then at least he'd have parity in numbers.

Maybe.

"Have we heard anything else about how many of those frigates they have, Kelsey?"

"No, Sir. We have heard of a new unit that was formed. All attack ship pilots. That unit has twenty-four pilots."

"OK, so three squadrons, maybe."

"Yes, Sir. If that's what this new unit is doing. I have some doubts there, because I haven't heard they were spacing, and I would have expected to. No shuttle trips to orbit or anything like that. With the battle groups, we did hear."

"So we don't really know what's coming, or even if it's coming."

"No, Sir. But those long-trip supply ships are worrisome."

"Well, I have my orders. If it looks like the Federation is

coming to the Deneb Republic, I'm to pull eight battle groups here to Gloucester to protect the government. That plus our frigates, all here to fight off the Federation."

"They may get handed their heads, Mitt. Especially if the Federation has more of these super-frigates than we think."

Prendergast nodded. This had the potential to turn out very badly. And Robertson would blame him.

Damn John Robertson to hell. He had started all this, by poking the Federation. Best to leave a sleeping bear lie.

But no. And then he had blamed High Admiral Hugo Biarritz for the disaster at Meredith. Biarritz, who hadn't been seen since, by the way. He was likely dead, and his family hadn't even been told.

Prendergast shook his head, then sighed.

"What's the status of Operation Medusa?" he asked with a nonchalance he didn't feel.

Donahue raised an eyebrow, but answered matter-of-factly.

"We are a go on that anytime you want. I'll check with Donny and make sure."

'Donny' was Admiral Donald Stillwagon, Prendergast's chief of naval operations.

"We should probably get ready to do that, Kelsey. While we still have some time to prepare."

"All right, Mitt. I'm on it."

Donahue left, and Prendergast considered his options. He was popular in the Navy, and he relied on that now.

Medusa. There was only one way to protect yourself from it. Cut off its head.

Deke Sharp got a call request from Admiral Jurgens.

"Sharp."

"Kurt Jurgens here, Deke."

"Hi, Kurt. Have your boys left yet?"

"No. Getting close, though. Which brings up a request."

"Uh-oh."

"Nothing big, Deke. I want to reactivate you and Admiral Fuller for a few weeks."

"We can't go anywhere, Kurt."

"I know, Deke. That's not what I need. We think the Deneb Republic has a dozen or so of the same type of ship you had at Meredith. We need to exercise our people against them. I thought the way to do that would be to have you and Suzie, together with Admiral Rodgers and Captain McGrath, serve as red team against them in the simulator."

Oooo. That was nasty.

Sounded like fun, actually.

"I think we can do that, Kurt. Maybe four hours a day, anyway. That lets us keep our commitments here as well."

"That's fine, Deke. With what the two of you, Shooter Rodgers, and Mad Man McGrath can dish out, I think that will be enough to get them up on their toes."

"All right, Admiral Jurgens. We're in."

"Thank you, Admiral Sharp. Admiral Rodgers will be in touch."

Rodgers had to give it to Jurgens. The man understood how to motivate people. Putting Attack Force 101 up against Sharp and Fuller, with himself and McGrath thrown in, would get them to give their best effort. Give them enough of a challenge to take the Deneb frigates seriously, so that when they arrived in Deneb, they would be ready.

Rodgers put in a call to Admiral Sharp.

Sharp, back on active status, accepted the call with his avatar in uniform as a vice admiral, the Federation Cross for Valor prominent at his neck.

"Sharp."

"Darrell Rodgers here, Admiral Sharp."

"Hello, Admiral Rodgers. Are you ready for war games yet?"

"No. Another couple of days. We're getting ourselves together for departure. We're faster than our support forces – who've left already – so we're not in a huge hurry."

"Just let us know, Admiral. We're here for you."

"Thank you for that, Sir. And your call signs?"

Sharp thought for a moment.

"'Sharp Edge' and 'Suzie-Q'," he said.

"Roger that, Sir. And we should probably have a strategy meeting before we take on Blue Team."

"Let us know, Admiral. Propose some times. We're generally good here."

"I will, Sir. Thank you, Sir."

Captain McGrath called the meeting.

"All right, everyone. Take your seats, please."

When everybody was seated, Admiral Rodgers came in. Everyone stood.

"At ease. Be seated," Rodgers said.

"I'm told we're all ready for departure?"

There were nods around the room.

"Yes, Sir. That's our status," McGrath said.

"Very well. When we break up here, all eight squadrons will space at squadron flank speed for the envelope. Tiers one and two piloting. Tier three, you are to stand by for relief as needed.

"Who's closest to Deneb right now? Two squadrons?"

"That would be us, Sir," Billy Bob said. "Us and Blondie, I

think."

"Yes, that's right," Blondie said.

"All right. Commander Thomas and Captain Stevenson, once in the envelope, you will turn toward Deneb and accelerate at one-half power. Everyone else will form up on you, except that Captain MacPherson and Commander Crosby will take lead when they overtake you.

"These two formations of four squadrons each will match velocity and then accelerate at three-quarter power until we overtake our support ships. At that point we will slow down so as not to be too far in front of them when we drop out of the envelope.

"Our transit should take about five weeks."

"What do we do in the meantime, Sir?" Holliday asked. "Hang out and play cards?"

"No, Commander McAllister. We're going to play some war games in the simulator. A little something Admiral Jurgens has set up for us."

"Why do I sense some evil shit coming?" Hot Bitch muttered.

"Because you have good instincts, Commander Crosby.

"The Deneb Republic, per our intelligence, has some new frigates of their own, copied from what we showed them at the Battle of Meredith. Do they have our improvements? Likely not. Do they have other improvements we don't know about? Likely so.

"So Admiral Jurgens thought it would be good for you to get some combat practice in the simulator against other frigates not unlike your own."

"Who will be piloting the Red Team ships, Sir?" the Scotsman asked. "Will we be fighting each other?"

"No, Captain MacPherson. The Red Team pilots will be

Sharp Edge, Suzie-Q, Shooter, and Mad Man. That is, Vice Admiral Sharp, Rear Admiral Fuller, myself, and Captain McGrath."

"No shit," Hot Bitch said, and slammed her hand down on the writing arm. "Hot damn! This is gonna be fun."

"Yes, Commander Crosby. Admiral Jurgens is giving you the nastiest Red Team pilots he can come up with, so that when you get to Deneb, you'll be able to beat those guys in your sleep.

"But you don't get to beat up on your commanding officers until you get those ships moving, so let's get ourselves up into the envelope and under way.

"Dismissed."

It was the weekend, and Sharp and Fuller were out on the patio. Tim and Daphne had taken Thomas into town for the afternoon. Some children's party or something.

"So we're going to be Red Team?" Fuller asked.

She adjusted Jackie a bit, and the infant woke up and began sucking again.

"Yes. Admiral Jurgens wants us to push these guys so they don't get surprised when they get to Deneb."

"Sounds smart," Fuller said.

"Well, the transit will take their ships five weeks, and, in the meantime, they're just sitting around. Best to use the time keeping sharp. They've practiced against battle groups with your simulation, but not against the new frigates."

"I'll have to work up some things, D.K. Variations on the frigates we had at Meredith. I can't imagine Deneb didn't make any modifications."

"We also need to work up some tactics against our new ones. Those modifications are going to make them tough nuts to crack."

"Oh, I think I can come up with some things."

There was deviltry in her eyes, and Sharp shuddered.

"Remember. We don't want to convince them they can't win, Suzie. That would be bad."

"Oh, they'll figure it out. I'll get started as soon as this one goes down."

"And then we need to practice with Rodgers and McGrath."

Fuller nodded.

"It'll be nice to see them again. It's been a while."

Jackie was finished tanking up. Sharp took the infant from Fuller and burped her, then put her down in her bassinet under the eave for her nap. When he got back to his chaise, Fuller was in virtual terminal working on the simulation.

Eyes closed, she had a smug smile on her face that raised the hairs on the back of Sharp's neck.

Sharp and Fuller met Rodgers and McGrath in the battlespace display of the simulation Fuller wrote in D Branch's data visualization engine. They were all wearing shipsuits.

"Good morning, gentlemen," Sharp said. "It's good to see you again."

"And you, Sir," Rodgers said.

There were handshakes all around.

"Before we start practicing, Admiral Fuller has some things to show us. Things she came up with for these exercises."

Sharp sat in one of the outer observer chairs, and Fuller waved to the two central command chairs, of the simulation. Rodgers and McGrath sat.

"Out there as Blue Team are two or three squadrons of your current frigates, with the modifications that were made to the design after the Battle of Meredith. The Red Team frigates, the

276

ones which you command, are the unmodified ones Admiral Sharp and I spaced at that battle.

"I have various flavors of the Red Team frigates, believing it naïve and dangerous to assume the enemy has not enhanced his frigates as well.

"Let's go over what some of those modifications are. We'll use some combination of them during each of the exercises."

Fuller spent almost an hour going through various modifications. The four then spent several hours attacking the Federation Navy frigates with two squadrons of the D Branch prototypes that were in the Battle of Meredith, using various combinations of Fuller's modifications.

When Rodgers and McGrath logged out of the D Branch simulator, McGrath looked around the Operations Room. No one else was looking at them. All were in virtual terminal.

"That woman is devious as hell," McGrath said.

"She's the top official corruption investigator on Ariel," Rodgers said. "Probably in the whole Federation. She's spent her entire career studying how people cheat."

"Well, she learned how to do it, that's for sure. Geez."

Rodgers chuckled.

"Are any of the modifications she came up with impossible for Deneb to have implemented?"

"Well, no. Not really."

"There you go, then. And if our people can beat her, they can beat Deneb. That's all I care about."

Under Way

The lead squadrons of Attack Force 101 entered the envelope and turned toward the Deneb Republic at half power. Behind them, the other six squadrons raced to catch them. Their computers worked to match velocities as they came together.

The squadrons of Hot Bitch and the Scotsman passed the others and moved into the lead, each with three squadrons arrayed in a triangle behind them.

The squadrons came up to three-quarters power and raced off after their support ships, two battle groups with supply ships for long missions.

The attack on Deneb was under way.

They were in the Operations Room. All twenty-four members of the frigate crews were there, seated in the command couches they used when spacing their squadrons in virtual terminal. They also discovered now why there were twenty-six couches in the Operations Room. Two in the front were marked reserved for Shooter and Mad Man.

Rodgers and McGrath stood in the front of the room, dressed in shipsuits. The display on the front wall was in split screen, and displayed Sharp and Fuller, also in shipsuits.

"All right, everybody," Rodgers said. "Today we will start exercises against Deneb frigates. Red Team pilots will be Admiral Sharp and Admiral Fuller as one crew, and Captain McGrath and I as the other crew.

"As we don't know what sort of modifications Deneb may have made to what they saw at the Battle of Meredith, we have various upgrades we will use in these exercises. As in any real confrontation, you won't know what those upgrades are until you run up against them.

"Bear in mind, what upgrades those ships have will change from one exercise to another, so you can't carry your findings from one exercise to the next.

"Our format will generally be two squadrons of our frigates against two squadrons of theirs. We don't know how many squadrons they have, but we'll exercise like this for the time being.

"That means two crews will fight our ships every exercise. For the first exercise, those crews will be our first two crews, Commanders Crosby and Roberts, and Captain MacPherson and Commander Sturgeon.

"The rest of you will occupy observer chairs on their flight decks. Each crew will be the only apparent observers on the flight deck, as the system will replicate system views for each crew. You will not be able to comment to the crew fighting the exercise. They won't even see you.

"The two Deneb frigate squadrons are protecting the conventional Deneb fleet behind them. We need to take out those squadrons to get at their fleet. That is the mission for the exercises. Take out the Deneb frigate squadrons.

"Any questions?"

It had been what they were expecting, so there were no questions. Rodgers looked around the room, then nodded sharply once.

"All right, then. Let's go."

Rodgers and McGrath took their seats in the remaining two couches, as, on the display, Sharp and Fuller did in theirs.

In reality, Sharp was on the sofa in his office, while Fuller was on a sofa in the big living room of the country house in West Coast Village.

Sharp and Fuller, Rodgers and McGrath, sat waiting as the Federation frigates slowly approached. This one was all Sharp's.

The Federation frigates had redundant communications. In addition to the quantum-entanglement links back to Meredith, which was being hooked through the Federation Navy's new computation facility, they had radio and whisker-laser communications.

It was the radio communications Sharp was passing to the massive – and recently upgraded – D Branch factoring engine. Could he decrypt their communications in time? Space battles developed very slowly due to the distances involved, and it might work.

Sharp relied on most people not using large enough encryption keys, which made the factoring engine's job easier. He was also running it in parallel across multiple communications streams among the ships of the two squadrons of Federation ships.

There it was. One of them, anyway.

"Channel open. It's all yours," he said.

"Downloading," Fuller said.

"Sharp Edge to Shooter. Beginning attack run."

"Roger that, Sharp Edge," Rodgers said. "Holding position."

"Here they come," Hot Bitch said. "Just one squadron."

"Tracking Bogey One," Slick replied.

The enemy vectors continued to develop.

"They're aiming to pass between us," Slick said. "Designate other squadron Bogey Two. Maintaining position."

"Guns free. Targets of opportunity. Begin jinking."

Both Federation squadrons began rotating their ships right and left as the Scotsman also started jinking his squadron.

"They're jinking as well," Slick said. "Guns as yet ineffective."

Hot Bitch nodded.

"They have the same shields we do. But they probably don't have the ability to close off their after aspect. We'll see if they give us the up-the-kilt shot."

The two Federation squadrons were firing nearly continuously – and ineffectively – as were the ships of the single Deneb squadron advancing.

As the Deneb ships passed through the Federation formation – one division through each squadron – Slick got a message from the simulation.

Software update on-line.

"What? I just got a software update message. It propagated across the squadrons."

"Find it," Hot Bitch said. "What did they do? And how?"

Slick was working furiously at his console, trying to isolate the source of the update.

"It came in on radio frequencies."

"Shut those radios off," Hot Bitch said. "What does it do?"

"Radios off. Working on it."

"Restore the previous software."

"I'm trying," Slick said. "They locked it somehow."

The Deneb frigates curved around behind the Federation formations. They were still firing.

"They shut off the after-aspect shield closure," Slick said.

Hot Bitch tried to jerk her squadron out of line with the Deneb ships' guns, but it was too late.

Each Deneb ship got a clean up-the-kilt shot into two Federation ships as they crossed the rear of the Federation formations.

"Federation ships destroyed. End of simulation," a voice announced.

There was a noisy lunch, then an after-action review.

"What did they do?" Rodgers asked.

"They shut off the after-aspect shield closure and then shot us in the fucking ass," Hot Bitch said.

"Pungently put, Commander Crosby. And how did they do that?"

"They inserted a software update in the frigates' control software over the RF radios," Slick said.

"Can they even do that, though, Sir?" Sparky asked. "Aren't those channels encrypted?"

Rodgers nodded.

"Indeed, they are, Commander Combs," Rodgers said. "But Admiral Sharp was able to use D Branch's factoring engine to decrypt one of the channels, and Admiral Fuller inserted the code modification."

"That's not fair," Dogbone said.

"Why not, Commander Sturgeon? Do we imagine the Deneb Republic has no decryption capability?"

Rodgers raised an eyebrow and Dogbone quieted.

"What is our solution?" Rodgers asked.

"Turn off the RF radios during combat," Holliday said.

"Use longer encryption keys," Sunshine said. "Make the factoring harder."

"Don't allow software updates without confirmation by crew," Giraffe said.

"Those are all good ideas. So which ones do we implement?"

"All of them," Hot Bitch said. "Just in case."

Rodgers nodded.

"I concur, Commander Crosby. I will leave it up to you to update the software this afternoon.

"Next exercise is tomorrow morning, for crews three and four. Captain Johnson and Commander Combs, Commander Hemler and Commander McAllister, you're on deck.

"Dismissed."

Two squadrons of Deneb frigates waited, as before. Two squadrons of Federation frigates approached, as before. But this time, the RF radios of the Federation frigates were shut down. They were running communications completely through the quantum-entanglement connection to Meredith.

Also, software updates had to be approved by a crew member. There would be no external command that could propagate a software change.

Fuller had a new modification to bedevil the Federation crews with. Missiles. But they were very special missiles. Behind the warhead, in front of the missile body, there was an intermediate chemical charge.

"We're ready?" Sharp asked.

"Yes, we're ready," Fuller said.

"Sharp Edge to Shooter. Beginning attack run."

"Roger that, Sharp Edge," Rodgers said. "Holding position."

"Enemy in motion," Giraffe said. "One squadron. Designate Bogey One."

"Tracking Bogey One," Sparky replied.

The enemy vectors continued to develop.

"They're coming straight at us," Sparky said. "Designate other squadron Bogey Two. Bogey Two maintaining position."

"Guns free. Targets of opportunity. Begin jinking."

Both Federation squadrons began rotating their ships right

and left, as Derrick also started jinking his squadron.

"They're jinking as well," Sparky said. "Guns as yet ineffective."

Giraffe nodded.

"Well, what's it gonna be?" he asked. "They gonna ram us?"

"Missile launch," Sparky said. "Forty-eight incoming. Tracking. Two missiles on each friendly."

Having launched their missiles, the Deneb frigates veered off their vectors, to evade closing with the Federation frigates.

"Believe it or not, they missed," Sparky said. "All missiles will pass well under us. Automated gunnery is ignoring them."

But as the missiles approached the point where they would pass under the Federation frigates, one in each pair of missiles pitched upward suddenly, and the intermediate charge detonated.

The missiles exploded, propelling their hot warheads up into the path of the Federation frigates. The nuclear warheads detonated directly in front of the Federation ships. The soft systems in the Federation frigates were destroyed, and the hardened systems were disrupted and went into reboot.

The second missile in each pair passed under its Federation frigate, then pitched upward suddenly. The intermediate charge detonated, catapulting the nuclear warhead up until it was directly behind its target, where it detonated.

That nuclear explosion was decisive, because there was no after-aspect shield closure. The hardened system that would have closed the after aspect of the shield was still in reboot.

"Federation ships destroyed. End of simulation," a voice announced.

After another noisy lunch, they had their after-action review.

"What did they do this time?" Rodgers asked.

"They popped up a nuke on us to reset our systems, then popped up another one behind us to take us out before our systems could reset," Giraffe said.

"Which meant we had no after-aspect shield closure," Sparky said.

"Correct, Captain Johnson, Commander Combs. How were they able to do that?"

"The gunnery system ignored the missiles when it saw they were going to miss us," Holliday said.

"Also correct, Commander McAllister. Now how are we going to fix that?"

There was silence for a few seconds, then Derrick spoke up.

"Adjust the target priority on the guns. Live missiles are always a priority, even if you think they're going to miss."

Rodgers nodded.

"That would be my position as well, I think. Commander McAllister, let's say you take the lead on getting that software fix incorporated."

"Yes, Sir."

"For the exercise tomorrow, it's teams five and six. Captain Stevenson and Commander Crockett, Commanders Thomas and Sonnenfeld, you're on deck."

Blondie, Lefty, Billy Bob, and Sunshine all nodded.

"Dismissed."

Again and again over the next three weeks, Sharp, Fuller, Rodgers, and McGrath put Attack Force 101 through hell. Sometimes one Deneb squadron was involved, sometimes both. Sometimes it was Sharp and Fuller, sometimes it was Rodgers and McGrath. Every time, the Federation pilots made minor changes to their software, or their methods, or their assumptions.

Gradually, they started winning – destroying the Deneb frigates – sometimes with horrific losses of their own. Those losses came down, too, as they gained experience and refined their methods.

Finally, Sharp and Fuller were able to tell Rodgers and McGrath they had done what they could.

"We've taught them all we can, Admiral Rodgers," Sharp said.

Fuller nodded.

"I have no more good ideas, either, Admiral. They're too good now to hurt in any serious way."

"Very well. Thank you very much, Admiral Sharp, Admiral Fuller. I think we're in a much better position now than we were three weeks ago."

"Glad to help, Admiral Rodgers. Go get 'em."

"Aye, Sir."

Rodgers saluted and cut the connection.

Political Decisions

Federation High Commissioner Geoffrey Dunleavy looked out the window of his office, though his thoughts were miles away. Light-years away.

He and Foreign Commissioner Jean-Marc Lacombe had divided the Federation Council between them, to goad, persuade, and cajole the Council into going along with the administration's plans with regard to the Deneb Republic. They had three weeks until Federation forces could no longer be withdrawn before an incursion into Deneb space.

It didn't help that those plans weren't final yet.

Dunleavy sighed.

Might as well get on with it.

Dunleavy started with Earth. It would be hard to get Earth's support for his plans, but how hard it was would tell him how difficult the rest of his task would be.

Earth always had a chip on its shoulder that the other human planets had much preferred to sign up with the Federation of Human Planets rather than the Earth Confederacy, given they were uneasy about Earth's clear aim to be dominant in its own political organization. Its name in the title announced that loud and clear.

Ultimately, Earth had signed up to the Federation of Human Planets rather than be left out. As a sop to its feelings of primacy, it had been given two votes on the Federation Council as the 'Heritage Planet.'

Which way it would go on this issue was a matter of some concern to Dunleavy, for Earth was hard to predict. Its decision would be dependent on its history, but how the current Councilor from Earth would interpret that history was up in the air. There was enough history there that any issue could go either way, depending on what the current Councilor from Earth decided to concentrate on.

Dunleavy laid out the current situation and the Federation's options to the current Earth Councilor, Baltimore Hitchens III. Barry – his chosen nickname for his unworkable first name – was initially skeptical.

"It's clear you want to do something military about this, Geoffrey, as your options include only one non-military response and three military responses. I am in general, as you know, opposed to military adventurism."

"How many non-military responses are there, Barry?"

"Clearly more than one, Geoffrey. There is to do nothing, of course, as if their pitiable incursion, which we dispatched so handily, were beneath our notice. There are also diplomatic sanctions, commercial sanctions, banking and market sanctions – why, any number of ways to register our displeasure."

"There is also the troubling intelligence that they are building their own powerful frigates, Barry."

"Yes, these troublesome little ships of yours. D Branch ships, you said?"

"Yes."

Hitchens nodded.

"That makes sense. D Branch is always fielding one- or two-man teams to trouble spots. Fast, small ships fill the bill nicely. Whereas the military types measure their importance by how many people are in their chain of command. Big capital ships with thousand of spacers aboard fulfills their needs better.

"I suppose the big-ship people are upset about these tiny warships."

"Oh, yes."

Hitchens nodded.

"That makes sense, as well."

Hitchens considered. He held his hands together, his splayed fingertips each in contact with the fingertips of the other hand. He tapped them to each other as he thought.

Hitchens sighed.

"You know, Geoffrey, Earth history is full of military adventures that went terribly awry. I worry about this one no less. However, Earth history is also full of cases in which a political entity let it be shown to be toothless, either militarily or in its lack of will to use its power, and those didn't work out so well either.

"Now, I know there are people here who would prefer we do nothing more than send them a stern letter. There are also people here who would encourage you to send enough of the Navy out there to stomp their navy into little dust bunnies. Which, from your briefing to me, you think we could do.

"I am, like yourself, more moved toward a middle ground. It would certainly be beneficial, from our point of view, to be rid of this Robertson fellow. He seems like nothing but trouble to me. Whether we can destabilize him enough to accomplish that within the scope of military action I am willing to countenance is another matter entirely.

"I will, therefore, go along with you to this extent. We must teach these people a lesson. Damage enough of their navy, in addition to what we have already done, to prove to them and others that we will not be attacked with impunity.

"However, we must leave them enough of a navy to be a bitter pill for their more aggressive neighbors. Like you, I worry about the Dorian Confederation and the Kingdom of Groton. A war between them over the pickings of the Deneb

Republic would do no one any good.

"And if Robertson can be destabilized enough to be toppled, I would make a serious effort to be friendly with the resulting government in Gloucester."

"Really, Barry?"

"Of course, of course. Robertson is clearly the problem. He made the decision to attack us. If someone is to replace him, let's be friends with him. That would likely cement his power. Why, it may even give us an ally against our mutual troublesome neighbors."

That was an angle Dunleavy hadn't thought of. Hitchens went on.

"There are many such cases in Earth's history, Geoffrey. When the victor in a war maintained frosty relations with the defeated, a second war often followed. But, in the cases where the victor and defeated became friends, why, they were often the most beneficial of allies."

"Thank you for that, Barry. It is an angle I hadn't considered."

Hitchens nodded.

"I think it a worthwhile project, Geoffrey. Why, we might even come to consider Mr. Robertson's ill-considered incursion a providential act."

"I will keep an eye out for the possibilities, Barry."

"Excellent, Geoffrey. Excellent. And, given that you and I are now of a mind on the issues we are currently presented with, I would be willing to speak for your plan in Council."

That was unexpected. And welcome. Hitchens was a gifted orator, and known to be able to go either way on most issues, depending on how Earth's history tilted. He was also respected, even liked, by most on the Council. For him to be solidly behind Dunleavy's plan was a huge plus.

"I would appreciate that, Barry. Thank you."

Hitchens just nodded, made a little wave, and cut the connection.

After two weeks, Dunleavy and Lacombe compared notes. They had a majority on the Council. Perhaps even enough of a majority to counter a motion to circumscribe Dunleavy's actions. Leave him a free hand to seek the best outcome.

It was worth a try.

Almost a week later, and with the deadline looming, they brought the matter to the floor in a closed session of the Council.

Of course, 'floor' in this case was a metaphor, as all Council members attended in virtual terminal in a simulation of the Council's actual chamber, which had not been used in decades.

In the final speech, Hitchens was eloquent in his support. He concluded with a flourish.

"And so, ladies and gentlemen of the Council – my friends, one and all – I find the administration's approach to this crisis to be well-considered. Moderate, measured, and with a greater likelihood of a beneficial outcome than any of our other options. I therefore urge you to support this measure, as I myself enthusiastically will."

The measure passed, and a motion to circumscribe was defeated.

The bar outside the Gloucester Naval Base was busy tonight. Michael 'Red' Tucker brought a fresh beer down the bar to the chief petty officer seated at the corner.

"Here you go, Chief. Sorry about the delay. You bring all your buddies tonight?"

The chief petty officer chuckled.

"No, Red. They're all down on planet leave. We got eight battle groups in Gloucester now, and so they got sixty thousand guys they're rotating through planet leave."

"Sixty thousand guys? Geez. I better go draw some more beers then. See you later, Chief."

That information went out to D Branch that night over the quantum-entanglement radio embedded in the coffeemaker in Tucker's kitchen.

"It's Gloucester, Kurt," Deke Sharp said. "They've got eight battle groups there now."

Admiral Jurgens nodded.

"That makes sense. First priority of an authoritarian government is regime protection."

"So now what?"

"We space for Gloucester. We can direct the squadrons now, with the comm method you shared with us."

"And your orders?"

Sharp half-expected Jurgens to demur on operational security grounds, but he was forthcoming.

"The Council has given Dunleavy a free hand, and Fender's passed on that free hand to me."

Sharp raised an eyebrow, and Jurgens caught the meaning.

"I can tell you, Deke, because you're in the chain of command. I left you active for the duration, you know. I'm hoping I can have you observing the action when we get there."

"So I'm the CO of Attack Force 101?"

"Officially, yes. Rodgers is in charge, but they like having you as the official CO. The crews have given themselves a nickname based on it. Swords. The Sharp Swords."

Sharp chuckled.

"I see. So what are your priorities, Kurt?"

"Teach them a lesson. You will not attack us with impunity. At the same time, leave them enough of a navy to defend against the Dorian Confederation and the Kingdom of Groton."

"Makes sense."

Jurgens nodded.

"Oh, and one other thing. If we manage to destabilize Robertson, try to make friends with whoever replaces him."

"Unexpected, but that's a really smart move."

"I think so, too, Deke. I just think it's unlikely."

"Be a coup if we can pull it off, though, Kurt."

"Yeah, well, their coup has to happen first."

"You got that right, Kurt. In any case, I'll be there for the finale. Keep me informed."

"Will do, Deke."

Rodgers got a call from Jurgens just as Rodgers was about to call him. Their forces were approaching the frontier with Deneb, and he had to make the decision to call them off or proceed soon.

"Good morning, Admiral Rodgers."

"Good morning, Sir."

"Admiral Rodgers, this is your official notice that penetration of the Deneb Republic has been approved. Written orders will follow."

"Yes, Sir."

"Further, your destination in the Deneb Republic is the capital planet, Gloucester. We have intelligence that eight battle groups and at least three divisions of frigates await you there."

"At least three, Sir?"

"Yes. Three divisions were operational some weeks ago, and three more divisions were in construction. We do not know their current status. So you might have three squadrons of them to deal with."

"I understand, Sir."

"That said, we don't want to destroy their whole navy and leave them to the mercy of the Dorians or the Grotons. We need to teach them a lesson, but not destroy them.

"And if their government falls over this, we want to try to make friends with the new guy, whoever that is."

"Sir?"

"Our view is that John Robertson makes all the decisions over there. Our problem is with him. If he's out, then we don't have a problem with the new guy. Friends would be better."

"Ah. I see, Sir."

Jurgens nodded.

"Watch for opportunities, Admiral. Be flexible, is what I'm saying. But not with Robertson. He's the guy who's trouble."

"We'll see what happens, Sir."

"Admirals Sharp and Fuller will be along. You're in command, but you can lean on their advice. For that matter, I may stop in myself. Not to jiggle your elbow, but to be of use if I can."

"Yes, Sir."

The eight squadrons of frigates had caught up and passed their support ships, then throttled back so as not to leave them behind. The whole fleet's velocity continued to increase as they continued accelerating.

They passed over the frontier into Deneb territory and kept going.

They had made a course adjustment, however. They were on course for Gloucester.

A SHARP EDGE

As the Federation fleet drew closer, their envelopes were easier to localize by ships in the envelope in the Deneb Republic. When they passed by the Deneb Republic planet of Burton on the way to Gloucester, a ship inbound to Burton got a good look at them.

That information – and the sensor scans – were sent on to Gloucester. From them, one could determine position, velocity, and mass of the envelopes of the Federation fleet.

"Seventy-six envelopes!" John Robertson shouted. "And sixty-four of them are frigate-sized."

He paced around in his office as he raged.

"Eight squadrons. Eight! And we have what? Three divisions?"

"I believe we have three squadrons, now, sir." said Joshua Peabody, his aide.

"That hardly even makes a difference against eight full squadrons."

"We don't know for sure, though, Sir. It may be a feint. They may not all be super-frigates."

"I bet they are. That bastard. That fucking bastard Prendergast lied to me. He *lied*. He said they only had seven of those damn things."

"We have to wait and see, sir. We don't know for sure."

"All right, Joshua. We wait. But if eight squadrons of those damn things drop out of the envelope here, Prendergast is *dead*. I will *enjoy* watching him die."

Prendergast listened to the recording in his office. He had had the foresight to place a pickup in Robertson's office while waiting for Robertson to show up for an appointment. Simple little thing, disguised to look like a time-release plant-feeder stick, in one of the potted plants in Robertson's office. The sort of thing everyone saw and ignored.

"...But if eight squadrons of those damn things drop out of the envelope here, Prendergast is *dead*. I will *enjoy* watching him die."

Well, there it was.

Prendergast, too, had seen the sensor data from Burton. He had no doubt it was eight squadrons of super-frigates. That plus two battle groups with support ships. That's what it looked like.

To support the super-frigates, most likely. Resupply them with reaction mass for the trip home.

There was no doubt they were from the Federation. Their velocity was testament to that. It took a long time in the envelope to build up that kind of velocity, so there was no way those ships were internal to the Deneb Republic. They had come from outside the Republic, and the only thing in that direction was the Federation.

Which meant that, when the Federation fleet dropped out of the envelope, he was a dead man. His children would grow up without a father.

For that matter, so were all the spacers in the Deneb fleet. He had analyzed the recordings of the Battle of Meredith extensively. If he was right, at least half of those Federation frigates were remotely piloted. With that many, they could just spear the sixteen capital ships, like they did the two attack-ship carriers at Meredith, while the rest of them picked off the sixteen destroyers at their leisure. Sixty-thousand-plus dead.

Tens of thousands of children growing up without fathers. Without mothers.

Unless....

Prendergast made a call, voice only.

"Yes?"

"Medusa is confirmed. When the Federation fleet arrives."

"Roger that."

Prendergast cut the connection.

Now to see if it worked.

Attack

Following the commands they received over the envelope communications system, the Federation frigate squadrons made a coordinated U-turn to the right of their incoming vector. They began thrusting against the envelope, and their velocity decreased rapidly.

Behind them, the manned support ships saw their U-turn and copied it, aiming to drop out of the envelope well behind the front-line frigate squadrons.

They were all gathered in the Ready Room. Lunch had been served. There was an air of tension in the room, as today was the day.

The day their ships arrived in Gloucester.

"Good afternoon, everybody. Let's take our seats," McGrath announced.

They were quicker to be seated and quiet down today. Some people were still noshing dessert, but most were all done with lunch.

Admiral Roberts entered.

"At ease," he said as he walked in.

"OK, today's the big day. These are your final instructions for the attack on Gloucester. Admirals Sharp and Fuller, myself, and Captain McGrath will all be observing. Admiral Jurgens likely will as well. So you need to stay sharp for new orders. Your general instructions are as follows.

"We have made our turn and have been decelerating against the envelope. That has decelerated us quickly toward normal spacetime. We'll come out a little further from Gloucester than a normal approach. That's to make sure we keep all the enemy ships in front of us as we exit.

"We are expecting eight battle groups, with a vanguard of up to three squadrons of frigates like our own. We will deploy one more squadron against their frigates than they have. That will give us a tremendous advantage in getting those up-the-kilt shots. By this time, you've practiced against both frigates and battle groups, and I expect no problems dealing with any of them.

"However – and this is the big however – we think the Robertson regime in the Deneb Republic is in serious trouble. A short victorious war is the usual response of an authoritarian regime that's in trouble at home. That's what he tried for last year, and it didn't work out. He ran into Admiral Sharp's force instead. That made his domestic problems even worse.

"Now, having a force like ours show up, with the ability to wipe out what's left of their navy, may be enough of an impulse to kick over the whole rotten anthill. We're going to be watching for that. Big invasions sometimes result in governments falling, and we have our hopes in that regard.

"So we're going to come out of the envelope, touch up our formations' positions a bit, and then sit there. Let them make the first move.

"Now I know it's fun to go running in there and blow stuff up. And we're good at it. That's what we train for, after all. But we're going to see what happens when we show up. We don't want to kill sixty thousand of our fellow spacers – and that's what they are, even if they're on the other team – if we don't have to.

"So we're going to let them form up. That will just gather them all in one place for us and make our job easier if it does come to blows. But the first offensive move will be up to them.

You'll get orders to go hot when it's the right time.

"In the meantime, let's decelerate, drop out of the envelope, and look all scary and shit. All right?"

There were nods and grunts and 'Aye, Sir's from around the room.

"Take your positions, everyone. We will drop out of the envelope in thirty minutes.

"Dismissed."

Everybody got up and headed for the Operations Room. There were trips to the head for many on the way, then they all settled down into their command chairs.

Rodgers and McGrath took the two reserved command chairs at the front of the room.

When Attack Force 101 logged into their battlespace displays, there were no views through real-time sensors. The engine-modulation technique for communicating to and from ships in the envelope didn't have anywhere near that kind of bandwidth.

Instead, what they saw was a computer simulation based on the reported positions and velocities of the ships. Their view was in the velocity direction, so they were looking out the rear view of their ships as they decelerated, thrusters first, toward Gloucester.

In front of them was the Gloucester system. They could see the sun and the gas giants, though the planet of Gloucester was still too far away to see.

They were coming in fast and decelerating hard, as was usual on exit from the envelope. As they watched, the gas giants passed behind them and the planet Gloucester became visible, rapidly approaching but slowing as their speed fell.

They dropped out of the envelope and everything froze. The

display refreshed with the actual sensor data as it came in from the frigates over quantum-entanglement radio. Tactical data began to fill in, too.

The crews of Attack Force 101 adjusted their ships' positions, using ships' thrusters to gather squadrons up from the slight scramble that always accompanied dropping out of the envelope. They rotated ship, to face their opponents.

The battle groups behind them adjusted their formations as well, and rotated ship to face the enemy.

Rather than spring to the attack, they waited, watching as the Deneb battle groups, in orbit about the planet, got their ships under way and spaced out to meet them.

They also noted three squadrons of frigates heading out from the planet to take up position between the Federation force and the Deneb battle groups.

"Look at that! Just look at that," Robertson raged.

"It's very imposing, sir,"

"It sure as hell is."

His display, echoed from one of the Deneb ships advancing away from the planet, showed an octagon of eight squadrons, each of which was an octagon of eight ships.

"Arrest that lying asshole Prendergast. Bring him to me."

"Yes, sir."

Why did a totalitarian regime's secret police always have black uniforms? Prendergast wondered.

Probably so when they arrested someone in the dead of night, they were harder to aim at.

It wasn't dead of night right now in Stroud, the capital city of Gloucester. It was early morning when the secret police squad showed up at Prendergast's office. Four enlisted and an officer, all dressed in black with the skull collar pins of the secret police.

The officer walked up to Prendergast.

"High Admiral Prendergast?"

"Yes."

"You are under arrest, Sir. Please come with me."

"Of course."

Prendergast waved them to the door and followed them. When they went through the door into the hallway, all five were cut down with a hail of bullets from six men to one side of Prendergast's office doors.

Five other men, standing behind them, waited, dressed in the same secret police uniforms as Prendergast's late escorts.

"You ready, Commander?" Prendergast asked the leader.

"Yes, Sir. This way please."

Prendergast sent a signal, then followed his faux-Secret Police out of Deneb Republic Navy headquarters.

The rifle companies of the battalions of the First Regiment, Capital Division of the Deneb Republic Marines waited in their ready rooms. They were all dressed for the party, and assault shuttles idled on the tarmac outside.

A three-second-long buzzer sounded, chilling the blood.

"GO! GO! GO! GO!" first sergeants shouted across the Marine portion of Gloucester Fleet Naval Base.

Marines jumped up out of their seats and ran out the doors of their ready rooms and into the waiting assault shuttles.

The assault shuttles did not take off immediately, though. They were waiting for the second signal.

It was a short drive to Robertson's residence/office complex, officially called Capital House. The black Secret Police van was waved through the gates. Deneb Republic Secret Police did not show IDs. No one dared impersonate the Secret Police.

Until today, anyway, that had been true.

Prendergast was walked through the complex until they came to the chairman's office. When he was walked through the doors and saw that Robertson was present, he paused and used virtual terminal to send a second signal.

Robertson misread Prendergast's hesitation.

"You damn well better hesitate to face me, you lying bastard. Look at that. Look at that!"

Robertson pointed to the display on the wall of his large office.

"Sixty-four fucking frigates. Sixty-four! We don't stand a chance against those bastards. All because of you and that fucking Biarritz. Well, now you're going to join him."

Prendergast had had enough. He turned to the faux-Secret Police officer standing next to him.

"Your sidearm, Commander."

"Yes, Sir."

The officer drew his sidearm and extended it to Prendergast, grip first. Prendergast took the sidearm, thumbed the safety off, and took aim at Robertson, who stared goggle-eyed at the weapon.

"Goodbye, Mr. Robertson."

Prendergast fired two shots to the center of mass, the heavy platinum slugs hitting Robertson in the sternum. The massive wound channels extended through his heart and he went down.

Peabody stared at Robertson, then turned, eyes wild, to Prendergast.

"Goodbye, Mr. Peabody."

Two more shots, then Prendergast handed the weapon back

to the officer.

"Secure the room until our people get here. We don't need any loyalists ruining the party."

"Aye, Sir."

The officer directed his men to the doors, then replaced the magazine in his weapon with a full magazine.

When the second signal was received, twenty-seven assault shuttles of the Deneb Republic Marines leapt into the air, turned, and hurried into the capital.

Eighteen of them headed to Capital House, while nine of them headed to Secret Police headquarters.

The eighteen assault shuttles that landed on the Capital House grounds discharged almost fifteen hundred Marines, who began a penetration in force of the building, clearing it as they went.

The Secret Police, so long unchallenged, were not a match for Marines in full combat loadout. Sidearms and snappy uniforms were no match for short-barreled assault rifles and body armor. Remotely piloted grenades, too, the few times it came to that.

The nine shuttles dispatched to the Secret Police headquarters broadcast orders over Secret Police channels to remain in barracks. A few of the Secret Police tried to exit their quarters only to be met with rocket attacks. This proved an effective discouragement to the others.

One at a time, the nine shuttles set down around the Secret Police headquarters and disgorged a total of over seven hundred Marines. They set up a perimeter around the Secret Police headquarters. One shuttle took off again and took up position as air cover, watchful for any organized resistance.

There was none.

In the former chairman's office, Prendergast sat behind the desk, went into virtual terminal, and called the commanding officer of the Deneb Republic fleet.

"Giscard here."

"Prendergast. I have things in hand here, Gaston. Take up your positions to oppose the Federation fleet, but do not initiate hostilities. Defend yourselves if you have to, but under no circumstances are you to make a hostile move. Let me see what I can do here."

"Aye, Sir."

"Probably best is to not even go to general quarters. Do not arm weapons systems. They can see that, and it will help me in negotiations."

"I understand, Sir."

That done, Prendergast switched to the interstellar network connections to the Federation of Human Planets and tried to raise the admiral of the Federation fleet.

Maybe he could save his personnel.

Victory

Sharp, Fuller, and Jurgens were sitting on a simulated flag deck watching the Deneb Republic fleet assemble.

"DV. Are the Deneb Republic ships at general quarters?" Sharp asked.

"Based on available signs, they are not at general quarters."

"DV. What signs are those?"

"Targeting radars are not active. Weapons systems are not armed."

"Interesting," Jurgens said.

"However, the capital of Stroud is currently on this side of the planet, and sensors have detected assault shuttle activity and small explosions in the capital."

"DV. Can you localize those sensor readings?" Fuller asked.

"Based on the map of Stroud published by the Deneb Republic government, the assault shuttle activity is at Capital House, John Robertson's residence and office complex, and at Secret Police Headquarters. Small explosions have been detected at Secret Police headquarters."

"OK, now that's *very* interesting," Jurgens said.

"Is it happening, I wonder?" Sharp asked.

"Sounds like," Jurgens said.

"DV. Are there any inbound communications at Federation Navy headquarters from Gloucester?"

"Checking Navy computers. Yes," the voice said. "There is a call request inbound from High Admiral Mitt Prendergast of the Deneb Republic Navy. He is requesting the admiral of the Federation fleet currently in command in Gloucester."

"You take it, Deke," Jurgens said.

"Me? Why me?"

"Because then you can escalate it to me. Rodgers could take it, but rear admiral is the wrong grade to take the High Admiral's call."

"OK. Fair enough. Monitor and let me know on a private channel if I'm screwing up, Kurt."

"Got it," Jurgens said.

"DV. Put High Admiral Prendergast's call request through to me."

"Requested from Federation Navy computers. Completed. Transferring Prendergast call request."

The call request came through to Deke Sharp, and he accepted the call. His avatar was in his vice admiral's uniform, the Federation Cross for Valor at his neck.

"Vice Admiral Sharp here."

Prendergast looked at Sharp in his display. He was in vice admiral's uniform, but without all the honor ribbons one normally saw. Prendergast did recognize the Federation Cross, however. They didn't give that away for nothing.

Good. Not a lightweight desk warmer, then.

Of course, he would have been unlikely to characterize Admiral Sharp that way anyway. The man had an edge about him. This was a man who had done things. Hard things. Even unsavory things.

Maybe Prendergast's wild play had a chance after all.

"High Admiral Prendergast here. Am I correct in thinking you're in command of the Federation fleet currently in Gloucester, Admiral Sharp?"

"Yes," Jurgens' voice came to Sharp on a private audio channel.

"That's correct, Admiral Prendergast. Am I to assume that you are in command of the fleet currently arraying against us?"

"Yes, Admiral Sharp. I am in command of the entire Deneb Republic Navy. Actually, at the moment, I am in command of the Deneb Republic, though that is somewhat in dispute at the moment."

"Not John Robertson, Admiral Prendergast?"

"John Robertson is no longer Chairman of the Central Committee, Admiral Sharp."

"He stepped down then?"

"In a manner of speaking, Admiral Sharp. Mr. Robertson has permanently retired. For medical reasons, let us say. He discovered a previously unknown allergy to high-velocity platinum."

Sharp nodded.

"Yes, I have seen several cases of that myself, Admiral Prendergast."

Prendergast had no doubt on that score. Deke Sharp looked like the sort of fellow one didn't want to mess with. If one even had the opportunity. Which would not present itself twice.

"Having taken over from Mr. Robertson, I find myself the unwilling inheritor of the results of his policies, Admiral Sharp. It was not I who sent the Deneb Republic fleet to Meredith. That debacle was all on Mr. Robertson."

Sharp nodded.

"I had a role in that debacle myself, Admiral Prendergast. I was the opposition force commander."

Well, that explained the Federation Cross. Prendergast had to admire anyone who would take a dozen frigates up against eight battle groups for the first time. Now that everybody knew what those frigates were capable of, that was one thing. Taking them into battle for the first time against such odds was another thing altogether.

His estimation of Admiral Sharp jumped higher.

"Then you may know and can certainly guess that I have no desire for you to demonstrate once again just how effective your ships can be against the Deneb Republic Navy, Admiral Sharp."

"And so...?"

Prendergast took a deep breath and let it out slowly.

"And so we surrender, Admiral Sharp. You are clearly in control of Gloucester, and I have no desire to argue the point. Your instructions?"

"Your fleet is to resume its orbital positions while we discuss where we go from here, Admiral Prendergast. I will contact my superiors for further instructions."

"Very well, Admiral Sharp. I'll send those orders now and await further communications."

Prendergast called Admiral Gaston Giscard.

"Giscard."

"Prendergast here, Gaston. I have surrendered Gloucester to the Federation. You are to move your ships back to their orbital positions, back to where they were when the Federation fleet arrived."

"Aye, Sir."

"Make sure your group commanders understand they are on their parole. I've saved everyone from useless slaughter, but only if they all obey orders. We do not want some hothead kicking off a battle here. We stand no chance against them. No chance at all."

"I understand, Sir."

From the sound of it, the fighting was moving closer to Prendergast's position in the office of the former Chairman of the Central Committee.

"You guys better get out of those uniforms. Otherwise, you're likely to end up friendly-fire casualties."

"Good idea, Sir," the faux-Secret Police officer said.

He and his four fellows took off the Secret Police jackets and shirts, leaving them in Navy-issue T-shirts.

Prendergast sent a message to the commandant of Marines that his office was secure, and asked him to warn his men to avoid friendly-fire casualties as they reached his office.

When the Marines broke through to the office, he sent orders to arrest and detain the members of the Deneb Republic's Central Committee.

The crews of Attack Force 101 watched as the Deneb ships flipped ship and fired thrusters, heading back toward Gloucester orbit.

"We've won," Admiral Rodgers announced to the crews. "The Deneb fleet has surrendered to Admiral Sharp. Remain in place. Stand down your weapons systems."

"We don't get to shoot anybody?" Lefty asked.

"No, Commander Crockett, we don't have to shoot anybody."

"Then all that training was for nothing."

"That's not how it fuckin' works, Lefty," Hot Bitch said. "We trained to win, and we did. The best offense is being prepared to fight. Then you don't have to fire a shot, because nobody wants to fuck around and find out."

"That is correct, Commander Crosby. We won because we were prepared to fight."

The Deneb vessels continued to move toward their original orbital positions.

"OK, third-tier crews take command. Two squadrons per crew. First- and second- tier crews stand down. You have twelve hours."

The four third-tier crews each took two squadrons, while the sixteen members of the first- and second-tier crews logged out of the battlespace display.

Movements in space taking so long, it was by now late evening at the Meredith Fleet Naval Base. They had been at it all day.

There was dinner waiting, then they headed off for bed.

"We've won, sir," Jurgens reported to Defense Commissioner Bert Fender.

"Casualties?"

"None on either side, sir. No battle occurred. High Admiral Mitt Prendergast is now head of state of the Deneb Republic. Mr. Robertson was forcibly retired."

"Forcibly retired, Admiral?"

"He will probably have a very nice state funeral, sir. In the meantime, High Admiral Prendergast is in command, and he has surrendered to Admiral Sharp."

"Excellent. Well done, Admiral Jurgens. I will inform the High Commissioner. If Prendergast is now head of state, the High Commissioner would seem the appropriate channel for further communications."

"I agree, sir."

"Congratulations, Admiral. Fender out."

Federation High Commissioner Geoffrey Dunleavy called Earth Councilor Baltimore Hitchens III.

"Hitchens."

"Dunleavy here, Barry."

"Yes, High Commissioner. How may I help you today?"

"Your plan has worked out admirably, Barry. There has

been a coup on Gloucester. John Robertson is dead. The commander of the Deneb Republic navy, High Admiral Mitt Prendergast, is now head of state. I am about to call him. You anticipated something of the kind, so I wanted to speak with you about next steps."

"That is excellent news, Geoffrey. I did not so much anticipate it as point out the possibility, and am gratified it came to pass."

Dunleavy nodded.

"So now what, Barry?"

"Offer friendship, Geoffrey. A mutual defense treaty. A fair trade agreement. Normalization of relations. All that sort of thing. Such a relationship makes us both much more secure against our unruly neighbors."

"Can I offer your assistance to Admiral Prendergast?"

"Absolutely. I would be pleased to assist Admiral Prendergast as he takes on his new duties, Geoffrey. There is a great deal of history on Earth of such arrangements, and I have been a student of such transitions for a long time."

"Excellent. Thanks, Barry. We want to see this fellow be successful."

"Indeed. It is the best outcome we could have hoped for."

Prendergast had been going all day. With his Marines in control of Capital House, with the Navy resuming its stand-down positions, with the Central Committee locked up and his family guarded by Marines, he finally felt secure enough to take a break.

He fell asleep on one of the couches in Robertson's former office. Household staff brought blankets and a pillow.

It was over.

He had won.

Admiral Casimir Kaminski, Prendergast's chief of staff, worked through the night. Anything like the change of power that had occurred that day had a lot of loose ends to clean up. He had napped off and on during the day, during the long delays that were always a part of space-based movements.

Skill at such napping was a hallmark of senior naval officers in a space-based navy.

Kaminski was involved in a flurry of activity overnight on that first critical day. He moved his own office and staff to Capital House once it was secure, taking up the office of the late Joshua Peabody.

Kaminski made sure the Central Committee was well treated during their detention. It was always better to win such over to the new regime if one could, and that started with making sure they were well treated.

Kaminski directed the cleanup of Capital House from the battle that had raged when the Marines cleared the building. This was mostly gathering up all the bodies of Secret Police killed during the fighting. There was also the clearing of some debris and the assessment of repairs needed from the few uses of remotely piloted grenades against some Secret Police hard points.

Kaminski directed household staff to clean out Mr. Robertson's residence within the complex and prepare it for the new occupant and his family. Much of that would wait until the larger daytime staff arrived, but that was fine. By tomorrow night, Admiral Prendergast and his family would be in residence.

Kaminski also had a Navy computer team break into Peabody's and Robertson's computer files overnight.

Once they had broken into Peabody's files, Kaminski began reviewing Peabody's communications with other government officials. Based on those communications, he sorted them into people who might be trouble and people who would likely simply go along with the change in administration.

Those who might be trouble were arrested and detained by Marine details. He specified that they were to be treated well, pending interviews about their attitudes to the change in administration.

When Prendergast woke the next morning, Kaminski had the new government well in hand.

Kaminski reported in to Prendergast in the morning as Prendergast ate breakfast at his desk.

"You're amazing, Cas. Did you get any sleep last night?"

"I got several hours, Sir."

"An hour here and an hour there, if I know you."

"As you say, Sir."

Prendergast laughed.

So far, so good.

Negotiations

There were a thousand pressing items on Prendergast's plate that second day, but none more pressing than the relationship between the Deneb Republic and the Federation of Human Planets.

What would it be? Annexation? Subjugation? Independence?

Prendergast hoped it would be independence, but on what terms?

All of this was up in the air, and not really his to determine. The Federation was in the driver's seat.

Prendergast spent the early morning reading up on the High Commissioner of the Federation, Geoffrey Dunleavy.

He allowed himself to hope.

Dunleavy put a call request in to Prendergast mid-morning Stroud time. Prendergast accepted immediately.

"Prendergast."

"Good morning, High Admiral. Thank you for taking my call. I am Federation High Commissioner Geoffrey Dunleavy. I hope I am not being interruptive on what must be a very busy morning for you."

"Not at all, High Commissioner. Of all the things pressing in on me this morning, our relationship to the Federation is the most important. I am surprised, though, that it would be you calling me."

"Ah, but you are now head of state, are you not, High Admiral? In that case, as head of state of the Federation, I am the most appropriate person with whom to negotiate our future relationship."

Prendergast felt great relief at the way Dunleavy answered. Future relationship did not imply subjugation or occupation.

Prendergast nodded.

"You are likely right, High Commissioner. As for our future relationship, my sincere wish is for friendship. Mr. Robertson's attitude toward the Federation is not shared by the current government."

It was Dunleavy's turn to feel relief. He found himself liking this military man. Dunleavy generally got along with military types, as long as they were operational commanders and not bureaucratic desk warmers. And Prendergast's bona fides as an operational commander were well known.

"That is my sincere wish as well, High Admiral. Imagine how much better we could both do for our people as friends rather than enemies. And, as friends, I must insist that you call me Geoffrey."

Prendergast nodded.

"Please call me Mitt, Geoffrey. For my part, I thought this whole adventure of Mr. Robertson's was ill-advised, but he was not open to input from his military commanders."

"I understand that Mr. Robertson is no longer involved in the government. Is that right?"

"Yes, Geoffrey. I shot him, for treason. That is, for acting against the wishes and the best interests of the people of the Deneb Republic."

"Well, I hope he has a lovely funeral, Mitt, but I cannot admit any sorrow on his passing. Let us discuss, then, how our two great nations might move forward from this point."

Almost an hour later, when Prendergast got off the phone, he couldn't believe his luck.

Kaminski was there.

"How did your call go, Sir?"

"Well, Cas. Very well. I can hardly believe it."

"Excellent. Your wife and children are here now, Sir. Would you like to eat lunch with them in the private dining room in the residence upstairs?"

"Yes. That would be splendid."

Prendergast looked around his office. At the multiple doors leading from it.

"Where is it, by the way?"

"This way, Sir. There is a private stairway."

Kaminski opened a side door of the office. Prendergast passed through and found a stairway to the residence portion of his wing of the complex.

His wife Elise Fischer met him in the hallway at the top of the stairs.

"Thank God you're OK," she said, hugging him.

"I did call, Elise."

"Oh, I know. But that's not the same as seeing you."

"The Marines treated you all right?"

"Oh, yes. They guarded the house all night, then transferred us here this morning in an armored car. They were very nice about it."

Prendergast nodded.

"We were all worried that someone would try to target you."

"We were very well guarded. Come. They were putting out lunch when Admiral Kaminski signaled you were coming upstairs."

Fischer led Prendergast down the hall to the dining room. Staff was standing by with lunch in covered chafing dishes.

"Daddy!" their youngest, Joanie called out.

All the kids came up to hug him. Their mother's worry had

signaled to them that things were very up in the air. Seeing him all right was a big relief.

"I love you, too, you guys. I love you, too. Come on now. Let's sit down and have some lunch."

When they were seated, staff served them. Some judicious choices had been made, considering children were among the diners. Lunch was spaghetti and meatballs with buttered and toasted Italian bread.

It felt good to be with his family, have a normal lunch with them. It reminded Prendergast again why he had taken such an insane risk.

Then again, as it was clear Robertson was going to execute him, what choice did he really have?

After lunch, Prendergast made his excuses.

"I have to get back to work, Elise."

"I know, dear. I'll be fine now. I just needed some reassurance things were going to work out."

"It'll be fine, dear. We're over the toughest part now."

Prendergast kissed her, hugged the kids, and headed back downstairs.

"All right, everybody," Captain McGrath said. "One squadron at a time, we're going to head back to our support ships and restock with reaction mass for the trip home. Team nine, you're up. Pick a squadron and let's get them headed back.

"Once you're topped off, set course for home and depart Gloucester."

Once back downstairs, Prendergast sat at what he now considered his desk and considered. He was considerably more relaxed than this morning. Not an empty reassurance to Elise, they actually were over the toughest part.

Word had spread like wildfire through the Navy that he had saved the lives of the fleet by surrendering Gloucester rather than simply throwing their lives away against the Federation fleet. That went a long way with them. He had been well liked before, but that appreciation had hardened in his favor.

The Secret Police was the one big thing he still worried about. The one armed force that could be a center of resistance.

Kaminski came in when he was back from lunch, and Prendergast asked him about it.

"We're proceeding as you ordered this morning, Sir. We are letting them out of the Secret Police headquarters a few at a time. We are confiscating their badges, their uniforms, and their service weapons. We are then sending them home on their parole."

"Are you sending them home naked, Cas?"

"No, Sir. We're issuing them shipsuits for their trip home. We collect a busload of them for their area of the city – north, east, south, west – and then we drive them home. They're to bring out and surrender their spare uniforms when we arrive at their home.

"We're explaining to everyone before they leave that as long as they behave, their prior service will not be counted against them. If they are picked up for any sort of resistance to the new administration, however – or if they try to impersonate police officers in any context – their actions when they were Secret Police will be used against them."

"That should keep most of them in line, I would think."

"I would think so, Sir. Especially since we have broken into the Secret Police files, and we have extensive records of just what specific individuals were up to."

"Do we let them know that?"

"Oh, yes."

"Good. The people who would be the most likely sources of trouble for us are probably the ones who have the nastiest records."

"That's likely true, Sir."

Prendergast nodded. What next?

"Sir, I have to ask. What happened during your phone call?"

"Oh. Sorry, Cas. Yes, you must be consumed with curiosity. But I had to have lunch first. See Elise."

Kaminski nodded.

"Of course, Sir. But now..."

"It was a call from the High Commissioner of the Federation. We've agreed that the Deneb Republic and the Federation of Human Planets will be friends going forward."

"Friends, Sir?"

"Yes. Peace treaty. Mutual defense treaty. Free trade. Free travel. Free immigration. Everything I could ever have hoped for and more."

"But why, Sir? They had us over a barrel."

"Mr. Dunleavy is a man of vision, Cas. That's the only thing that explains it. He thinks the best long-term situation for the Federation is for our two star nations to be friends, and I for one am not going to argue against it."

"No. No, Sir. I get that. But... I just can't get over it."

"The Councilor for Earth is going to call me this afternoon. Mr. Dunleavy offered me his assistance as we get things together here. I hope to get more insight into their thinking when I talk to him.

"In the meantime, he is withdrawing Federation forces from Gloucester."

"Yes, Sir. I was going to mention that, while you were at lunch, Federation squadrons began moving back to their support ships for reaction mass, presumably before setting off for home."

"That fits in with what Mr. Dunleavy committed to me, Cas. It's what I expected, but it is nice to see."

It was nearing mid-afternoon in Stroud when the call request from Earth came in. Prendergast accepted.

"Prendergast."

"Good afternoon, High Admiral. My name is Baltimore Hitchens III. I am the Councilor for Earth on the Council of the Federation of Human Planets."

Hitchens had the air of someone who was very satisfied with himself, and Prendergast thought this conversation would likely go nowhere. The best he could hope was not to break anything he and the High Commissioner had already agreed to.

"Good afternoon, Councilor."

"Oh, do call me Barry, please, High Admiral. If we are to be friends, let us start off on the right foot."

"And you should call me Mitt, Barry."

"Excellent. Mitt, the High Commissioner asked me if I could make myself available to you as you considered the task before you, and I am more than happy to do so. You see, on Earth we have ten millennia of experience in all the ways government can and cannot work. I have been a student of these matters for some time. If you have any questions for me, I would be pleased to answer them the best I can."

"I guess my first question is, Why is the Federation being so generous to the Deneb Republic? Your navy very much had the upper hand on us, and I would have expected a less, well, magnanimous approach."

Hitchens nodded.

"I had some small part in convincing Mr. Dunleavy that was the best approach in the circumstances, Mitt, so I can speak to this issue."

Wait. This was Hitchens' plan? Prendergast reassessed the Councilor from Earth. Perhaps his apparent self-satisfaction was artifice. Protective coloration, as it were. Or a cultural thing. Prendergast didn't know much about Earth.

Hitchens went on.

"Consider the alternatives, Mitt. The Federation could consider the Deneb Republic a conquered territory. Rule it as a subjugated people. Would the people of the Deneb Republic be happy with such a plan on the long term?"

"No, Barry. Not at all."

"You see. We would be building in a future war or wars, one of which you would ultimately win."

"We would?"

"Of course. People do not fight as long or as hard to subjugate someone else as the subjugated fight to free themselves. Then again, we could annex the Deneb Republic. I ask you again, would that work on the long term?"

"I don't know, Barry. Perhaps."

Hitchens shook his head.

"It would not, Mitt. The people of the Deneb Republic have, at this point, no culture of democracy. No experience with it. Whereas we in the Federation are quite comfortable in our system. Oh, we have our differences, and it can seem quite rancorous at times, but we successfully blunder along in apparent chaos. In addition to a method of government, it is often a source of entertainment.

"But annexing the Deneb Republic to the Federation would throw a wrench into the works. Your people would ultimately be the end of us. Do you see that?"

"Yes, Barry. I suppose I do, now. We would not know how to react to the machinery of your system."

"And would break the machinery thereby. Exactly. And so I advised the High Commissioner. No, the most stable long-term relationship between our two countries, based on millennia of history, is to simply be friends."

"You make what appears so unusual to me seem the only rational possibility, Barry."

"And so it is, Mitt. As mankind has proved again and again. I advised Mr. Dunleavy of the possibility, and thus he has acted."

"Well, thank you for that, Barry."

Hitchens spread his hands and bowed his head briefly.

"But I now have another problem," Prendergast continued. "Without a system imposed from without, I am left to ponder the system I would install here. I suppose you would recommend a democracy of some sort."

"Oh, no. Not at all, Mitt. It can't work, for the same reason annexation to the Federation can't work. Your people have no experience with such a system. You've inherited a strong-man form of government, and, over the medium term, so it shall remain. To borrow a phrase from fishing, High Admiral, you've caught it, and now you must clean it."

"I can't install a democracy?"

"No, Mitt. Not knowing how to work it, people would be unsatisfied with it. Eventually a strong-man would emerge, and people would be happier. This is clear from a study of mankind's history here on our native planet."

"Then what am I to do, Barry?"

"Rule in the manner people expect, but build the systems of democracy as you do. Be the strong-man they want, until they have the experience to make a more subtle system workable."

"Can you give me some concrete steps there, Barry?"

"Of course. You have a central committee now, correct?"

"Yes."

"Keep them. Call them the Central *Advisory* Committee, however. Let them propose things to you, then you decide. That is the actual system as it was under Mr. Robertson. Make it official.

"Similarly, form an elected council, something like we have here. Let them debate things, argue about solutions, vote on them, and then pass them to you. But you make the decisions. In the meantime, they gain experience with debate and argument and voting, and your citizens gain experience with elections.

"Over time, this council will gain the experience and the customs required. You can acquiesce to their proposals more often. Cede more control to them. Eventually, make them the sole legislative power, while you retain the executive authority.

"Ultimately, you can step down and the executive authority can itself be an elected position.

"It is the work of, at a minimum, ten years. Perhaps more like fifteen or twenty. But it is the only way to build a democracy that endures, Mitt. The only way that has always worked."

Prendergast considered, and Hitchens was content to wait. It was not what Prendergast had anticipated. Being strong-man for the next ten or twenty years. But he could see Hitchens' point. It was a sobering realization. Finally, he broke the silence.

"But will people stand for it, Barry? To trade one strong-man for another?"

"Right now, Mitt, it is a question of, Is this strong-man better than the last one? Here, instead of someone who started a war, we have someone who has constructed a peace. Instead of someone making enemies, we have someone making friends. Instead of someone who rules with no input from the people at all, we have someone who has advisory bodies, one of whom is elected, to which he listens. It is much the better situation, but still comports with the culture and habits of your people."

"It seems simple when you put it that way, Barry."

"It will work out, Mitt. You will see. You will take your fair share of criticism, and I can't promise you that history will be kind to you, but it is your best way forward. And we will help."

"How can the Federation help, Barry?"

"Not with the government. That can't work. We can help with the economy. Any number of our wealthy will want to get in on the investment boom that will accompany such a loosening as a free trade agreement between our countries. A booming economy takes people's eyes off of government, thereby giving you a much freer hand."

Prendergast nodded. The path forward was becoming clearer.

"And my title going forward, Barry?"

"Pick something new, Mitt. Not Chairman of the Central Committee. Let people know change is coming, in the simplest possible way. President, perhaps. That one has a long history."

Prendergast took a deep breath and let it out slowly.

"Thank you for your time today, Barry. You've certainly given me some things to think about."

"I'm happy to oblige, Mitt. Know that I am always here for you, as you go forward."

Prendergast nodded. Hitchens was much more than he had at first appeared, and Prendergast was grateful.

Cleaning Up

Dominic Trask was watching events in the Deneb Republic with a great deal of interest. He knew the political considerations. He knew the Federation would take some action to redress the Meredith Incursion. It had to, to avoid appearing weak and attracting predators.

What form that action would take was another issue. Of course, those in power would not be forthcoming about it until after it was over, so he kept on the lookout for signs that something had happened.

He knew the Federation had let out the contract for a large number of the new frigates. That he knew from his involvement with General Ship & Fitting. Gabriel Artino had not been able to tell him everything, but Trask could read between the lines.

The big tell was something Trask recognized immediately. The sudden and forceful exit of John Robertson from power in Deneb, replaced with someone named High Admiral Mitt Prendergast.

Such changes often signaled opportunity to a savvy investor. The trick was to get in early. Become the first mover. But for that Trask needed information.

How high in the Federation government could he reach to get someone who would be honest with him?

Trask placed a call request with his old friend, Admiral Jurgens. Whatever else Jurgens was, he would never be a good liar.

"Jurgens."

"Good morning, Kurt. Dominic Trask here."

"Good morning, Dominic. How are you today?"

"Good. Good. Thank you. I was calling to congratulate you."

"For what, Dominic?"

"For your success in dealing successfully with the Deneb Republic. I assume the recent change of government there was as a result of some successful event, likely precipitated by you Navy folks."

"Yes, well, I can't say much about that. I can tell you, though, that your advice to manufacture more of the little super-frigates was well considered."

"I appreciate your position, Kurt. And I'm glad my advice worked out for you. Let me ask about something not likely to be confidential, however. What sort of fellow is this High Admiral Prendergast?"

"The new leader of the Deneb Republic? He's a pretty well grounded fellow, Dominic. I like him. Of course, he's from the same background as I am. Chief of their navy. You know. I think Mr. Robertson tried to move against him, and High Admiral Prendergast objected."

Oh, so that was what had happened. Trask nodded. Leave it to somebody like Robertson to move against someone competent and come up hard against it. That had clearly been a mistake.

Trask had done some background work on Prendergast. In his early fifties, he had married late to a somewhat younger woman. He had three young children, and was considered a devoted family man.

What would relations be like with someone like that?

"His accession to power in Deneb is certainly to be welcomed, then, I would think, Kurt. Why, it could set the two countries on an entirely new path."

Jurgens nodded.

"I can't say much about that, Dominic, but I will say you have a rare appreciation of the possibilities in many situations. You know who might be able to tell you more? The Councilor for Earth. Do you know Mr. Hitchens?"

"Oddly enough, I do, Kurt. Earth is often a difficult investment opportunity. 'Meddling by the colonies' they usually call it. I've had the occasional conversation with Barry Hitchens, and he's assisted me in avoiding some difficulties."

"You might want to chat with him, then, Dominic. He may be able to be more forthcoming than I can."

"All right. Thanks, Kurt. And, once again, congratulations."

"Hitchens."

"Good afternoon, Barry. Dominic Trask here."

"Well, hello, Dominic. Nice to hear from you. Some minor investment difficulty I might assist you with today?"

"Yes, actually, but not on Earth this time. Barry, what's going on with the Deneb Republic?"

"Ah. Yes. That has been a matter of no small concern lately."

Hitchens tented his fingers and considered, then spoke to his hands.

"I believe it would be improvident of me to discuss specific events, Dominic, but I can speak more generally. It has long been my opinion, from an extensive study of the millennia of history we have available here, that long-term peace between nations is only possible within the context of friendship."

Hitchens looked up from his hands to catch Trask's eye.

"I find, to my great satisfaction, that that point of view seems to be gaining more widespread traction of late."

Trask nodded. That was all he needed. Oh. One more thing.

"Barry, you wouldn't happen to have the private mail

address of High Admiral Prendergast, would you?"

"Why, yes, Dominic. I believe I do. Yes, here it is. Coming over now."

"Thanks, Barry. I appreciate it."

"No problem, Dominic. Good hunting."

Hitchens winked, then cut the connection.

It was First Minister Prendergast's third full day as ruler of the Deneb Republic. He was wearing a business suit to work now, not his navy uniform. He had promoted his chief of operations, Donny Stillwagon, to High Admiral of the navy.

He had selected the title 'First Minister' rather than 'Prime Minister' or 'President.' Prime Minister Prendergast and President Prendergast both had an unfortunate alliteration. He also thought it would be easier to step down as First Minister. It just seemed less permanent, somehow. Less pretentious, anyway.

He was simply the First Minister of the new government of the Deneb Republic. There would later be other ministers, like Minister of Defense, Minister of State, Minister of the Treasury. He was thinking of who those other ministers might be now.

Prendergast's Chief of Staff, Cas Kaminski, had put him in touch with John Robertson's former department heads. He had spoken to each of them in turn. Most were delighted with the change in the government. They had lived in terror of the petulant and childish Robertson.

Having someone as moderate and mature as Prendergast in charge was fine with them.

Kaminski came in from the outer office.

"I have a call holding for you, sir. I think you should take this one."

"Who is it?"

"A fellow by the name of Dominic Trask. He claims to be the richest person in the Federation. I checked him out, and he is who he says he is."

"The richest person in the Federation?"

"Yes, sir. That checks, too."

"All right, Cas. Put him through."

Kaminski nodded and left his office. The call request came through within seconds, and Prendergast accepted.

"Prendergast."

"Good morning, First Minister. My name is Dominic Trask."

"Good morning, Mr. Trask. How may I help you?"

"My understanding, First Minister, to the extent I can pry any information out of anyone on this end, is that the Deneb Republic and the Federation are to be friends."

"Yes, Mr. Trask. That is my understanding as well, surprising as it is to me."

"Surprising, First Minister?"

"Yes, Mr. Trask. Your navy showed up here in overwhelming force, in the form of eight squadrons of the new super-frigates. Do you know of them?"

Trask nodded.

"Yes, it was one of my companies that built those ships over the last year or so."

"Well, then you know that eight squadrons of them was simply an unbeatable opponent. Mr. Robertson blamed me for being unprepared to meet such a force, and tried to have me executed."

"Oh, my."

"Yes. So I shot him and took over the Deneb Republic in a coup d'etat. I then surrendered to the Federation fleet, and, of all the unlikely possibilities, High Commissioner Dunleavy offered me peace and friendship between our nations."

"And you have consolidated control now, First Minister?"

"Yes, Mr. Trask. It turns out that most of the people who worked for Mr. Robertson in the prior government prefer the current administration."

Trask chuckled.

"Knowing something of the late Mr. Robertson, I am not surprised, First Minister. I think I can shed some light on Mr. Dunleavy's remarkable offer, however. Baltimore Hitchens III is the Councilor for Earth in the Federation Council. It is his well studied position that long-term peace between nations is only possible in friendship."

Prendergast nodded.

"I have spoken to Mr. Hitchens, Mr. Trask. He has been most kind in offering me his counsel as we move forward."

"A generous offer, First Minister. Barry Hitchens is a man of rare wisdom."

"So it would seem, Mr. Trask. And your purpose in contacting me today?"

"If we are to be friends, First Minister, that implies many things. One thing it implies is a large increase in the carry trade between the Deneb Republic and the Federation. You need ships, lest all that carry trade transit in Federation hulls."

Prendergast nodded. He had had some thoughts in that direction as well.

"And?"

"I wish to invest in the Deneb Republic, First Minister, by building a major commercial shipyard on Gloucester. I would build you a fleet of cargo ships to equalize the capabilities in trade."

"And you would make a great deal of money."

"Of course, First Minister. But I will make a great deal of money in any case. I would rather make a great deal of money hiring your citizens to build the cargo ships you need there than to make a great deal of money hiring Federation citizens to build cargo ships here."

"You're a Federation citizen, Mr. Trask. Why would you rather invest in that shipbuilding here?"

"Because the long-term interests of the Federation are in peace, First Minister. An equalization in the carry trade, cross investment in each other's businesses, and more interwoven business interests are all conducive to friendship and disincentives to war."

"And you make a great deal of money either way."

"Yes, First Minister. Of course. I have to make money just to keep even, to compensate for the government's inflation of the currency."

"Your government inflates the currency, Mr. Trask?"

"All governments inflate their currency, First Minister. Some more than others, but they all do it. It is basically a free tax. They issue more money, and prices go up. They then blame the inflation on price gouging, big business, or the rich, diverting attention away from their own responsibility. That goes all the way back to Rome. So I have to make more money continuously, just to keep even."

"How did Rome inflate the currency, Mr. Trask? Weren't they based on specie? Gold coins and the like?"

"Yes, First Minister. Both gold and silver. They diluted the gold and silver they minted their coins from. With lead and other cheaper metals."

"Well, I hope to shrink the government and not further inflate the currency, Mr. Trask. A police state is an expensive operation. There are many things I can cut."

"I would be pleased to advise you on those matters, as well, First Minister, if you have any need. I am not uninformed on the issues."

"Let's stick to the investment plan, Mr. Trask. And I would invite you to call me Mitt."

"And I am Dominic, Mitt. Very well, let's get into some details about how this could work."

They spent another hour on the phone. By the time they were finished, Trask and Prendergast had hammered out the broad outlines of an investment plan.

The call request came in from Elizabeth.

"Sharp."

"Hi, Deke. Dominic Trask."

"Hi, Dominic. What's going on?"

"I have reached an agreement in principle with First Minister Prendergast of the Deneb Republic to build a shipyard on Gloucester. They're going to need cargo ships for the interstellar trade, and we're going to build them there."

"Sounds like a good deal, Dominic. Congratulations."

"Thanks, Deke."

"You know, I've spoken to then-High Admiral Prendergast."

"You have?"

"Yes. I accepted his surrender."

"Excellent. Well, then, you know what sort of person he is. We've made a deal, and I expect him to keep his part of it."

"I would, too. I think he's pretty much a straight arrow."

Trask nodded.

"So I want you to advise me on this project as we go forward. I'll compensate you in stock."

Sharp's eyebrows shot up. That had the potential of being insanely lucrative.

"Are you sure, Dominic?"

"Absolutely. I owe you one, Deke. At least. So this is one

way to even the tables. I always even the tables. There's also an opportunity to get in on this deal if you want."

"I wouldn't be able to contribute much, at least on your scale of operations, Dominic."

"Put a consortium together on your end, Deke. You and your friends. I will personally guarantee you do not lose money."

"He said that?" Fuller asked later.

"Yes. 'I will personally guarantee you do not lose money.' His exact words."

"Oh, my. Well, in that case, I think we should go in whole hog, D.K."

"Not worried about diversification?"

"Not with Dominic Trask's personal guarantee."

"He said me and my friends. Who all would that be, Suzie? Daphne and Tim for sure."

"Lydia and Paul. Oh, and Otto, for that matter."

Sharp nodded.

"Yeah. Tim's a corporate big shot here in New Destin. Not a lightweight in terms of his ability to consult on the project."

"Yes, and Lydia is as good a finance whiz as I've ever seen. Let's get everybody on board, and let Dominic know they're available to help."

"OK, Suzie. Sounds like fun."

Dominic Trask never had to cover his personal guarantee.
The venture was insanely lucrative.

Epilogue

After fifteen years as head of operations of D Branch, Deke Sharp retired. His assistant for the last two years, Matt Deckard, took over as head of operations. Sharp was now in his early fifties.

Otto Pasha, too, retired as head of D Branch. His position was taken by the long-time head of the intelligence division. Pasha had just turned seventy-five.

Suzie Fuller retired as Principal Investigator for Official Corruption on Ariel. She was not replaced, as the corruption issues that had plagued the planetary government had been resolved, at least for the time being.

Mitt Prendergast stepped down as First Minister of the Deneb Republic. He turned a smoothly running executive branch over to the Deneb Republic's first elected president, in a new government dubbed the Third Republic at the suggestion of Barry Hitchens, the former Councilor for Earth.

On the occasion of their near-simultaneous retirements, they were invited to Dominic Trask's beach house for an extended vacation.

Trask himself, now seventy-seven, had stepped down from most of his business activities ten years ago, leaving them in the charge of his son-in-law, David Sachs, his daughter Marie's husband.

Trask and his wife Janine were now in semi-permanent residence at the beach house.

For their transit to Elizabeth, Trask sent one of the new private yachts being built in Gloucester to pick up Sharp,

Fuller, Pasha and his wife, Duplay, Hansen, and the five kids. With six cabins, there was enough room for them all.

The ship was a hybrid of sorts, based on the super-frigate design. Using the huge powerplant of an attack-ship carrier, it was fast. Leaving off the heavy cruiser's guns, the missiles, and the nose gun, it was lean enough to mount the much larger cabin, while maintaining twin shuttles for trips to the planet. Those shuttles, too, were a bit larger, to accommodate enough seating.

Never one to skimp when it counted, Trask sent a separate private yacht to Humphreys to pick up Lydia Thompsen, Paul Camden, their three children and their spouses, and their grandson. Sarah was now twenty-four, and the twin boys were twenty-two.

For his part, Prendergast and his family – his wife Elise Fischer and their three children, now in their early twenties, plus one son-in-law and a grandchild – took a government yacht from Gloucester to Elizabeth. Prendergast figured the new president was just as glad to have the long-ruling First Minister of the Second Republic out of the way for a while.

They all converged on the beach house, though the shuttles had to take turns on the landing pad in the front yard.

Dominic Trask's 'beach house' was the size of a large country club. Having nearly thirty guests in residence in the guest wing did not stress either the staff or the facility.

As for Trask, he was in his element. Entertaining so many friends all at once, he was having the time of his life.

Trask, Pasha, Sharp, Hayden, Camden, and Prendergast were sitting around a patio table on the main patio of the house with cigars and beverages. It was sunny, with a cooling, on-shore breeze. Everyone had just had lunch.

After a quick bite, the kids had gone back out to the swimming raft, and were jumping off the raft and splashing in the water. The sound of laughter carried across the beach.

The women were out in the water, too, though they were staying away from the commotion around the raft. Fuller, Duplay, and Marie Dubois were swimming out to the breakwater. The older women – Janine Dubois, Elise Fisher, and Muriel Pasha – were swimming closer in.

The young adults were sunning on beach blankets, watching various grandchildren playing in the sand.

Sharp sighed.

"Your kitchen hasn't suffered any over the years, Dominic."

Trask smiled.

"I think they may have gotten even better, Deke. But they certainly haven't backslid."

"That was remarkable," Pasha said. "I've had the luxury of being spoiled over the years, but that was truly wonderful."

"It was great after five weeks of ship food," Prendergast said.

"Yeah, that was a long trip for you, Mitt," Sharp said.

"Yes, but, after the last fifteen years of orders and reports, subordinates and retainers, it was nice to just be alone with my family. My wife, my kids, my grandson. What a luxury."

Sharp nodded. Yeah, he could see that.

The men sat and drank their cognac, smoking their cigars. It was a wonderful day for the beach.

As Sharp watched the children play – his and Suzie's two, Jacqueline and Bernard, Duplay and Hansen's three, Thomas and Evelyn and Stephen, and Sachs and Dubois' two, Monique and Gabrielle – his mind wandered.

It had been a hell of a ride, the last thirty years. Being part of D Branch operations, getting blown up and reassembled, taking out the pirates, subduing and ultimately overturning the Robertson government of the Deneb Republic, and running D Branch operations the last fifteen years.

Also in there was facing down the Deneb Republic Navy in a dozen frigates, working up the Federation Navy attack force, and then turning the war around and building a shipyard on Gloucester.

Every invested couple here had contributed. Management expertise, or financial expertise, or ship expertise. The newer ships – like the yachts – had benefitted a lot from Sharp and Fuller's experience spacing the original super-frigates. Many of the old annoyances had been designed out of the new ships.

They had all done stupidly well with the venture. All would be considered wealthy now, though nowhere near Dominic Trask's stupendous riches, which had only grown larger from the shipyard project.

As for Sharp, he was still bound to his prosthetics. He still had the ritual of washing his prosthetics, salving his stumps, going some nights without prosthetics installed so the skin could heal completely.

Sharp still had prosthetic genitals, though they continued to work properly, and his love life with Fuller had not suffered much with age.

He also had a number of internal devices to regulate various functions, like the internal cardiac defibrillator and the ventricular assist device.

Sharp had consulted doctors during his normal check-ups to try to determine if his modifications increased his lifespan or decreased it, and they simply didn't know. He was a one-off.

In the meantime, Sharp enjoyed life. He enjoyed marriage to

Fuller. He enjoyed their country house. He enjoyed their kids.

He was determined to enjoy every single day, because he didn't know how long he had.

Then again, he supposed nobody else knew how long they had, either.

Please review this book on Amazon.

Author's Afterword

This is probably the last book of Deke Sharp. Of course, I don't know that for sure. I might get an idea for another book in this series, but the story arc I wanted to tell is complete. How Deke Sharp did, after all, survive his encounter with pirates. How he came back from disaster. How he found love, retired from ops, settled down, had kids.

How he lived a normal life after being a D Branch field operative for so many years. After being nearly destroyed in an op gone bad.

This series was cathartic for me after my medical issues of the last year. Four times in the emergency room with life-threatening medical issues. One *very* close call. Two surgeries. Lots of powerful meds. Rehab.

Deke Sharp was in much worse shape than I, and he came back. I could, too.

My own medical experiences informed some of the content here, especially in the first book. Much research was done as well. I always want the non-SF portions of my books to be as accurate as I can make them. The science-fiction part is for fun, and to allow me to place my characters in interesting situations.

To allow me to pose questions and explore answers that the real world hasn't yet presented.

Love, honor, duty, and loyalty – the pillars of civilization and my persistent themes – are all here. The biggest example in this book is that Deke Sharp won't even consider having children until and unless he is out of field ops, out of duty to his wife and children.

It is all of the above – love, honor, duty, and loyalty – that drive the D Branch field operatives to stand in the way of eight Deneb battle groups in a handful of frigates, to protect the planet Meredith. When push comes to shove, they are not found wanting.

Suzie Fuller is right in there with them. She will not stand aside while Deke Sharp goes off on his own to face that terrible challenge, despite his effort to shield her from it. Her love, her duty, her honor, her loyalty demand it of her. She is not found wanting either.

Again and again, people throughout the book step up to the challenges they face. Dominic Trask, Daphne Duplay, Kurt Jurgens, Rodgers and McGrath, Hot Bitch Crosby and Scotsman MacPherson and the rest of the crews. Even Mitt Prendergast.

Each of them does their part to make the world a better place for everybody, often at great risk to themselves.

Deliriously hopeful? I think not. Humanity doesn't change much over time. Nobility is always there, given the right circumstances, with the right encouragement.

I simply dream of the future, and then I write what I dream.

I hope you enjoyed this series.

Richard F. Weyand
Bloomington, IN
March 25, 2025